C000043334

Seven Islands of the Fog

Thomas Terraforte

authorHOUSE®

AuthorHouse™
1663 Liberty Drive
Bloomington, IN 47403
www.authorhouse.com
Phone: 1 (800) 839-8640

Published by AuthorHouse   05/06/2015

ISBN: 978-1-5049-1120-7 (sc)
ISBN: 978-1-5049-1121-4 (hc)
ISBN: 978-1-5049-1119-1 (e)

Print information available on the last page.

Imagination

A little bucket jumping rope
A little box flying string
An assortment in a wrapper
Spinning Effortlessly
Change Form, Change Structure
A Hand, a Ball of Twine
A Tiny Imagination with a start
For you or me to unwind

Thomas Terraforte

Contents

Chapter 1

Triton

A mystical Sunday morning on the marsh of a grassy town park, the fog rolls in, obscuring the trees and accentuating the burgeoning light. A lone person steps toward the fog, keeping pace with their shoes. The wind picks up, a far turn to the right and the fog shifts contrasting the direction of the wind. A step and the grasses are clear, another step and the fog thickens. The lawn slowly begins to freeze. One step and the fog is clear. 'One Step... and ... One Step... and ... ahhh;' the misty clouds are no longer fog but clouds and the feeling that of falling; falling through a frozen sky to where the land looked like a map. This map is covered with peaks in the center and on the outskirts. This falling is mountainous and hilly. The light illuminates the dimensions of the terrain; one single ray reflected the symmetric mirroring of the mountaintops. Farther in the distance one can see the ring of mountaintops give way to hills in the center where an enormous congregation of statuesque mausoleum gazebo structures dots the landscape. The clouds are full of even smaller dots, dots in motion. The dots stream across the sky in a near straight line. Each maneuvering dot seems crossed in the center. The magnification increases, the dots' crosses separate and expand. These are not crosses, these are wings and what they are attached to aren't dots at all but people. Winged People flying to and fro, some carrying packages; some holding children; like a busy city street in the sky. One-hundred feet separate opposing lanes and each of the sides have a triple section. The people fly at a level of one-thousand feet above the ground level base of the mountainous region.

On this day, one particular man stands out. He is troubled and whereas most of the population flies slowly; he is laid out and racing. The man's feet extend flat revealing three toes. His speed seems to be at least two and a half times that of the next fastest flyer. He windes up and down, side to side, through the crowds. Clenched in his right-arm is a shoebox tied with a bow. The first instinct of an onlooker would be 'a gift', not this package. On the island of Triton shoeboxes signify important business and this must be more important than most. Boxes hold distinctions by left or right hand bow ties. The box the messenger carries is adorned with one center bow and a left hand charm. Gazebos dot the peaks, the very center of each emblazoned with the overflow of one great gazebo. The meeting place of all, unlike those seen on the ground; the top mountain gazebos have three general openings in triangle symmetry. The floor is an inverted sunken pyramid with row seats. No one takes the floor; all are in consultation with each. Lucius sweeps through the inward entrance without even a glance toward the throng of wings lining the marble aisles. Dropping down into the very center of the pyramid, He sweeps up barely missing the heads of the first row, leaving the box at the very center. All eyes focus on him during his upward ascent and about face.

"What is the meaning of this," a Triton at the very center stands to the attention of all. The Triton man is a chancellor, the leader of the mountain. Chancellors always sit on the outward facing side of the middle of the congregation. On this day, the other two congregations were centered by chancellors from the outer islands, a small and large piece of land to the north of Triton. The two other chancellors sit in observation over the proceedings.

Lucius takes one step forward from the center and lifts his long hair, a custom of gazebo matters. He clears his throat out of respect for chancellor Robbins, a long time friend and associate. "There, they are...," Lucius holds his box above his head for the review of the attendants. "They just arrived from a meeting on Scio," Lucius feels the stare of the audience and yet keeps his focus on his box, clearing his throat the messenger continues his thought, "... no one has seen them." "The war assessment on Scio," questions Robbins from his standing position." Why bring it here, The

Angel's Guild or the Triton Delegation should have it first." Lowering his box to chest level, the messenger looks toward the statesman. "What they say directly concerns you Chancellor Robbins." With a swallow the messenger feels for his friend," That is all I know; I brought them to you first. I don't know who saw but I grasped a gamble in transporting them."

The chancellor sits considering the gravity of the situation and the sacrifice on Lucius's part. "Very well, we will have to vote per our charter." The visiting sub-island delegation easily stands for the chancellor, having so little clout in the formal Triton delegation. With very little objection and the wandering eyes of some leering angels in the shadows, the chancellor hears the roll call of the page. The Angels that is what they called themselves, the mystical wizard's guild of Triton. Angels wandered the island with even respect as political delegations, in some cases more. "All in support raise your hand," The page calls out and then puts a foot on several lower steps to count the number. When the page reaches the majority, he returns to the top step and calls the announcement. "Lucius the messenger will present his message."

No scissors... No fingers..., Lucius being the messenger is required to make an Angel's Chant over the box, while hovering in mid-air. Lucius places the container on the center where he stands and rises with his wings to a center viewing height. The wings crease on a quarter length of each span. In a surprisingly effortless motion, Lucius slowly rises to the center of the crowd. "Mitto Venio," the messenger calls to the air. The box shutters on its corners; one edge then the opposite then the adjacent then the opposite. Then the box stands on a short side and begins to spin, slow at first and then fast. Lifting, ever so slowly off the ground, the spinning begins to reach a maximum with the loss of friction. The dark coloration of the box starts to lighten to a bright white light. The rays reached as high as Lucius's feet. Then the light dims and softens patiently revealing a parchment. An old antiquated looking paper with a bow at the left side drifts ever so slowly to the floor.

A page of the congregation to the chancellor's side ceremoniously rolls the scroll and runs the scroll up to him. The only comparison to this brief ritual is in tennis when a runner keeps running past the exchange. The page puts the scroll in the chancellor's hand on his left side; passing the

3

chancellor and standing at the top of the step. The pages are instructed never to leave until after each vote and each scroll is read.

Quite in contrast, the chancellor is supposed to begin reading, soon upon receiving the scroll. On this day, He put his self-interest first and reviews the scroll once, before beginning. Clearing his throat out of respect for the document, the chancellor begins to read.

To My Honorable Friends on the Island of Triton:

It has long been known that the Tritons are one of the wisest and most trusted of the member states involved in the current treaty construction. The currents have gone sour with border states fighting over the territorial boundaries on the island of Scio. In Fact, A Battle for the Southern Lands wages as I write. To this I make a formal request, To the Guild of Angels and every Chancellor of Triton for the presence of my trusted friend and shrewd negotiator, Chancellor Robbins. This message has been sent with a fast messenger and provisions for a ship to see the chancellor safely through the treacherous waters. Hurry my friends, the island grows worse by the day and your presence may bring some much needed solace to the discussions.

Signed,
Grand Parity Tumult

The runner quickly descends the staircase and upon receiving the parchment quickly says an incantation. Once again, The parchment is a box.

Lucius descends to his position in the center and turns toward the congregation, as the chancellor began to speak again. "Page, see this package to the Guild and instruct them that I am on my way to port with Lucius, where we await further instruction." The page bows and moves from his position on the top stair. The crowd clamors in discussions. Lucius walks to the location of the chancellor and pauses. The two men step to the page location and walk toward the open air landing outside the gazebo.

The two men let their feet drop from under them and the breeze from behind sweep them off the mountain. The page can be seen just getting off the ground, as the crowd disassembles. Far from the hurried business of mountaintop congregations is a small northern village. A vast array of hills, where a huge castle can be seen emerging from the precipice of an ocean. The Castle is the Angels Guild. The Village is an industrial town. There are boat builders in this town but the boats they build are unlike anything seen on any island. They aren't so much boats, as leveled platforms with cable attachments. This is AboveBoard, Pop. 2,001.

The boats of the town can be seen for miles in large columns, stacked precariously close to the shoreline. From the shoreline of Aboveboard, two small islands can be seen. On the larger island, one can see huge objects blocking a view of the horizon. These are Whirly Birds, 'The Largest Birds in the World.' One Bird can fill a normal city block and the platforms were for them. The birds and platforms composed the Assault/Exploration Force of Triton and they were unrivaled for domination of the Northern Sky.

The boat builders have a guild and, on this day, all work has stopped for the great conference. "If peace breaks out will never fill our orders," shouts one man. The words echo through the quiet of a simple wooden meeting hall with lined wooden benches and a place to speak in the very center front. "Peace will never exist over the seas," shouts another. "Quiet down, the guild will now come to order," the guild clerk began and then started the laborious task of reading the role call. After all were silenced, the guild chancellor steps forward for his pronouncement. "The Rumors... well they're just rumors but boat production will not cease with the conflict. The Angels have assured me that negotiations will begin ... following a peace settlement, for production on the other islands." A lone voice from the back shouts, "What are Dragoons going to need a boat for?" The Hall fills with laughter at the suggestion that the large, intelligent winged creatures of the south would need a boat at all. "OK, OK, my friends, we will do what we always have done and turn our construction trade to the best use we can. I have lost two sons to the conflict and I am not about to lose another. Meeting adjourned." The meeting disembarked in usual routine. Two Dark Figures from the rear of the room waited... waited... waited for all to leave.

Then they shimmered. Shimmering is the magical ability to teleport, one particle at a time. The ability is called shimmer because it looks like someone fading down a mirror image. When they reappear, they are in the great hall of the Castle De Angelis. This is mid-day and the hall resembles a crypt. No one enters for congregation except on approved meetings. The eclectic ways of Angel Spies are coordinated by the Minister of Local and Foreign Affairs, a human well-versed in the traditions and ways of the castle. His office resides just off the great hall. The minister's office is the size of a large living room with a large meeting table and a side view of the wetlands surrounding the castle base. The angel's know to sit at the far end out of respect for the minister's position. In one the angel's left hand is a folder with the name Lucius. The angels clear their throat, a gesture allowing the minister to speak. "Marcus and Magis, you are my two best and I have an important assignment for you. The Triton Delegation and the Formal Angelic Administration have been informed by the Grand Parity of Scio that a certain peace settlement may be possible despite the ongoing conflict. A Triton named Lucius and Chancellor Robbins are on their way to deliberations. I want you to track them and keep the castle informed. Now, I have been entrusted to give you a rare artifact on Triton, 'A Letter Sender.'" The minister puts what looks like two large envelopes on the Table. "The red one stays here and the blue goes, with you. All you need due to operate the sender is write a letter and put it in the envelope." The minister with a blank paper insertion demonstrated his speech. The envelope closed, the paper reappeared in another envelope on the side of the table. "The letter enters the envelope; it will reappear on the other side in mine." The minister seemed well elated with his ability. "This will work both ways, vice-versa." The minister forwarded a hand to the angels. "Now, and this is important, if these two men are captured or detained for any reason. You are to stay with them incorporeally and continue correspondence. Gentleman, in a way, you are responsible for their safety, even though your first duty is to the castle. Understood," The Angels nodded. Magis put the folder he was carrying on the table. The minister led the two angels to the door. Shimmering is strictly unallowed in the castle administration hallways. Marcus and Magis have to be careful concerning their proclivity toward the castings. "Marcus and Magis be safe and Godspeed." The minister waved a hand to the departing angels, since reaching his office entrance to the hall.

In the course of such a formal meeting, the minister usually turns toward his office. Today, his business would bring him to the leader of the Angel's Guild Arch Angel Spring Shine. The minister wound down a hall and up stairs to another level where the office door consisted of huge double doors with beads running the side and the width. Spring Shine is a credit to his name. He is wise and optimistic, even not as the leader of the Angels; he would have made a good chancellor on one of Triton's Congregations. Spring Shine believes Angels should be felt rather than heard and recognized the longstanding policy of secrecy that has earned the castle its respect.

"Afternoon, Minister, I hope all went well with your meeting." The minister caught the hinging doors and then released them and finding himself a seat in front of an even larger desk then his own. "Yes, they are the best at what they do," offered the minister, referring to Marcus and Magis. The minister held his vest to preface and then continued, sitting on the archangel's visitor chair. "I am here to discuss quite another matter." "Go ahead," The Archangel prodded. "THE WINGS OF TRITON were sent to Scio. Do you think our most precious artifact is safe in such a place?" The archangel only got involved in important matters to the castle. The wings are of such a nature. "The famed <u>THE WINGS OF TRITON</u> is thought to be the very magical item enabling all Tritons their flight ability." Springshine gets the facts in the air before discovering the minister's answer. "The Wings have some minimal magical protection and are guarded on the central volcano on Scio," The Archangel stated. "For what purpose could we possibly have in ever allowing them to leave?" The minister looks at the archangel's table, eyeing a strange bit of wording on a manuscript. "The wings have a dual ability!" The Minister and Archangel seeming to both lean back as the Archangel espouses. "The people of Scio need to see the other islands trust them... for a possible path to a more prosperous day." Spring Shine paused momentarily before continuing and offered candy on his desk to the minister. The minister halted the gesture, still listening. "The wars will end, and where will Scio find an alliance?" asking and then answering his own question, "With the very nation of Triton and the Angel's Guild who trusted them during time of crisis." The minister coughs before posing his question, "Does anyone in the formal delegation know?" The Archangel leans in giving an answer, "No, The wings are our responsibility and we can get a constructive diplomatic utilization of them; instead of having them collect dust. Still you bring a good point, maybe someone should watch them. We will consider the matter tomorrow at our monthly meeting; Day minister." "Day Archangel," the two parted. The minister toward the door and spring shine toward the window.

Far on the western shore, Lucius and the Chancellor make their way to a tavern. The sign on the placard reads "The Swabbed Deck." As a strange peculiarity to the sunny seaside town of oblique, there are no Tritons in this bar. The bar and its keeper are merchants from the great island plateau to the south, the island Tantamount. TM's as they are called on Triton are looked down on by most of the other islands. On Triton, they are given equal respect with all visitors. The precarious close location of Tantamount to Triton makes their mutual cooperation a matter of pragmatic diplomacy. The TM's never get involved with any political situations on other islands which make them easy companions to the Tritons. The chancellor grabs Lucius by the collar, a social and class distinction marker. Lucius wears purple, indicating a messenger of some import. The Chancellor wears yellow and green, indicating a man of import on a major mount. "Let me talk, maybe it would be better if we use a non-descript means of transport." Lucius thought the chancellor meant one of the many merchant captains, frequenting the establishment. The chancellor caught much attention; many in the bar new of him personally or, at the very least, the significance of his rank.

The TM captains being few in the bar became the only one's not looking over the chancellor. Lucius began observing the bartender utilizing a lever press on strange half-fruits. "What do you call them round fruits," one of the captains asks. "There called an orange. They come from some place called Florida." The bartender lifts his head and looks toward the wooden panels of the walling. Robbins viewing Lucius at the bar walks right through the bar and enters the kitchen beyond. The kitchen is a small room. In that small room is the owner of the establishment, one Mr. Finkle Charm going over the laborious task of matching figures and totals in his log book. The entrance of anyone could startle the fragile man. The entrance of a chancellor stood the man right out of his chair.

Finkle Charm recalling a memory of his youth a long a merchant ship, He nervously stood at attention awaiting orders; his hands moving and fluttering down to his side. The chancellor took him off stance by offering his hand. "Mr. Charm, my companion and I are in need of transport and, my memory serving me correct, you have a whirly bird." Mr. Charm shook the chancellor's hand a few more times then etiquette requires. "Why, yes sir, no ship, just a bird," Finkle turned toward his log entries and reviewing a column titled "Whirly," he put his nose toward the possibilities. "Perfect, we would like to rent your whirly bird for a month. We'll pay whatever fare market price," Lucius stood quiet as the chancellor advised. "Oh no, I can't charge a chancellor, you boys just bring the bird back in one piece and maybe come tax time, I'll get some relaxing service." "Unfortunately, that is not our department; we will pay for the bird. Thank You, Mr. Charm." The chancellor returned to a more rigid distinctive demeanor and one more characteristic of his station. Mr. Charm directed the two travelers, down a ridge to the side and out the back door. The wind blew the door open at the exact moment Finkle gestured with his finger. Lucius being first through and perusing the scene, there, several feet in front of him, a cliff met the floor. The cliff gave reveal to a grand disparity in the geological shelf. The village and the bar easily met the sands in front of them and yet the digressing of the cliff to the sands below graduating, but extreme, at maybe 100ft, also met the ocean's seem. The final drop off totaling 500ft for the cliff facing bottom, the swirling and falling currents near the bar amaze most any visitor.

On the first of these levels is a house and stables where Mr. Charm resides. The stables are huge and in compartments. They have to be, to house whirly birds. The style is a colonial cottage with an overabundance of rounding edges and subduing colors. "Just go down and see Victoria. She is the keeper of the whirly birds." Mr. Charm didn't point with his head; his gesturing became a function of his tilting torso. "Thank You, Sir." The chancellor was going to make a promise of payment and yet knowing how these travels can be, he wisely held his tongue. The men walk toward the center of the level with stables. The cliff gives only moderately and holds firm with each step. At the center of the level, there is a beautiful Triton girl with an enormous whirly bird. The grounds being mostly dirt in front of the stables, the dirt got all over.

Victoria being a beautiful voluptuous Triton girl, with a very silly heart, Lucius stepped forward to receive the bird. Extending one hand toward his beak, Lucius slid his hand over the beak. The bird turned a head to the side. "Hey, don't touch him until after his feeding." Victoria scolded while pouring bucket water from one container to another. "Mr. Charm sent us for the bird," Lucius interjected. Victoria forming a stance with both hands at her hips, she let the Triton know, "Well then the bird will receive you, when he is ready." Lucius's curiosity became piqued, "What exactly do whirly birds eat?" With a half sigh and a half turn of her head, she looked down her nose to the side, "Whirly Bird Food, Of Course!" "Of course," Lucius replied before turning to the chancellor. "The delay chancellor..." Lucius turning his head from the chancellor toward Victoria," I am sure this won't take long." Victoria's eyes began rolling, then she took the huge beast to the cliffs and let him get his morning flight. The bird gave a 'caw,' and then with an eye toward the ground began powering straight up and then out. Chancellor Robbins was then at a loss, "Where is he going?" The chancellor put a finger toward his mouth in question. "Silly, before a big journey, they fish... fill their bellies and then he'll be ready for you... after he poops... oh and I get his saddle on." With that, Lucius and the Chancellor sit down on the rocks and admire the view. "This shouldn't delay our plans," The Chancellor gave a despondent look at the view from the west coast, since finding a comfortable place in the bottom center of a stone. A fidgeting Victoria could not sit still to admire the view; company was scarce and regal at that. "What are your names?" A brief silence followed Victoria's Question. "If I am to trust you with my bird, your names aren't too much to ask." "I'm Lucius," he responded with a double pointed arm gesture," And this is Chancellor Robbins." The officers of Triton didn't exist with the conversation, Victoria kept continuity all bouncy and bubbly, "My Bird is the fastest on the coast; he won the Tantamount 500 twice and the Triton Cup once. Of course, I don't race him; I don't want to race him...." Victoria shivered and kept continuing, "... not anymore, they're mean to him sometimes. Oh, His Name is George but he doesn't respond to George. There is a 'G' on his back. If you want his attention, you just push it." The Chancellor rubbed his neck and began calming the girl. "Thank You, Victoria," the chancellor chimed in. "Oh, I was rambling... have you ever scaled these cliffs, they're kind of fun... oh... oh." With that she found a rock beside them and sat.

The Bum Sat... the mouth didn't. "Really, watching the stables is kind of boring. Occasionally, I'll ride George to the cliffs of my hometown. I'm from Summer Island, the smaller of the two islands. You know that and George, of course, is from <u>An Hour Behind</u>. <u>An Hour Behind</u> is the name of the larger island where whirly birds come from; so named because a mad man once terrorized the island by stealing everyone's clocks. When the clockmaker finally built or rebuilt everyone's clocks. They were set to the wrong time. Many months went by before the mainland of Triton began realizing and ever since the island kept their time and their name. Summer Island is mostly a Triton Resort Island." The morning flight of George skimming the water's face could be seen in the distance. George looking relatively small on a horizon with a very dominant sun showing through the middle of wave crests.

George, finally, landed after four hours in flight. Victoria took him by the reigns and after allowing him his time, saddled and plucked him. Victoria gave an explanation to the men observing from the rock," The birds aren't brushed like horses; they are plucked of any dirty or problematic feathers. This is a skill and somewhat of an art, as this can affect their aerodynamics." Victoria's grooming became very intensive, including feet, wings, and tail.

The intensity of her cleaning increasing, a question began to surface to her attention, "Can I come? There is nothing here for me." Victoria inquired. Lucius gave a flat smile sigh, the chancellor got off his rock and gave a touch of the air, "OK, on one condition," the chancellor's tones changing, he knew in the short time of their acquaintance she was eager for adventure, and her skill made her worth while. "You drive the bird, you care for the bird, and if I say so, you get off the bird." Victoria's excitement mostly began reaching her arms, in containment of her mouth, "Anything to get off this rock," Victoria's own feathers fluttered in the breeze. She had the manner of a person who had been working there sometime.

The three riders brought a very unusual saddle for the task. Lucius and the chancellor carried the saddle from the barn per Victoria's instruction. "The saddle being somewhat like a rock climbing harness attaching to a giant horse saddle; the harness provides for four passengers and the driver,"

Lucius gave a foot for Victoria's climb on the bird while the chancellor gave a knee to Lucius. With hardly a word, Victoria pushed the George Button. The whirly bird ran and jumped, steering a coarse south, with some coaxing from the driver. "We are going to have to make one stop at Tantamount, so George has enough energy for the trip to Scio. Victoria is a different person as a driver, and Lucius and the chancellor are kind of glad she was along. Victoria, she was ecstatic.

Chapter 2

Tantamount
"The Island of Merchants"

One morning the fog appears near someone's work. Spring mornings can sometimes see people to work in a haze. Rolling fog is a rare occurrence and makes presence most often during spring and fall. England and Brazil experience such fog in their city streets and business places. Such instances give rise to detective stories and thrillers. People seeming to disappear in the fog and then reappear moments later can be common occurrences. If you ever see the fog at your work, try walking just right of center. Of course you will need an open glade for this and a part of work; no one seems to bother with.

Walking just right of center on the side of some busy building, you will find the fog continues for miles. The ground stays level and even, a dirt trail emerging with an upward slope. Walking thus one dreary morning, you may find a tavern with a picture of a ghoul. "The Tavern of Lost Souls," is a popular spot to find work, on merchant ships in the western seaboard of <u>Tantamount</u>. The tavern is home to many captains and taverns are where all business on Tantamount is conducted. Rumors circulate on other islands that men from Tantamount are drunks and pirates. The truth is that long ago Tantamount was used by the island of Ignis, as a penal colony. One day, the protectors of Ignis (A social class), just decided to ignore Tantamount and since the residents of Tantamount were not much for politics, they stayed a merchant trading post run by five families who mostly built stuff of use to the trading captains. They are in order of wealth, the Bonzis – maker of ships, the Ehleta – maker of houses, the Lonswi – maker of weapons, the Triswi – maker of ale, and the Tenswi – cattle ranchers. Only the Ehleta, the Triswi, and the Tenswi have become prominent on the other islands.

The owner of the <u>Tavern of Lost Souls</u> is a man named <u>Paul</u>. Just Paul, he doesn't give out his last name and the captains have learned not to ask. Paul is not open to questions but on some odd nights, he'll tell you stories that will make your hair flee from your scalp.

The bar is solid oak, giving each captain the secure feeling of their moorings. The tables are wagon wheels and barrels; each barrel is securely fastened to the bulk head. One room to the side of the bar is for recruiting captains and all trade matters are handled via a handshake and a contract at the wagon wheels. "I'll give you fifty head of cattle for your weed ale," one captain asserts. Another begins to quarrel over the price of an Electric Eel. Paul keeps a tidy bar and if he taps you then you cease quarreling. Some captains quarrel even just to get Paul's Tap, signifying the best price. Paul Taps are a popular colloquialism lending to the fame of the bar and it's owner.

On this particular night, a man named rider is looking for a crew of men for salvage, deep water salvage off the island of Scio. The war still rages on Scio and men like rider have learned, retrieving the waste of war is a good living. The men are lined up around the block, because they know, captain rider is recruiting. Rider's ship is called," The Long Shadow of the Deep," a vessel more suited to the navies of one of the other islands. In all his travels neither rider nor his crew had ever seen its likeness or it's equal. Some say the vessel comes from the mysterious seventh island. Rider is very silent, he is just glad to have a vessel that can outpace a surface fleet underwater and still have enough space for countless treasures.

"The Long Shadow of the Deep," is the only underwater vessel, aside from the sometimes fantastic creatures infrequently seen in southeastern Tantamount waters. The ship is extremely efficient, operating on a power source kept secret by the famous captain. One popular idea among the trading captains is rider got the ship from sea creatures. The true origins are known only to rider and add to his mystique. Rider usually gains the notice of the trading captains as he barters in magical artifacts and ancient ruins. The value of rider's cargo is detailed and kept secret with <u>John</u> his first mate.

"You have an hour," Paul told the famous captain. "That's all I NEED," rider stated in return. Although his crew changed periodically, his first-mate john, his second-mate Hanz, and his engineman Robert, never did. This was rider's way of keeping his vessel. John was Helm and fire control, and Hanz looked after the crew. "Captain, You never did say what we were after." John put to Rider's Ear. "You will all know what I am after, when we are underway." "Understood," the response came from his staff and more than a few men waiting in line. The Signup Sheet took only forty-five minutes and many familiar faces paraded by, making the captain feel a sense of ease. Rider relaxed enough to look around the bar. The bar's construction is a forte of the Ehleta. The face of the bar where Paul resides displays a picture of Tritons fighting with winged monsters over the island of Tantamount. The side posts have a striped coloration. "Huh," Rider spoke to himself although the people in line thought he referred to them. John his first-mate grabbed rider's shoulder. Rider gave a wince. "I thought I saw something moving in the post at the bar." "Don't drink washbe before recruitment, captain." The captain didn't drink the strange intoxicant known to southern waters. His smile returned in mere moments and his energy for recruitment. "Next," rider put to the crowd. The nervous sailor's lining up, continuing to put their signatures on the recruitment papers.

Meanwhile on the very northern edge of Tantamount, Lucius leaps down off George and flies in a scouting direction for a landing site. This is engrained in the messengers of Triton and Lucius knew his job very well. The northern town of Deblesque is moderately populated and mostly used as a lumber yard for the Ehleta, who control the northern quadrant of the island. There is a large whirly barn, one of the biggest ever seen and a smaller horse barn on one side with a huge multi-story ranch house on the other. Victoria thought to stop here for replenishment because she knew the stable keeper and he is quite the authority on whirly bird care and preparation. "Look, once we land, I'll ask my friend, Donald, if we can stay the night." "Little one," that is what Robbins took to calling Victoria. "Little one, we have only two days to reach the conference, can George fly fast." "Silly," that was her only response as she took George into a dive. Robbins held on for dear life, Victoria's driving did not keep the stomach steady.

Directly upon landing, they met Donald and Lucius. Donald reached out to hug Victoria and the embrace seemed liked old friends reunited. "Wow, how you've grown; I remember when you were just an obnoxious student with a lot of questions I couldn't answer. Donald turned to address Lucius and the chancellor. "Is she still a spit-fire?" The chancellor looked at Lucius and took his turn, "She keeps us guessing. Thank You for putting us up for the night." "Anything for my star pupil, George and I are old friends too." The bird turns and much to Lucius's surprise, the only one not too much for whirly bird travel, he cawes to the wind. Lucius discovering that whirly birds have intelligence let alone a personality. Lucius stroked the bird and began to see similarities in their wing structure; A distant thought being if they were related.

George took to the stables with great vigor, only yielding to Donald's somewhat familiar hand. Most of the whirlies kept busy in a nesting posture or else in some quite social cackle. "Are there different breeds?" the chancellor broached, following a close second into the stable. "Oh yes, there are five different breeds on that crazy time island, you can usually tell by the color of the feathers or the size. "Has there been much word about the wars just south," the chancellor in stylistic attitude began testing the waters to get information. "None, not a peep," the keeper gave managing a hand on the stall door. They usually have a messenger run a word, now and again. I just know that our birds are not for that." Donald began reaching into his shirt pocket where a work order sat. He handed the work order to the chancellor showing several recent orders. "Oh what are they for," Robbins could be inquisitive although usually he restrained himself. Robbins examined the paper in interest. "Like everything on Tantamount, transport. We have several harnesses from Triton and they seem to work well for carrying cargo. Just an aside, I suggest you give George till tomorrow afternoon... if you want a nice long distance out of him." Robbins returned the work order to Donald and he put the paper in his shirt pocket. The chancellor noticed a few scratch marks on the side of the barn wall. He began realizing the marks were too small for whirly birds. "Are you having trouble with domestic animals?" The chancellor realizing sometimes information came in the most out of the way observations. Donald wipes the sweat from his brow and gripping his outer fingers, trusts the information to Robbins, "A couple months ago, a wizard and a cat visited and inquired about a whirly. I have never seen a humanoid cat; I thought some of those captains were telling stories. Those big cats are very similar to house cats and every once in awhile need to dull there claws. I wish he didn't use the side of my barn." The Chancellor felt the deep gash in the woodwork and gave a reassuring pat to his host.

The group retires to relaxing quarters. The main house containing a quite unusually large lounge for a country setting with just a few hands and Donald's wife on staff. "Thank You, for letting us stay here to night," Victoria trained on this ranch and so knew most of the people in residence. "Don't get too comfortable," Lucius cautioned. "We need to work on preparations in the morning and I know the skies of Scio, well enough to know calculations should be made in advance for navigable flying." "Then right to bed with you," the chancellor patted Lucius on the back collar. Donald smiling a walk toward his house gave the biggest grin he could muster. Inside the front door, he got quickly to the work of showing everyone their rooms. The front parlor to the right of the door held many chairs for relaxation and a moderate country fireplace. The chancellor gave a reassuring look to Donald. Donald just sighed. Donald's wife ran a letter to her husband. "What do you have there, another inquiry on a whirly?" "Looks like tickets." Donald looked up, as the parlor clears of residents and guests. The tickets included a letter and Donald read the invitation out loud to his wife. "The letter is about the wizard from a couple months ago, someone is inviting us to a water volleyball match in a place called Subsa and the letter is telling us to bring the Ignis contract we have in our possession. The letter continues stating, 'the wizard, we met a couple months ago, will help us get more horses for our ranch.'" "Well, we could use more horses," Donald's wife avowing with a smile. Donald grew half impatient with the letter in his hands, "I know, we could use more horses and the wizard was nice." "Then make the inquiry," Donald's wife was one of the best ranch wives around, forceful and direct with a kind heart and a big smile. Donald winced and then resolved himself to inquire. The fire crackled in reassurance of his decision.

The next morning saw Lucius and Victoria, up early at," The Whirly Center," that is what Donald had named his ranch and partly the reason it had been used as a training center for years. Victoria shouted to Lucius running past his half opened door and then paused at the parlor entrance. Victoria gripped the door for Lucius's walk outside and turned to the inside stairwell for a second. She thought maybe she would see a familiar face running down the stairs from the time when she was still in training. She didn't. The wood on the banister seemed to move and the oddest of things, blink. "What are you looking at," Lucius inquired of the inquisitive girl. "I thought that I saw something moving in the banister. "You have quite an imagination," Lucius offered as he headed for the brisk morning. Victoria put in a trot toward Lucius as they found the front yard up against a cliff facing. Lucius walked Victoria to the ridge of the high cliff looking out over Deblesque. "The winds of Tantamount seem to give George's wings more lift," Lucius put to the whirly keeper. Victoria nodded," the reason Donald put his farm here." Right before the edge of the landing sat a large flat boulder, on this he laid out his map of Tantamount and the surrounding seas. "We will avoid most of the trading routes, if we cross inland and then dart out, just below Crescent City. Most of the sea captains will either be taking direct northern routes or direct southern routes, at the very worst a northern diagonal to Ignis." Lucius made a line across the map with a messenger pencil." We will take a southern diagonal which will place us just south of Ignis, away from the traders and the southern wars." Victoria just listened, she saw Lucius as an expert on what he did and that gave her a somewhat relaxing attention span.

Everyone at "The Whirly Center" ate breakfast at the same time, a comparable affair to most ranches. Donald's Routine was set and there had to be some unawareness of the guests to keep to the schedule. The chancellor saw everyone dart about in the morning rushing from one job to the next. Not wanting to be useless, he set upon preparing George. An out of the way task for the chancellor but his youth had seen him to the northern lands of Triton more than once. After some considerable time in preparation, the chancellor saddled the great beast, with a sudden shiver and a cold wind George moved slightly. The chancellor turned his head in time to see the stable wall shimmer a bit. Robbins shrugged off the notion realizing Triton had several watchful eyes.

Lucius and Victoria settling on their course heading marked each landmark on the map. Victoria had but one question for Lucius. "Why are we avoiding the operating routes of Tantamount?" Lucius stood at attention to reply," In instances of important business or travel, all main thoroughfares are to be avoided when possible," Lucius had such a stolid look. Victoria just rolled her eyes playfully. Victoria very rarely used her wings but the giddy mood entranced her. "Let's Fly!" She and Lucius practically flew right onto the back of George with only the slightest of motion showing Lucius's concealment of the map. The chancellor shook Donald's hand and the three were off on a heading directly south of the barn.

The flying was fast and laid out for two miles. A large monument dotting the center of Tantamount's landscape in the unofficial capitol of the center province ruled by the Tenswai. Victoria swallowing the sloshes in her mouth, spoke," Lucius can we take George on a flyby of the cattle ranches." Lucius nodded reluctantly, "A few dips, only a few." The chancellor also knows of Lucius's role in the planning and takes this moment to mention the subject. "Tell me Lucius, which will be our approach to Scio." Lucius motions briefly for the map and then catches himself. "Chancellor, we will be approaching the northeast quadrant of Scio. There is a small archipelago there called emote. We will land there first; I don't want our presence on the island to be preempted by any disputes. I will scout the mainland approach before we continue on." Lucius grabbed the saddle keeping his station steady. The chancellor gives a listen," Excellent, now, if we can just get Victoria to leave these cattle alone;" Victoria couldn't stop smiling.

Most of the crew of the, "Long Shadow of the Deep," never having seen the vessel, knew only the vessel ran out of a port town called Crescent City. Crescent City being so named because the lowlands of the west side of Tantamount formed a crescent and this town is at the middle of the Arch.

Long docks and piers develop the water front with ships of all shapes and sizes. Some run by sea creatures as fantastic as above water sea horses and giant electric eels. All of the ships have reserve dock boarding, usually with great ramps or stand alone berths. Captain Rider has rather unique accommodations. Jutting just slightly from a rocky part of the shoreline is an outhouse with a picture of a wave and the silhouette of a ship.

The first mate does the honors, "All Aboard." As is commonplace with some newbies to the crew of forty-nine, some chuckles erupt. The first man to step forward is an engine-mate named Flink. He squeals at joy for being on the crew again, after an accident burned his arm. Flink, quickly disappeared into the outhouse, which really wasn't an outhouse but a long spiraling staircase to an Airlock. The Airlock only had two windows but what they revealed always slowed boarding. The ship was not solid but rather an interlaced lattice of metal. For many layers did the lattice structure tend, making a man wonder if the ship would leak. Not only didn't the vessel leak but the vessel had an unusual trick. The vessel has two buttons at the helm (Left Tail, Right Tail). In an emergency, "The Long Shadow of the Deep," can fishtail around a direct collision. The shapes of the ship are full and slender resembling a sword or a barracuda.

The Long Shadow of the Deep is equipped with ballasts and can even surface. The airlock preserves the splendor and grandeur of the ship and usually fills the crew with a sense of awe. The strangest part with regards to the ships origins is that all metal deposits are scarce in the seven islands. The ships hull doesn't rust indicating a rare metal or else a magical spell.

The only space large enough to contain the crew besides the mess hall is the cargo staging area. Hanz hurries the crew to quarters and calls a whistle to meet in the cargo keep. Sometimes a hunt has to include the crew; this was one of those times. Most of the initial boarding usually got the crew anxious with room selection and job detailing. On this day, the large meeting in the ships center hull became an inspiration in discovery.

"Gentleman," Rider starts curtly, but loud enough for everyone to hear. We are after a very rare treasure on a small island just northeast of Scio." John brings forth a map and stands it on a large easel. "Usually, I say usually, because we have gone to land before... (Rider pauses and clears his throat) ... like I said usually we salvage the ocean. However, the recent wars on Scio have created a lost artifact. One the Tritons would be after; if they knew it was missing. Gentleman, we are after the famed, "Wings of Triton."

Flink, being naturally curious and still a little excited, stumbles to his feet, "Uhh... what are the wings of Triton?" Most of the crew laughed but then most of the crew enjoy keeping their silence. Rider occasioning upon the opportunity, "My man, Flink did you say how quickly you entered that port-a-john. Well, you would have entered at twice the speed if you had wings. The famed <u>Wings of Triton</u>, as legend has it, is what initially gave Tritons their power to fly. This is the prize that will make crews everywhere envious. Gentleman to your stations, the hunt is on and I expect one-hundred percent out of each of you. When you ride the Long Shadow of the Deep, you ride a legend, and today you ride into history."

Chapter 3

Ignis
"The Island of Fire"

Alone person walks into a night of thick fog, backlit from incandescent lamps. The wind picks up, slowly stirring the cavernous fog and yet does not permeate the thick soup. Whoosh, the man is bent over and pulled strait up in the air, where he lands is the island of Ignis with fire's burning, he is now on the island of fire.

Two warriors are locked in an embrace. Each warrior wants the other to yield. One stands his ground and antagonizes. The other pushes to his stalwart shelter and dares. "Your fire is weak," he prods. "Yet my shelter is too strong for you," the other retorts. The pair spent the hour casting burning rocks at each other and now digress to pride recognition. Their homes are mud huts but the most well guarded mud huts in the world with each warrior spending hours on a personal arsenal of weaponry. A town square is called to attention, adjacent the combatants. "Here ye Here ye," calls out the red dressed protector. The protector stands on a flat wooden platform and swings a spear in the air as a call to his order. "Experiential 8 will now read the monthly mandates." The warriors listen as a fur coated short frail elderly man carries a podium from a horse drawn cart. The mud affecting his boots is scraped on the platform, as the podium is brought to level with the hand of the protector. The short experiential has a small box and stands on the box, while opening a large folder at the podium. The experiential clears his throat and looks over the page for a moment and then reads to the onlookers. "The monthly mandates for personal contrivances are: remember to eat in the morning, remember all bodies are not to be kept near food supplies, remember to tend the crops each day, and remember to look for Indilep's call for militia or those of other off island non-political opportunities. Hair should be kept at shoulder length and roads should be free of weaponry or dry goods." The experiential walking to the front quarter center of the platform; puts an Ignis flag on the podium. The man then commences with entering his horse drawn wagon and departing the village. The two warriors looking at the mud tracks, the horse carriage make and watch them extending to the northern hills. A blueberry bush standing between the two men cause a side glance observation from each of the men. Each warrior looks at the other and then the bush. Each in turn grabs a few of the messy sweet morsels for their mouths. In a brief few seconds, the eating increases. In a few more seconds, the warriors are each ripping the branches off the bush. They are hungry. There concentration only gets a momentary cessation at the sight of a man in an all grey jogging suit crossing the dirt path in front. The left standing warrior looks at the other, "The Fog!" The other warrior shrugs and keeps eating.

The east coast of Ignis is filled with a group of protectors sent from the ruling class of Ignis. The warriors collect crops and fish for independent means and the individual identities on Scio make for antagonistic social interactions. The protectors keep the peace, as a middle class of Ignis, under the authority of the experientials, the highest caste to the north.

Experientials ride to both sides of Ignis and visit the poets of the western seaboard. The poetic culture seems quite unusual as with thousands of residents, almost none say a single word. The experientials take the silence of the poets as a sort of subtle protest against Indilep but regard the western peace as quite enamoring. The fact neither the warriors nor protectors cause the poets much disturbance is a modern miracle of the island. Some say the poets don't work but they gather and build as productive as any of the islands and in some cases more.

Ignis is ruled based on a caste system and the leader of the island is a man with the family name, "Indilep." The ruling elite live in a separate colony to the north of the island, guarded with woods and mountains. Food is plentiful on Ignis, so people tend to mostly solitary affairs.

Indilep's family has ruled Ignis for as long as most of the other islands can remember and much longer than Tantamount. Some believe the split between the Poets and Warriors was a result of a massive battle leading to Indilep's Family Ascendancy.

Flashback:

The central road dividing the two halfs of Ignis is known as the chimney and was over a thousand years ago the sight of a great war. Ignis society is clan based and the east and west are divided into an eastern alliance and a western alliance. The eastern alliance feuds with the west over fishing revenues and the result is both sides planting huge self-sustaining crops and orchards. The profits sag on the island with the overabundance of supply and each side blames the other for the Ignis economy. The chimney, the great north-south highway, is based in a valley between two very long and straight mountains. In the day of the war, the mountains didn't exist. The chimney was along a flat path and the exact point of contact for the eastern and western alliance. The warriors were nobility and rode astride on huge horses with long lances. Each side paraded colors on their horse leads and followed a disciplined training.

Both sides declared their refusal to yield. This distinguishment of pride reached even to the bugler and drummer. On a dry warm day, the economic feud turned into the center of the island. The two sides fought. The battle raged for months and almost looked as if there wouldn't be a resident left on the island. One man hit the ground, another fought in their stead. The very large food supplies kept fueling the battle when most others would have seised. The legend goes when there were only 60 men and women left on each side, Indilep's family attacked. The Indileps didn't attack with weapons, they attacked with chains. Many soldiers lost their life clamping the enemy to the ground. Once in chains, the Indileps tasked the shackled soldiers with burying each and every body on the field. The result was the two long rock formations on either side of the chimney. The half-exhausted and half-dead troops were allowed their half of the island with the provision Indilep's family controlled the northern tier of the island. Many visitors to Ignis believe the shackled soldiers were the poets. Indeed the shackled soldiers were the eastern warriors. Over many generations Indilep's family grew in distrust of their western allies and disbanded the western alliance. The poets resulted, as the Indileps were always harder on those loyal to them and all of them were quite intelligent. The Indilep family put into place the current caste system as a way of maintaining maximum freedom with maximum control.

On this day, word of the Triton mission to Scio has leaked and Indilep addresses' his experientials in the matter. The voice of Indilep echoes through a great hall of brick stone architecture and an enormous fire place, leaving his experientials working on a long black table with fixed black leather seats. A small breeze usurps the enormous parabolic doors at the entranceway causing the fire to uproar. "The colony on Scio needs our governance, for one they are closer to us then any other island. Two," the face of Indilep grimaces, "The colony obviously needs to get rid of the southern island squabbles." Indilep's look turned from grimace to scoffing, as he steps toward the center of the great chamber. "Big Winged Dragoon Beasts fighting with wizards and humanoid cats, the strong hand of Ignis will calm the waters of any discontent on the outer islands." "What about self-governance. The Tritons always seem to push for self-governance," a very brave and weary experiential dares. Fire wells up in the eyes of Indilep, as the experiential speaks to another island's cause. Indilep regained his composure before speaking. "The Scions are great thinkers, we have poets on Ignis. The hand of Ignis should usher in a new era of peace on Scio." The brave experiential seeking to curry favor, offered a suggestion. "We already rule the north; we could engage the beasts and wizards in the south." "Not yet," Indilep replied. "We will push our advantage, once we clear them of Scio." "Do you think the Scions will object," the experiential chimed, finally wearing out his welcome. "Not the Scions, I am concerned with. I am concerned with our winged neighbors and their Angel's Guild," pacing Indilep considered his options. "The matter is of to much import. I will leave immediately for Scio and secure peace on the island before the Tritons put a foot in the matter. Move our reserve troops to the south of Ignis. We will strike when the iron is hot."

Indilep caught his royal caravan to the south, leaving the meeting hall empty. The large hall door remains open during Indilep's departure and the snow piling to the foot of the door housed a wall of experientials watching Indilep and their breath. Each of the experientials realized the northern mountains of Ignis were colder than the other islands. Each proceeded to managerial tasks with a slight shiver. "Cold... brrr."

The cold winds of the northern mountains lead to the vast chimney highway spanning the north-south route. Far in a grove on a western hill overlooking the highway a man sits on green grass and writes:

The Sun's Ecstasy

The Light which burns with all we meet
The Hand's not shook, the look so meek
Lead our lender on his race and bring to mind the higher keep
Kinder deeds are yet to do
And greater hands and feet still chew
For one day the wars will rend
When the poets conquer the last known end

As the man finished writing another man walked a near six inches from his position and neither man touched or acknowledged the other. They each had the look of a people staring directly into the sun.

The wind picks a flower seed and carries the seed to the central south. The air warms as the seed flies. The sparks of a fire mix with the traveling packet. Loud voices begin to rise from a slow hum to a crescendo of clamor. The voices then calm and relax in formation.

The Sixth Battalion of Ignis is considered to be the best fighting force in all the islands. The regiment wears Ignis red colors and has a special weapon, nickel plated swords. When wielded the sword is effortless and effective. The army itself carries an armor to protect them from their own weapons. Since, Ignis is a place of individual prowess, the army gathers recruits through contract and food rationing. The sixth army is an expeditionary force and holds station at the southern tip of Ignis. Over and Over again troops are told of the time when Scio was Ignis property. The leading general's name is Mecos and apart from Indilep there isn't a more determined man on the island. Each day, Mecos drills his lieutenants and puts together live fire tests of an invasion. The northern half of Scio is already under Ignis control. The word would have to come from Indilep for the invasion to begin. "Ready swords," a lieutenant issues.

"Ready," the troops respond. "Battalion advance," Mecos administered the order carried through a chain of lower officers. A dual flank advances on each other. Hundreds of Ignis troops whip searing lunges at the torso of the opposition. Each armament heats up with the fiery torches, in short combat the fire is tolerable. The armament leaves most of the soldiers in hand to hand combat. "Ready Battle Boats," the order again comes from Mecos to a serious of lieutenants. The very plain battle boats are floating barges with rowing oars. "Scio is only five miles offshore. Very close," Mecos tells his second. "Very close."

Chapter 4

Scio
"The Island of Knowledge"

True Knowledge comes from observing life in a way nobody ever has. In much the same way many scientists have observed fog and the way glare interacts with the fog. If you were to look at the Fog on some off Sunday morning. You might experience what could be called a loss of focus in your eyes. Most people dismiss the phenomenon but a rare group of people stay out of focus. Just when the fog looks a little off it will start to clear and an even smaller group of you will find yourselves on the island of Scio.

From the center of the island a large volcano jets out of the epicenter. The volcano is located near trees and grassy knowles. There aren't surrounding hills, only a surrounding crater with gradient increases toward the surface. The point of entry to the volcano reveals a large office complex stretching forty percent, the second half of the volcano. A man with an oversized cranium boards a flat flying panel with two air balloons and a propeller. He carries a box bound for the small archipelago of Scio, Emote. The wind picks up and hurries the man off the volcano. The only dirigibles in the seven islands are on the Island of Scio. Since, all the other islands were granted some innate physical quality; the grand thinkers of Scio had to rely on invention. Laboratories for all the physical sciences reside in the volcanoes heart and cubical buildings in modern structures form a grid pattern with streets made of unusual elements and with differing physical characteristics. Some city streets are slippery and propel fast sliding sleds while others have more texture and allow the inhabitants elastic walking surfaces. Scio has all the traits of great societies and yet does not overly complicate their lives with the many inventions, they discover. One and two person balloons with fan propellers, allow the islanders to travel around the far ends of the island. The large volcano in the center makes Scio, one of the interesting aerial views in the Seven Islands. Scio thinkers come in all shapes and sizes. Any question with regard to the physical world is answered on Scio. This is part of the reason Ignis, Cat's Wall, and Dragoon are always seeking control of the island. Ignis believes Scio would be a stepping stone to control of all the islands. Cat's Wall and Dragoon each believe Scio would give them an edge on the other. Scio is so named because its occupants have unusually large craniums. Since recorded time, the Scions have been held in esteem as knowledge keepers and some of the wisest people living in the islands of the fog.

Our story continues a little off Scio on Scio's protectorate 'Emote' with some unusual visitors on even more obfuscated business. Marcus and Magis, two of Tritons most aspiring Angels walked onto the precipice of the Temple of Emote. 'Emote' gets its name due to the reputations of the inhabitance as being too emotional for the strict intellectual business of the mainland. The Inhabitants of Emote became local experts on rare magical artifacts and the keepers of a time of many rare artifacts the bigger islands didn't want lost in any conflict. Marcus and Magis knew of the Wings of Triton being brought to the temple when even the Castle de Angelis was now in the dark. Marcus and Magis had a reputation of quick learning and secretive behavior.

The High keeper as he is known on emote is a man named Celebus. Celebus is the High keeper of the Temple, all artifacts are protected by a force shield, the source of which is a carefully guarded secret on emote. Only captain rider and the Angels guard their secrets as well. Marcus and Magis might have needed introduction but their chosen method of travel, shimmering, told Celebus of as much their station in life. The temple is a Romanesque marble business center with huge open spaces and many exhibits. "Oh Angels, I didn't think you would have returned so quickly for the wings." Marcus cautioned Magis from speaking; Magis knew Marcus's gestures and so stayed silent. "Of Course, I will need papers before I can release such a prize artifact." Again, Marcus gestured, this time Magis knew what he meant exactly. Magis left the room and opened the letter sender. Writing a quick note, he put the note in the letter sender. The Letter Sender itself is a curious artifact; some say that time is different on one side than the other. Some contend that time actually stands still for the sender and the recipient. In any event, Magis did not have to wait long for two official parchments. Carefully, he opens one with his name on it.

To Marcus and Magis:

The Angels Guild and the Triton Delegation were uninformed that the Wings of Triton still resided on Emote. Never mind that this is not your mission, find those Wings. Retrieve with this letter and one of you return with them, while the other continues the mission. You will both receive due recognition for this action.

Guild Archangel Spring Shine

Magis led the gathering into the grand hall, as the letter passed to Celebus. The entirely marble hallways bore a tan, white, and black distinction; the distinction being pervasive through the entire structure. "The wings are kept in a special exhibit room and I keep Trent busy, my lead guard with constant inspections. You will find the wings in order just there." Celebus pointed to a back inlet in the sides of a marble structure. The wings were encased in glass. Marcus was seeing the wings for the first time and squinted as he kept seeing a concentrated light touching the end of the wings and didn't fathom the location of the source. Magis, always the silent leader, touched Marcus on the shoulder as he stood in front of the pair of wings with a human frontal metallic hold. Celebus remarked, "There is only one magical item in all the seven islands, claiming to create an entire race." Celebus's eyes widened, "... magnificent."

East of the temple was the eastern shoreline an approach for Tantamount ships and the blending of routes, as outlined from Lucius. George was visibly fatigued from crossing over water for a long distance. Victoria was also an expert caretaker and she put down on the very edge of the coast of emote. "This is a small fishing village, on the eastern coast, called Past Time." The chancellor let Victoria know. Lucius flew off the whirly bird before George's Feet even hit the pavement. Within seconds, one could barely see Lucius on the horizon; a horizon with many rolling hills on a beautiful sky blue day.

"My turn at hospitality, little one," The chancellor winked at Victoria. Victoria smiled attentively. The elder statesman, righting his clothes gave Victoria the information," Just on the outskirt of <u>Past Time</u> is the manor of a retired Tantamount captain. Lawrence is his name but his fame being as Captain Skimmer." Robbins finds a walking stick on the side of the road and stabilizes his foot passage. Many similarities can be drawn between captain skimmer and captain rider, as they both went in search of lost artifacts. Only Captain Skimmer kept his activities above the sea floor. The chancellor briefed Victoria, on their brisk walk to the country mansion concerning his knowledge of the ship captain. The Chancellor and Victoria walking alongside a wooden fence in a picturesque path with farm crops and animals, they enjoy a congenial attitude, "We are old friends; he used to visit with my family estate on Triton." The chancellor caught Victoria's wondering eye viewing the grand expanse of nature. "Victoria, pay attention, there are very few friends who welcome you with open arms every time you see them. Lawrence is such a man and I leave an open invitation when he travels abroad, although he seldom does." Victoria gave a sly grin, "Does he have any really good artifacts?" "Some of the best, Victoria," the chancellor replied gesturing toward a running rabbit crossing a mud crevice in the road. "And if you are on your best behavior, he will show them to you."

The mansion looked on approach to be a massive plantation, only with no crops and a central structure made of Triton marble and oak wall seams. To the right of the mansion lumber stacks grew large and huge water barrels gave the plantation workers opportunity to stretch the lumber. "It looks as if there is somewhat of a lumber and shipbuilding operation going on," observing closely Robbins began reviewing all the great characteristics on the estate. "All the people of the estate wear strange purple uniforms with a marked on 'S' on their right sleeve in gold. All of the residents of the compound make Aristotelian bows and curtsies as they pass," Robbins gave an upward smirk, seeing his words come to life before his eyes. Victoria gave a cynical word considering the Tantamount reputations," If indeed Captain Skimmer is a pirate, he is one of the most aristocratic of his type." Robbins patted Victoria's hands down toward her side. The chancellor could have rang the doorbell, stepping on to the raised and covered rectangular platform. The door remained wide open to friends and plantation personnel. The butler wears a suede suit with many buckles and talks with an accent native to emote. With a wave of his hand, he ushers them to a sitting parlor, a very formal waiting room. "Little One, Lawrence is considered to be one of the wealthiest people on emote, so we must mind our manners." Victoria gave a check of her own feathers. Robbins also gave a look into Victoria's feathers. "Oh please, I'm fine," Victoria smiled with her usual aloofness and then sat on a side stone.

The chancellor being as important as he is and a good friend, Lawrence didn't keep them waiting long. The greeting consisting of a hug, with actual affection and a handshake with Victoria sitting on a pale white wooden entranceway step, Robbins got his hand palm up in Victoria's manners. "Getup and greet our host," the chancellor let his arm swing toward the door arch. "I hope this isn't too much trouble for you, Lawrence." Lawrence gave a somber emotionless expression with the words not expecting to his causes, "No, In fact, I haven't shown anyone new my estate in at least a year. I have a few new items from a recent visitor, maybe you have heard of him, Captain Rider." A blank look crossing the face of Lawrence's visitors gave them an escort through the home.

They started their tour by walking through a great hall with magnificent paintings and arms from all over. They then entered what Lawrence kept referring to as his war room. Victoria's Eyes caught a glimpse of a black bracelet at the entrance. Victoria anticipating little trouble, she began to pick up the bracelet. She started to but the bracelet of immobility is aptly named. The bracelet multiplies all over the wearer's body and in this case the bracelet pinned Victoria to the front wall. She squirmed first left and then right. The larger bracelets seeming to extend from the surface of the wall, gave an expansion in width and size reaching around Triton wings and skin. The bracelet is also unusually quiet, nobody heard Victoria scream. Only quiet reminiscing of old friends could be heard in the space.

Lucius on the other hand had quite an opposite feeling. Although, the wreckage of the northern wars on Scio became most evident on the scenery, peace had broken out in the northern tier. The view being commensurate with a rebuilding and revitalizing effort; the smiles of Scio shining like the dawn, as people everywhere rebuilt bridges, dams, and river-ways. Being confident of his approach, Lucius began his turn toward emote. "Just a half-a-day and we will have succeeded." No one heard his words, but a small house being rebuilt on a remote hill echoed his effectual charm.

Emote is rather another story. The trade routes are starting to catch up with recent events and more and more ships can be seen in villages across the emote perimeter. Lucius, approaches to the north end of emote; the ships diminish with only one gigantic fish emerging from the water. Was it a fish, too far to tell, he lowers his wings to rendezvous with his compatriots.

"They are not just going to give us the wings," Captain Rider asserts. Rider could have entered the front of the temple for them but the window for the wings being at the temple became slimmer and he wasn't sure the next time an angelic magical item of such magnitude would be within his grasp. The quartermaster of his ship snapped to and opened the weapons locker, "Which ones, sir?" Rider's arsenal looked comparable to a small village starting a large war. "Stealth is our best option, Dragoon's tail for each of the landing party and for me the weed sword." The dragoons tail were small guns that fired stunning barbs akin to dragoons themselves, the barb would render any victim unconscious for 24-48 hours. As for the weed sword, the sword is a very strong make which rendered the wielder a shadowy obfuscation as long as he/she maintained a grip on it. The weed sword is a more recent addition to rider's treasure and had come from an abandoned underwater settlement.

Victoria likewise understood feeling abandoned; Alert, Awake, and yet somehow invisible to the two men who now began talking about tea and the parlor. She still was a Triton and like all little Tritons learn, one must use your muscles before you can walk or fly. "Tap, Tap, Tap," She could just make the edge of her wing flutter slightly against the edge of the wall. She wondered if the sound seemed louder to her then the chancellor and the captain. "Tap, Tap, Tap," She did find the more she relaxed, the more the noise could be heard, and the more she tightened, the more frustrated she became. Calmly she fluttered and after a minute, she could see the chancellor react. "Do you have a window hanging against the house or something?" "Oh No," replied the captain. "Must be the birds, let me show you my collection, they are quite rare and quite exquisite." By Now she was banging so hard, her wing tips started to bleed, ever so slightly they dampened the sound. The Chancellor was the first to notice. "Oh my dear!" he scrambled to her with a crude sort of knife, that he carried with him. "Chopping and dicing will do you no good," added the captain. "The Bracelet of Immobility only works with a magic word." Robbins circled his hands many times over in a loop. Quickening his regard while Lawrence gave a look of calm, "What magic word, hurry," the chancellor begged. Victoria realizing the chancellor did care for her; she stopped tapping and stood still. "Well, come on, come on," urged the chancellor. Lawrence put a finger across his chin, "Please, the magic word is please." Almost as soon as the captain uttered the phrase, she was just wearing one bracelet which she quickly removed and placed in it's stand. Talking only to the bracelet, she scolded, "Sarcastic Bracelet." Lawrence waving his arm from the group felt on continuation, "The bracelet isn't the only magical item in the house, best to watch your step." The captains warning seemed ominous to Victoria and as for the house, more enchanting then ever.

The approach to the temple was treacherous, guarded by high cliffs and dwellings. John was the first to lookup, "Is this really necessary?" "Necessary, if we want to escape detection," Rider gave a concerted look in a relative direction. Flink led the way; he climbed the first rock, then the second rock, then the landing and wound his way to the top. Hanz was fastening rope links when his jaw dropped. There stood Flink right beside the temple wall. "Who knew he could climb?" "I did," motioned rider to the log book. "Always hand pick your men, you may be surprised." "Well, he should have taken the rope then!" All of Hanz words fell on deaf ears, as the crew made Flink a little less self-assured. One by one, each of them climbed steadily and swift. Still they were all at least a minute slower then the soul of the crew, Flink.

The crew measuring each foot and hand hold toward the summit; they were having silent accompaniment, watching Flink from the sky. Lucius began having trouble locating Captain Skimmer's Estate. Recent times had taught him to look smaller then expected, the thing, he was overlooking is the grandest manor on the island. Out of the fade of his left wing, he caught the 'S' of one of the laborers. Swooping down, he became quite a site to the wingless inhabitants. Most Tritons didn't exercise their wings on emote. Lucius eyeing his placement while tracing the sky to ground with his stomach. The swooping through sparse, protective foliage kept the hapless people unaware with his imminent approach. Now a little way from his rendezvous and enjoying his fly, Lucius kept low to ground cover. The wings snapping and the suction blowing, the doors gave to reverse pressure. The Butler feeling the inward pull of the air, he became astonished but welcoming. He knew to expect Lucius. Lucius, he was always about the mission. The butler stood toward the left of the entrance hall and gave a wave toward the main hall. Lucius barely gave the butler a look of recognition and put his feet toward the approaching granite and marble with his wing tightening for theatrics. The elongation of the hall has a clean sparkling floor with many pictures and murals. The messenger gave retreat to his wondering feelings and gave an ear toward the rooms in the distance. Lucius marinating a perfect focus almost stood at stand still for a grand bronze statue on his right. The statue showed an angel and a man fighting over a rock. Lucius saw in the statue something new or familiar. The Triton gave his step only momentary pause and soon heard voices in a room on his upper left.

Victoria sitting and laughing in shock and relaxation got a calming impression and sat rejoicing while pouring tea with skimmer and the chancellor. The messenger's entrance being less theatrical then his entrance of the mansion, he chose access through the right of wood double doors with ivy designs. Lucius without even a nod in the host's location, an out facing sitting chair, begins a whisper in the chancellor's ear on entrance to the room. So intent on informing the chancellor, he didn't notice both Tritons had lost their wings. "Isn't it wonderful," Victoria said to Lucius since leaning toward a cushion in her seat. "Isn't what wonderful? . . . oh (noticing the lack of wings) ... oh..... NO! . . . what happened to you?" "So you are human after all," Captain Skimmer inputting from a near chair while getting biscuits on his plate. Victoria found persistence continuing toward Lucius from her chair, "Captain Skimmer gave us these robes which make our wings disappear, temporarily of course, still I never realized how light I could be without them." "Wouldn't you agree," Skimmer asserted. Victoria stood for a right and left twisting pose. Lucius finding the events all overwhelming; he shrugged off skimmers offer for similar treatment. "A Triton is not a Triton without his wings, thanks anyway."

"Do Tritons eat," Skimmer added with more sarcasm. Lucius didn't give ground to the captain's attitude. "When time permits, where are we exactly?" Lucius slowing his breathing brought himself calm. "We are in my parlor, the gateway between my magical artifacts and my historical antiques. I was just telling the chancellor, how wonderful this side of emote is..." Lawrence's head moving sideways with a bite of a biscuit," the north end usually has relaxed commerce and the towns' people treat me quite well." "We can stay the night," Lucius was not in command but he was beginning to learn the nature of the other two. 'Keeping a peace mission on Scio, peaceful, was as important as getting there,' Lucius reluctantly conceded to himself.

Flink was starting to get his militaristic airs on the emote mount. By the time the others had made the wall, he was scouting the entrance to the temple. Hanz signaled to Rider, "Where does he get his enthusiasm from?" "I'll take a dozen more, let's make this quick." Rider didn't slow his pace for chit-chat. There weren't usually many guards toward nightfall, still rider instructed his men to knock out the guards and wait at the temple's half-divide. The divide was the name for the sections of the coliseum structure known as the temple. They didn't have to go far; rider knew if the wings were here, they would be exhibited in the back divide of the building. No Sooner did the group enter then the walls sealed in around them. Celebus always alarmed divides, even empty ones. John never knew Rider to fail and so broached the Captain, "We can either fight our way out or do you have another idea?" "Whatever did happen to the wings we won't learn by force," Rider quietly indicated. "Instruct your men to keep their ears open, I'll follow to get you. Gripping the sword, the captain faded from view. Watching... all the time watching and observing. Nightfall came quickly, as Celebus came to claim his prize. He was always particularly proud of his security precautions. Magis accompanied Celebus and the temple security to round up Rider's Crew. Rider knew of his own popularity on Tantamount but he was well known about all the islands and, at least his crew, were usually recognizable. In any Event, Celebus did not wait for Rider; he took the lot of people to a more permanent holding cell in the basement. Rider's Eyes were mostly focused on Magis, Emoten Security is one thing, and Angel's magic another. Rider had one advantage, no one observed his presence. Magis raised his hand and began to chant, "Oh

No!" Rider said under his voice. Celebus grabbed at the Angel, "We'll wait till later, my security should be enough for now." Rider wondered why Celebus would stop an angel from helping; then again the Emotens were a fickle bunch. Rider saw his opportunity to get his crew out and he took it.

Morning came quickly on captain skimmer's estate, no one noticed. Victoria became quite fascinated with the prospect of not having wings. Lucius just withheld his disgust. He wanted to keep the groups path to Scio clear, so he pressed the others to the door. Captain Skimmer took the chance to be ingratiating," Victoria, you can keep the robe. You never know when not being a Triton may be useful. Here, I've got a few more fresh ones, so you will all have one." Skimmer shot a very lost glance at Lucius. "I also have quite enough of them," skimmer managed with an explanation. Victoria marked his retraction and smiled in appreciation. The Chancellor shook hands with his long time friend, "Til we meet again, the doors always open to you." "Likewise," came the chancellor's remark. The Group parted ready to face the day. As for George, the winged bird was similarly having a peaceful exit. The country had remained as Lucius had seen only the night before. George was on his fastest pace for the entire trip and the group would reach their destination before lunch.

"Chancellor," Victoria queried. "Do you think the war is going to end soon. . .? I am not really sure, I understood what they were fighting about." "Well, my dear," he said with an authoritative yet tactful mood. "The Island of Scio has always been a protectorate of one of the larger islands, and with so much history, several of the islands felt entitled to ownership. If the war goes on, most likely the Island will split but fortunately, we may be able to broker a peace which will allow Scio self-governance." "The Southern Islands are particularly difficult," he went on hitting a stride. "So all fighting must come to an end if Scio can exist." "I hope you succeed, chancellor," Victoria's naïve eyes gave comfort and fortitude to the old man. "Me too, Victoria, me too."

Reaching to the key holder, Rider grabbed at the keys. Rider had only let the guard sleep for fifteen minutes, he knew another fifteen; might see the guard awake again. Barely touching the tumblers in the lock, his motions ebbed and flowed with the breath of the sleeping guard. The noise of metal on metal made a discord and all held their breath until the guard's exhale. Tenuously, the gate creaked open; all tip-toed out. Rider took his grip off of the sword to reassure his crew. When all surrounded him, the group grabbed onto the sword, with the sheath covering the blade. Rider held the center of the sword. The party vanished quietly and quickly. Flink barely missed a stool at the edge of the door. The captain pondered why Celebus even gave Rider's crew the opportunity, too coincidental for his liking but the exploit made him smile anyway.

The journey to the ship became uneventful as even with the wars, security on emote was never very high. The crew settled into the ship and just as all had reached their bunks, a bell rang signaling the start of a new ship day. Another miscalculation, did not serve to make Rider's Reputation with his crew as laudable, as usual. The morning meeting, he hoped would. All officers were assembled in a meeting room to discuss the re-acclamation of the target. "Well what do we know, John?" Rider questioned his first mate. "We know the wings are not in the temple." "Correct," Rider bolstered. "Given the Presence of an Angel, we must assume Triton has regained control of them; which leaves us two options. Continue to search for plunder on the southern banks or head for Triton. Flink found himself passing the officers meeting and slowed to hear a word or two. Under his breath Flink could barely muttle, "I Never knew the captain to miss a target."

John and Robert started in with a little hesitation, "The Southern Banks!" "No," replied the Captain. "Triton then," Hanz found his voice with representation. "No, Hanz." Rider pushed follow through in his double speak, "I set forth to make the Long Shadow of the Deep, the foremost underwater artifact salvage vessel. Gentleman, I mean to keep to my agenda. "Set a Course for Dragoon, I don't mean to miss a second time." Flink hurried down a side passage with a renewed sense of pride.

"As for the wings," Hanz put forth. "The Wings ... The Wings... (the captain feigned stumbling) ... Why were the wings on emote? Why would an Island display their most important artifact on an island riddled with war and usurpation?" John felt a more honest twinge toward the captain, "No Idea, Sir." "Politics, "The captain continued. "Politics, my friend, Triton and Scio have a long history of cooperation and I believe those beating wings aren't the last sign of Tritons on Scio." "You think they mean to take the island?" logical as an engineman is, Robert rarely interrupted. "No, Robert, as much as the Islanders might prefer Triton control, the other islands would not bear it, especially Ignis. Mark my words, we will see more than a few Angels on our journey, more than the southern coasts are accustomed to and I mean to capture one. "Capture an Angel," John could barely express more than astonishment. Robert being more technically minded posed the obvious question, "What about the Shimmer?" "We are heading to just off the coast of dragoon, I think our next artifact might help to answer your question. We will obtain the atmosphere from Subsa. "What's an atmosphere?" Hanz really didn't know. "Not an Atmosphere, the Atmosphere. A long time ago, dragoon and Triton went to war over Tantamount. The Only chance the Dragoons had to stop the Angels was the famed <u>Atmosphere of Dragoon</u>." "I recall the tale captain but wasn't the atmosphere lost." The captain knew much more than the crew in these matters and put himself at ease. "I recovered a scroll which seemed to indicate a certain race of sea creatures who live off the coast seized the atmosphere to stave off war on the seas. "No doubt a deal brokered by one of our forefathers, "Hanz interrupted. "When recovered, the atmosphere will allow us to block the angel's power but only for a certain radius. So we are going to have to be sure, before we use it. In any event, the hunt is still on." Rider dismissed his officers and took the helm himself.

The grand parity like the chancellor met on a mountain top. However, unlike Triton, Scio had only one, right at the center. A desolate volcano made the perfect place to build the largest think tank on Scio. Many a visitor to the island journeyed just to see the marvelous volcano. The volcano is home to many of the strange experiments of the Scions such as something mystical called a helicopter. Labs dotted and filled the black conical mount. George set down and was held in a cave just off the volcano. The blackened rocky exterior turned steely and plated in the plasticized compound interior. Victoria was feeling her wings again and began to circle the great volcano before her duties commenced.

"Lucius," the chancellor beckoned. "Try to keep Victoria out of trouble while I meet with the grand parity. I know this is outside of your duties but the only wing print we need to leave is in that building." The Chancellor pointed to the cylindrical structure jutting out of the middle of the volcano. "Understood Chancellor," Lucius responded. Robbins began his lone drift toward the volcanoes center. The volcanoes central hall mirrored almost perfectly the current state of affairs on Scio. The representatives were arguing in fierce discussions while the Grand Parity and the viceroy of the Largest Island, Ignis, sat in quiet discussion. "Ah, Chancellor Robbins, have you met the viceroy, Indilep." "No, I haven't had the pleasure, nice to meet you." Indilep exchanged frustrated looks with the chancellor. "They always call on us as the wise decision makers," the Grand Parity addressed the threesome. "But we know Tritons have a long history of settling disputes." Robbins followed the tumble of his hand forward "I am honored to be here," Robbins curtly stated. In such situations, He knew listening would help more than talking. Indilep had some discomfort but appeared amicable to the meeting. "Ignis, of course is very proud of how the northern shore is coming along, we feel certain the southern shore will follow suit." Robbins was decidedly questionable about Ignis occupation of the northern shore and more so of the southern shore disputes. "Well, I can't begin here where there is little trouble, If you gentleman will excuse me, I have some work to do." Pressing his way forward, he set out to meet the now arguing delegates of the southern shore. Dragoon was a little larger island then Cat's Wall but both Islands were equally fierce. Dragoon was a dark land filled with pre-historic creatures; while Cat's Wall had some mythical creatures but mostly Shiny Headed Wizards of an indeterminately long tradition and a race of humanoid cats. Equally different are their points of view on Scio. The Dragoons who were dragon like humanoid beasts believed their destiny resided in ruling Scio. The Wizard's of Cat's Wall believed them selves direct descendants of Scio and took stake in preserving their ancestral home. As many who had come before Chancellor Robbins, there was more room in the wizards' argument then in the dragoons'. Yet, Years of Diplomacy had hardened the wizards against arguments. Still both sides expected the Tritons to talk to Wizard Melmo first and so he did. Broaching the red haze between the diplomats, Robbins felt the pressure overcoming them. "All Ancestral Homes must be revered," Robbins interjected. If there was one common mentality to Wizards and Dragoons, it was a weary eye to the winged-people of Triton. The Wizard's believed, they were a fanciful magical race to be respected. The Dragoons believed them to be a link between Dragoons and the more humanoid races. Still, An Ancient War raged between Triton and Dragoon and all diplomacy was suspect. "Yes," Melmo finally responded, combing his shiny hair with his hand. "We above all dislike the war but we cannot permit more dragoon incursions." Turning now to the Dragoon Representative, "Any Prize worth having must be worth having." Chancellor Robbins was well versed on both perspectives which gave him a chance at brokering peace. The Dragoon representative was a man named Kur and he was unusually likeable considering his somewhat gruff race. The half dragon and half man race were double the size of any other humanoid race. "The Dispute started with the actions of a Southern Wizard, we at Dragoon are taking the necessary steps to insure the southern shores prosperity." Kur had stretched his speaking ability to the limit as dragoons only spoke in symbols and grunts. The Dragon man even seemed weary. "Of Course," Robbins stated while listening. "We will not stop until the town of point rock is ours, so no further wizard disruptions can cause problems." Kur seemed to be reciting the second leg from memory as he was a close associate to the ruler of dragoon, NEA. NEA has a great capacity for speech. Despite Melmo's Anger, he let Robbins continue. "Then Point Rock is where we will start," Robbins shined in diplomatic flare. "If Point Rock is the issue then we can agree to stop all fighting outside of point rock." "Agreed," he stated, usurping the power of the dispute. If both men were going to have peace, each wanted to be first, so all three repeated at the same time, "Agreed." Robbins also knew diplomacy took time, so he settled on peace outside of point rock and the three would continue discussions tomorrow. Indilep seeing such quick agreement was put off but Tumult felt a pride at having chosen the right diplomat. Both Men stood in Awe. "What did you say?" Indilep insisted. "As of right now, all fighting will stop on the southern shore, except for point rock." Robbins was acutely aware, he ignored the ruler of Ignis. The humans of Ignis were a little jealous of the wise ways of Triton but all would benefit from the two outer islands cessation of hostility. The Grand Parity spoke first to Robbins and then to all. "We have prepared quarters for all diplomats. If there are any further needs, please feel free to consult with me or any of my envoys. With Tumult's words commenced the day's discussions. The fading of a shimmer could be seen just outside the hall.

Lucius was the only one to notice the shimmer. Messengers could sense angels but found like all important information; was to be protected. Lucius ran up the side hall just in time to see the chancellor. "Victoria is caring for George in his nest. Shall I stay with her?" "No," the chancellor stopped. "You and Victoria have been given quarters next to mine, tell Victoria to tie George up and join us for dinner." "At Once," the messenger replied. Lucius didn't speak of the Angel but his curiosity saw him down the same hall.

Magis was the one with view, this time. He sat atop the large volcano, sensing the satisfaction in the completion of his duties thus far. "Now, to write to Marcus..." He noticed that his old friend had arrived more quickly then others would have expected. On the other-side of the Letter sender was Marcus. Marcus was a quicker writer then Magis and being at a desk, as opposed to a volcano, helped.

To Magis:

> The Wings have been secured and the Arch Angel has installed around the clock security. He feels an eminent threat. He wants us to head to the Island of Dragoon and meet a wizard named Pembridge. He says Pembridge might have a more permanent protection spell for the wings. We are to meet Pembridge and bring him to Triton. I will meet you at a harbor town called Inswala. I will be at the main ship docks. Please be careful, Dragoon is not the safest place for Angels.

Your friend Marcus

Magis would fly the trip but only after he shimmered as far as the shoreline. The practice of having no one be aware of your movements is part of the training at Castle de Angelis.

Victoria had found Scio quite different then she remembered. She had been to Scio, only once before and found it a confusing place with all the outer islands represented in rather intense amounts. She didn't care much for the locals but Scio was a rather beautiful Island and with moderate amounts of Tritons, her wings still made her somewhat recognizable. She had also never seen all these laboratories on the side of the volcano.

Victoria saw the men in white coats building weird looking devices, on a side overhang of one of the laboratories, seemed a very serious place.

Coming in for her landing, she eyed Lucius impatiently waiting. Rare for him, he usually had a lot of patience for non-messenger tasks. "Are you ready for dinner?" "Quite," she responded. Tapping her wings, he smiled. "They work quite well, don't they," the chagrin caused a mutual smirk, on entrance to the volcano.

All of the representatives were at dinner, although diplomatic discussions were strictly prohibited at meal times. Melmo's dinner cloak was the subject of much whispering dialogue. The hooded cape had a star with a magical cat on a mountain top. The Wizard Melmo also represented a humanoid cat race on Cat's Wall and he had to make a show for the pride of the Island. The Only other astonishing affair was the live eating of raw fish by Kur. If you have never seen a dragoon eat, then you will quickly realize, table manners are not their forte. In Fact, Victoria and Lucius took in the scene with much compunction being the only non-delegates in attendance.

Of course before Lucius could stop her, "I'm having a lot of fun," Victoria burst forth. "Are we going to see the great caverns on Scio, I hear they have hidden secrets and treasures." "We are not on a site seeing tour, I'm afraid," Robbins was getting good at easing Victoria's Enthusiasm. "My Dear, we are hear for business." "Triton, just north of Tantamount," Melmo interjected. Lucius ignoring the jibe deciding to test the waters with Kur. "Have you been here long Chancellor Kur?" Not much dialogue followed as Dragoons were very focused eaters and a mere grunt of recognition could be heard. Indilep saw his opening, "We are all grateful to have your delegation chancellor Robbins, perhaps you would consider a trip to Ignis on your return." "Perhaps, the great fortune of our trip so far is more than we could have hoped for." The chancellor knew Ignis as one of the older of the islands holding much clout in Scio's fate, besides being a near neighbor to Triton. "I imagine we will see our trip to its conclusion and then think about other visits." The chancellor marked his words, realizing he held peace at arm's length. Turning to Victoria, "Have you had the deserts on Scio, fish cream is by far one of the most under rated of exotic desserts. "I'll try," Victoria stated reticently but with the first mouthful, she was starting to outpace Kur. The hall went silence with the eating of the group and the night appearing through a spherical opening.

Three Triton women travel with feet sliding on a slippery street with fast moving air cars, as the sun diffuses light across the volcano. The underside of each car is propelled forward through steam conveyance generated from the volcano. All of the very official looking women carry safety glasses and important papers. "Our lab is producing a substance to hold any material together." The lead Triton woman spoke. "Our lab is ahead of schedule, of all the other island designs," spoke a second. The last Triton women grimaced and looked at her work. The Triton wings made a low flying airfoil moving in and out of air cars and balloon boards. The light of their wings reflected up and contacted the eyes of Lucius.

The morning saw Lucius alone, watching the sunrise. Smoke slowly rose from the southern quadrant and Lucius with little work, again reflected on his wings. Quickly having a second thought, Lucius stood on his feet and walked to where George was nesting. He gave Victoria a break and cared for George, himself.

The chancellor's work was much less solitary and overnight a deal was struck by Indilep, not wanting to be outdone by the chancellor of a mere mountain on Triton. The Grand Parity consented to Indilep's Deal and the Chancellor spent the morning ironing out the details. According to the agreement struck, the hostilities would be completely stopped, pending the approval of both cat's wall and dragoon. The pact called for the Chancellor and all the delegates to meet on Dragoon and then Cat's Wall. The Document would be signed and witnessed on both islands before proceeding to Scio for preservation and enforcement. The overnight opportunity meant the Chancellor's trip was far from over and he considered if maybe a trip to Ignis would be a good idea.

Chapter 5

Subsa
"The City of Weeds"

Have you ever fallen in fog? A Quite unusual experience, especially, with a friend. The Closest two people of sharp vision can get without one being able to see the other. On Certain mornings ground fog can be, as thick. For a party, near a waterfront or pond, the situation can be more treacherous. Strictly speaking there is no land entrance to Subsa. Falling down in a fog, near a pond or a lake, one may in fact arrive at the underwater docking facilities of a vast below sea cave. Rider and his crew are probably more familiar with the Weed City than most. Tantamount trading vessels never entered, they just traded from a docking station moored in the middle of the vast sea between Tantamount and Dragoon. The Long Shadow is an underwater ship and as such was allowed the grandeur of a site thought myth by most of the islands' populations.

Subsa has no sea protection but the innate caves; which house the residents; and required each to have extremely adroit night vision. The light could only penetrate for the first forty feet on the path to Subsa and little beyond. "Captain Rider and the Long Shadow of the Deep... are requesting permission to dock on Subsa soil?" A pause was followed with a very static, "OK." Neither the submarine nor the city had radios. The side of rider's dock had a place to communicate before entering the city. Rider had to ask permission of the mooring captain, a kind of unofficial title of the weed in charge of trade with the islanders. Many giant sea horses and eels slowed or stopped at the coming of the Long Shadow. Even to the Weeds or maybe especially to the weeds, the long shadow was a quite formidable ship.

The site of the weeds ability to breathe under and above water was amazing enough for new crew members. The crew sat in awe of the magnificent city dome and peered through the side window at each Sea horse passing. Some wanted to see where the famous Subsa Weed Ale was made, others wanted to know the diet of the weeds, and a few of the crew believed the Long Shadow was built in Subsa. All rumors and talk, yet the ship was as excited as the captain about the business of the day.

The dock was an exact fit for the Long Shadow and entrance to the caves never was a long affair. Rider plowed through the muck and mire to make his entrance. "Don't the bilge pumps still work?" "At once Captain Rider," answered a shin named branch. The Shin are a very fast sloth looking race from dragoon. Branch was a retired old shin and was slower than most of his brethren. Rider found a use for him as docking attendant to his personal dock. The Shin's Pay was tied to docking fees and they very rarely, if ever saw each other. The Bilge Pumps were a remarkable idea from Rider himself; the pumps immediately evacuate any excess water to a buoy above the dock. The dock itself was steel reinforced, again drawing question as to his access to metal. In any event, the dock was able to withstand high external and internal stresses.

Rider was himself a celebrity in Subsa due to his vessel and already famous collection of artifacts. In addition to the weed sword, he had a less palatable item to the weeds themselves, known as the eye of weed. They were in actuality not even artifacts but rather inventions of a Scion captain who conducted underwater trading with the weeds. The Eye of Weed were glasses allowing the user to not see a dark damp cave but rather akin to the vision the weeds themselves possessed. Flink looked particularly silly as he always had trouble keeping his glasses on. The famed beauty of Weed Females also occupied the mind of the crew.

Rider had a more focused outlook, seeing as he was going to get the atmosphere from a highly political hold. Hanz secured the dock connection personally and informed the crew of their duties to civility and representing the pride of the Long Shadow. When all were prepped, a way was made for the captain to lead them. And he did.

The cave system was lit with a phosphorescent algae which was magnified by the retinal focus of the glasses. Other than the damp mildew smell, Subsa was like most large cities with an enormous population. Some might say close to a million. The Shear Size of some of the Subsa meeting houses boggled the imagination. Subsa had great malls where the latest fashion in scale wear was advertised.

Weeds having the ability to breathe above and below water meant they prospered from the many minerals and plentiful food supply of the sea. The actual taste of weeds varied from live fish to raw oysters, to those fascinated with cooking and even many of the land delicacies, such as cattle or lamb. The weeds grew mushrooms and spices underground and had discovered some of the best fragrances come from the island waters. The Sea also provided Subsa armies with toxins for weapons and giant sea horses and eels for reliable transport.

Subsa was built on steam vents from underground fissures. The feeling was always like being on the grounds of an indoor swimming pool. Over the years, the weeds mixed slightly but only with those who could function in Subsa society. The diversity consisted of Tantamount Traders, Wizards from Cat's Wall and the occasional Scion. Due to the natural air pocket created by the great city, the underbelly of the metropolis have waterways similar to city streets. Many seahorses drove carriages through the city streets. One could argue for the dominant sophistication of the society, creating the larger mystery as to their massive seclusion. Weeds were so rarely seen on some islands that they reverted to myth. One reason might be the many underwater sports and advanced forms of luminescent entertainment, which kept them proud of the Subsa Standard.

Rider knew of the Subsa Standard and took the advanced precaution of occupying his crews time with trading from the cargo hold and ships maintenance. Since Rider owned the docking port, he had some of the crew review the docking records. Any free time the crew were given was on a deadline and based on each man's time with the ship.

Rider set upon his task hailing, taking with him John and a very unusual looking luggage carrier. The taxi was a very fancy floating stage coach led by two sea horses. Currencies' varied in Subsa and sometimes one could get by with a net full of fish.

Subsa neighborhoods were segregated for islanders. At the same time as Riders trip, A Wizard named Pembridge was preparing potions only a few streets away. Pembridge's fame was as a dark wizard but in fact he involved himself with the very highest rungs of island society and even with higher rungs of experimental wizardry. His one assistant was a humanoid cat named Herbert. "No, not the lizard's tale, the swordfish spleen." Herbert was far from a good wizard's assistant and one could see their relationship was mostly one of companionship. Herbert was one of the few humanoid cats who enjoyed water and he took every opportunity to participate in Subsa sports. The Cat had quite a reputation as a water volleyball player. His demeanor remained somewhat servile toward Pembridge, not allowing his celebrity to go to his head. When asked about sports, Herbert's reply was always, "I enjoy the game."

"What is the potion for, if I may ask?" "Herbert, the potion is for us. We will need some protection on our journey; our mission is of the highest diplomatic importance. We cannot be stopped on Dragoon. Trust me, the Scions themselves would admire the shield potion and we only need the effects to last twenty-four hours." "So, we are going to Scio?" Herbert followed the Wizard's Adventures accurately. "No, my friend, we are going to a more important island." "Now make sure all our possessions are secure. I may need to spend the afternoon bartering for passage."

At roughly the same time Herbert was packing their belongings, Rider's Sea Carriage arrived at the Scuffle Center. The Scuffle Center was an administrative body in charge of dealing with magical situations, which may arise in Subsa or for any Subsa traders. The Magical Hand of the Subsa Shell, The Center had been in operation since," The Great Peace over the Sea," which was the so called effect of seizing the atmosphere. "If they have a whole governmental center built around your atmosphere, why do you think they will just hand it over." John was looking for some direction. "Do you think the wings are going to be any easier to obtain, the luggage carrier is our first step, let me worry about the details."

Scores of Weeds were always entering and leaving the Scuffle Center. The Scuffle Center itself carried a museum of artifacts and a history of great magical conflicts, as seen from the weed's perspective. The Building was ornately created by the mixing of large coral reefs and sea shells from the sea floor, making the Scuffle Center, one of the most eye catching of Subsa buildings.

"Can you tell me captain rider, why we are so blessed with your presence at this time?" A voice echoed from the back of a large meeting room filled with four officials and two guards. Rider entered the chambers of the top shelf of the scuffle center quarters, initially ignoring the voice coming at him. The room was a green marble walls with a black floor seats and table. Even for Rider, arranging such a meeting took planning. John actually wondered if Rider had planned the trip to Subsa before they set sail.

The magical blockade was a man named Quandor. He had his title because of his natural suspicion of all magic users, due to his actually having been a shin before being turned into a weed. In Subsa records there is actually no one who has ever been transformed into a weed and no magical text of any known knowledge was equal to the task. Quandor liked Captain Rider and others like him because they usually secured magical artifacts without him or his staff dirtying their hands with traveling or diplomacy.

"They're safer in my hands, what treats have you brought for us, Captain Rider?" Quandor was half sarcastic but always eager to take items off the market. "Actually no selling... How about a venture of astronomical proportions, beyond your wildest dreams?" Quandor just waited, not buying in to Rider's talk and waiting for substance.

Rider grabbed the far end of the table before allowing himself and his first-mate the chairs. "I'm here for the Atmosphere." The entire chamber went silent. Quandor immediately looked for any extraneous staff and dismissed them. "You want the Atmosphere? Not for good I presume." All in all, Rider's reputation was solid in Subsa. The Atmosphere was still an arm's length issue. "Correct, I only need to borrow the Atmosphere and as to the good of my possessing it, only time will tell." "Impossible!" You are speaking of an issue which resides slightly above my head, Mr. Rider." Suddenly, He was Mr. Rider. "I know the Subsa Council will defer to your good opinion. I have brought with me, my best magical wonders to keep the Subsa populace occupied in the absence of the atmosphere. I will only need the Atmosphere for a month, at most." "There is a larger issue here, Captain Rider." He was suddenly Captain Rider, again. Quandor inadvertently cleared his throat before speaking, "The Atmosphere is a magical item and presumably against only one race. We do not wish a problem with the flying people of the north." "You will have to rely on my discretion." "Ahh," came Quandor's suspicions. "There is the problem. The captain of a great ship such as <u>The Long Shadow of the Deep</u>, discretion is not the first thought to mind." "Well then if my assurance was given to the council to not bring the atmosphere to Triton would the council sit more comfortably?" "Indeed, captain rider." Quandor perused a paper in front of him revealing a vast array of items. The weed rippled his fingers across the table's surface in a recapture of command and then continued speaking, "We must also know why?" Rider made sure every eye caught his focus for his important words, "The Seventh Island." Rider's statement was enough to push the matter into over drive. Rider did not add anymore information and intrigue festered in the hearts and minds, even of the magical blockade. "I would need one further assurance, even knowing our long standing friendship." Rider was not even aware that he was considered a friend. "We need to know the Tritons will not be bothered and the Dragoons will not be involved." Rider was quick with a reply, "As to the second, most assuredly ... no Dragoons." "As to the first, well like you said there is only one race affected by the atmosphere." "Then Mr. Rider, I need your word Subsa will not regret a loan of this magnitude." "The word is Trust and the duration is one month," Rider's confidence was not counterfeit. Quandor reassured his own chest, "I will of course need a report of the atmosphere's use and any other magical artifacts involved, as well as a few extra trinkets to be granted on your return." "The least of our worries," Rider's energy beamed high and he stood with his first-mate. "Quandor, we need discretion to move the atmosphere, say tonight at close." "Okay, Captain Rider. One month and this information will have to be reported to the council." Captain Rider started to like having Quandor as a friend and wondered if retirement in Subsa might be an option. "Paul Tap," Quandor stated. "Paul Tap," Rider replied.

Captain Rider wasted no time in obtaining the atmosphere and recalling all of his crew. The long shadow set sail, figuratively having no actual sails. "Make ready a southwest heading," Rider shouted to the crew. John snapped to attention and made ready a course. "Flink, you are now on century duty, guard this box." Rider pointed to the ornamental package on the Long Shadow Dock. Flink, as did many of the crew, knew the package was important to the mission. In usual Flink Style, He resolved the box to a corner of the Long Shadow Hold and issued himself more weapons then were strictly sensible. Rider knew the box was, at least, safe on pain of Flink's life. A more comforting thought then many who saw Flink's behavior believed apparent.

Chapter 6

Dragoon
The Prehistoric Island

og sometimes gathers closer to tree-lines and bushes then anywhere else. In certain jungles there are breaks in the Fog around cave openings due to the cooler air mass. One Cave Entrance on a Fog driven day, may in fact lead you to Dragoon. The Island of Prehistoric Beasts holds more mythical creatures then any of the others and yet only two of them have advanced beyond survival behavior; the shin and the rulers of the island, Dragoons.

A misty fog rolls into a dock, next to a cave. The Tavern's on Dragoon are an eclectic mix of creatures. The bar maid, named Lily was in fact a sea creature, not a mermaid and not some sea mutation. She was a reflection of the famed beauty of weed females. Their skin color was a sort of aquamarine but their curves were an unearthly sense of sensuous. Lily only occupied a small space in the cave. Dragoons themselves had much girth so the Tavern was the size of a small warehouse. Another native to dragoon were the shin. Shin are sloth looking creatures with multiple legs, making them incredibly fast and near undetectable on the surface of dragoon. Wizards from Cat's Wall were becoming a more frequent sight in the bars, even with the wars. Both Wizards and Dragoons saw war as a proprietary activity and so could stand each other's company, except on battlefields. Dragoons were very secure in their dominance of the island and sometimes used a wizard or two to flaunt it.

The scenery was indeed cave like, with one wall connecting to the sounds of the sea. Most of the customers drank, washbe. Washbe was the mythical intoxicant brought to trade through the weeds. It's true origin was supposedly a plant growing at the bottom of the sea. Most of the Islanders had never seen the washbe plant collected and were suspect of it's strange intoxicating effects.

Two awkward dragoons sat on the far side of the bar, at an unusual side table; the table being suspended completely with clasps and a rod crossing in the diagonal center. "What are we waiting for?" Herbert asked his wizard friend. "Well, no one can see through our disguise, so the idea is to wait until we see who we are to meet." "How will we know?" Herbert was as full of questions, as Pembridge mystery. "Tritons are not a very common site on dragoon, we should be able to see them or feel them." "Feel Them?" Herbert announced. "Yes, Herbert, feel them, wizards aren't the only magical creatures." Herbert feeling particularly proud of his being a wizard's assistant decided to conjour a ball of light to illuminate the table. Pembridge grasped at his arms. "There aren't many dragoons who esteem magic and even fewer who practice. Give yourself some calm, and stay alert to who we are to meet."

As if the mere mention brought the two men into existence; Marcus and Magis strolled into the bar. Everyone from Lily to a motheater on the floor stopped in amazement. Not a single angel or Triton had set foot on dragoon since "The Great War", at least not officially. Marcus and Magis became the complete center of attention, the last place an angel wanted to be. Magis pulled out a scroll and read the words out loud," Twister Tongue by zone for candor font alone." Besides the Angels, only Pembridge would remember what actually happened. The Room began to swirl, as the minds of all in resident were wiped of the Angel's presence. When the swirling stopped, the pair were wingless at a table across from Pembridge. Pembridge put a drop of a potion in his and Herbert's goblet reverting them to original form. Pembridge and Herbert stood and moved tables.

"Mr. Pembridge is the scroll in your possession?" Magis began, already knowing to whom he was addressing. "Yes," Pembridge replied. "And they will remain so." Pembridge found the dragoon tables chaffing his pants. He adjusted his cloak. Herbert made an attempt to help the wizard and found his paw patted. After repositioning the seat, Pembridge looked the visitors in the eyes. "Very well, my consort and I have been instructed to bring you to the wings." "We are going to Triton then?" Marcus and Magis didn't forward an answer due to the approach of lily with drinks. The weed barkeep wore motheater fur in recognition of the island and carried a round tray. "Four washbes on the the house," lily put to the table. Magis waved lily from the table and then looked to Pembridge. "No, change of plans, we are going to Cat's Wall. An Emissary of the Arch Angel will be there guarding them." "And how will we travel?" Pembridge threw in. "The fastest way is flying although there are enough weed vessels or Tantamount ships to get us safely there. Marcus book us passage and we will leave immediately." Marcus made a quick dash out of the bar to make the arrangements. Magis led the wizard pair to an empty side passage of the cave. Pembridge had a lingering look at lily as the other two made a relaxed exit of the bar.

George spent the afternoon feasting on various lizards and crabs found in the dragoon woods. The Trees were the only non-prehistoric things on the island and the bird found the coolness of the island quite comforting.

Kur being as affable, as was possible for a dragoon, led the chancellor and his party to a meeting place on the coast facing Tantamount. The length was a mere mile from the bar where Marcus and Magis met Pembridge. A marked change had come over the traveller's temporary stay on Dragoon. For One, Lucius and the Chancellor had grown in trust of George's Obedience and Victoria with some respect for the island, showed a little more discretion. A few non-descript gestures seemed to keep Victoria from protocol disasters during her stay. The gestures nor the change in attitude were necessary on Victoria's Part, Dragoons did not prize the civil nature of the northern races. Kur's meeting place resembled a very large cave with a table. Occasionally, Kur would utilize the fireplace. A more cultured custom usually had visitors assume the dry temperate nature of the cave and enjoyed the boulder chairs. Boulder Chairs were known only to Kur and much of the reason he had advanced to a representative.

Indilep and Melmo were quick to arrive. The Wizard showed some flare and resolve in starting the Dragoon's Fire. Indilep felt more assured of his standing and differed to the Chancellor and Kur for the exact direction of the proceedings. The treaty paper consisted of a rock parchment for Kur's first imprint. The document was amendable to ink or the very basic wizard signature spell. The paper laid on the table as each in attendance put their name as affidavit. Lucius and Victoria were invited to sign as witness. Lucius declined, never letting the messenger get confused with the message. After all parties had signed, Indilep and the chancellor signed with the very oldest of contract stops. Then all were allowed to partake in the slaughter of motheaters, a ground dwelling mammal, to be eaten rare. Victoria and Lucius excused themselves, as the ritual was nauseating to most civilized species, although all representatives were required in attendance.

As Lucius and Victoria departed the meeting, four dragoons entered the cave. The head dragoon was a man named NEA. NEA was King of the Dragoons and bore witness to all diplomatic matters on the island. Kur gave a grunt at NEA's entering the cave. Melmo and Indilep stood fast to hear NEA's assessment. "Peace you say," he wasn't addressing Kur, he was addressing Indilep. Indilep suddenly seemed in agreement with Robbins. "There is no need for dragoons and wizards to fight over a rock." NEA's three dragoons grabbed the corners of the room. "Maybe as much need for Ignis troops on the northern tier." Indilep kept silent and the chancellor became the authority in the room. "Scio's people are very wise and we all benefit from their prosperity." "True," NEA never understood the need for conflict between Triton and Dragoon, unbeknownst to NEA, neither did Triton. "Sign your contract and then I have some business with my representative." Kur grunted. NEA held his position in part because of his linguistic ability. All heads bowed at NEA's departure, all didn't include Indilep and Chancellor Robbins.

Caves were the only homes on dragoon to the dragoons of a high enough rank. The representatives had to make provisions for camping in the wild out doors of a prehistoric world. Lucius brought the groups supplies to a clearing on a hill with a magnificent view of the northern lands of dragoon. In the distance, dragoons could be seen flying or carousing in small clusters. Victoria slept on her side, the woods being more ominous then any of the previous treks. Lucius and the chancellor had been provided provisions for camping. Formal delegations received better treatment on all the other islands. Most dragoons lived in perch tops and the shin in burrows. The Nearest actual house might be on the island of Scio. The nearest prepared shelter a bar or a shop.

The Woods also housed other smaller creatures from reptilian birds to herds of the tiny motheaters. Motheaters were fuzzy mop looking creatures and camoflauge was their only defense. Much of Dragoon had been uncharted by formal maps and only messengers such as Lucius would even have a reason. The Chancellor wondered if Dragoon Dominance was much the result of lack of competition. The Shin were in charge of the forest dwellings and felt no need to challenge the creatures of the firmament. Still, George and Triton wings stood out from the color scheme of the landscape. The Triton wings almost became reflectors against the dark dragoon sky. One of the reptile birds called ste'vans perched on a treetop directly above Victoria. Victoria rolled over flaring her left wing and sent the creature reeling down the side of a nearby slope. "Do you think we should try the robes? At least we could sleep." Victoria indicated not the first of many attempts on her slumber. There was no answer from the respite of the other three travelers. The Wood beat back the wind from the cliff faces and Lucius erected a tarp covering; created a solitary escape for the company. The scurrying of feet could be heard at changing intervals on the woodland floor. The Shin were a most curious bunch and yet they never joined visitors to their woods. The Shin preferred to watch from a distance. The Chancellor being attune to the noise of the shin, awoke slightly. The shin gathered on the other side of the branches weren't actually looking at the visitors. The shin were telling stories to each other. Three shin were nestled close around the wooded trees and without fire told many tales. The eldest shin started his tale with a wise look and a playful smile. "There was a magical shin and one day he decided he would go live under the water. Everyday, he went into the water a little deeper. Untill, he reached his arm and his waist. Finally, the shin went in above his head. We all thought he was gonna drown." "What happened," asked the younger shin. The older shin with a frank expression, looked the young furry creature in the eyes," He drowned." Lucius and the chancellor were both awake. Lucius obviously had a question on his mind and it had nothing to do with the shin. Lucius put a finger toward his lips as a man dressed in all black ran through the woods in front of them. The frightened man made screams and twists in the night breeze, running quickly off in the distance. The three camping Tritons gave simultaneous statements, "The Fog!" Lucius sitting up for the running man gave a continuing attention in the chancellor's direction," Do you think peace will come to point rock, chancellor?" The question was very out of place for Lucius, messengers never got involved with the message and rarely, if ever, felt comfortable enough to broach a question. "The Dragoons will most likely decide the affair, Lucius. The Wizard's will save face with our presence and more importantly for the first time in ages, the Scio Southern Coast will be a free province." The chancelor had the innate ability to be complete and formal day or night. "What of Ignis?" Lucius having succeeded with one question pressed on. "What of Ignis, Indeed. My friend, they will more than likely, if they are wise, seek a protectorate council; I Know I will. Good Night, Lucius." "Good Night, Chancellor." "Good Night, Victoria." "Shhh..."

Chapter 7

THE BARGE

Lucius sat up in the morning dew and dusted off his feathers, grooming was as important to the Tritons as the whirly birds. "Victoria, you have come with us farther then expected will you continue with us to the journey's conclusion?" Her reply was quick and full of energy, "I am actually having a lot of fun and I have never seen all the islands before, where to next." The ground was firm yet flexible sifts. Lucius gathered his official self from the morning light, "Most likely, Cat's Wall. Given the history between Dragoons and Wizards, the document will probably have to be signed twice and duplicates made for Scio, Cat's Wall, Dragoon, and of course Triton; Maybe Ignis, considering Indilep's presence. If we are to proceed to Cat's Wall, you may find the pleasant terrain abruptly halted. Still you may find some fun on our stop over." Victoria began tending her area before tending to George. "More gross food?" the words came from the side of her mouth. "Gross, yes," Lucius replied; "Better scenery, most likely."

This time George found himself the eager one for the flight and he swept the threesome onto his back. A lowering beak easily grasped the wings. The chancellor almost stood to halt the bird and then resolved to enjoy the ride. Wings have surprisingly few exposed nerve endings. George leapt off the mountain, scattering the Ste'vans; the birds flocked inward on dragoon. George made a huge deep dive in the valley and then turned about face toward the upturned coastline. The bird maintained a rapid pace and then George ducked low on the shores of dragoon. The huge mass of feathers spied food brought up from Subsa fisherman. The chancellor leaned in to nod at George's anticipation. The gesture was subtle and not required. The bird dives for a morning feast. George plucks fish after fish from mere inches to the waterline and holds steady the crew on his back. "Lucky for us he's a neat eater." The chancellor commented as George threw another fish in his beak. Then as if the bird took the chancellor's words in dare, George halted in mid-air and dove with the entire gathering, into the ocean. The entire group was drenched except for Victoria who was the last one on George. As the Whirly rose from the Ocean, he tendered a very large fish in his mouth. The Chancellor reached for the only dry garment on Victoria's bag. Lucius and Victoria realized the cloth garment; the chancellor grabbed and dove to stop him. The chancellor at a mere fifty foot height began to dry the bird with a robe. His attempt was working until, he reached George's wings. The wing quickly disappeared, sending the party into a one wing spiral. Lucius and veronica grabbed hold of the surface feathers. "AHHH...," Robbins held only the saddle. Recovering quickly, the chancellor saw the wing reappear and laughed at his own mistake. Lucius and Victoria were not amused; A new development for Victoria. The bird flew diagonally side to side until he was up right; Victoria moved to the front and began the group's journey westward.

Only a few hours into their across water journey, Lucius pointed to an object on the horizon. On a little skiff floating alone in a pile of naval scuttle. There lives a lone soul pining through the sea wreckage. If one were to draw a line from Dragoon to Cat's Wall to Scio, The flotilla of old naval barges would intersect in the exact center. Many know of the barges and many have searched through the debris. Yet, only two or three people in all the islands know of the inhabitant. Lucius is one of those few.

The naval barges are visible from many miles away, containing the remains of some one hundred plus vessels. As George enlarged the passengers' view of the flotilla, Victoria was perplexed. "I thought you said the view was better. All I see is floating trash." "Maybe you have never met the inhabitant," Lucius's words were as astounding to the chancellor's ears as to Victorias, "Inhabitant?" The chancellor chimed in, "You mean someone actually lives here?" A curiosity built up in the diplomat. "Not just lives here," Lucius answered. "The spirit is responsible for the barges existence." "The spirit, "Victoria asked. "Is he human or Triton?" Victoria supposed getting her bearings. "Neither, "Lucius narrated, "<u>She</u> is what many would have called a malevolent spirit." "'Malevolent,' why would we want to meet a malevolent spirit?" The chancellor was starting to have trouble following Lucius's meaning. "She was a malevolent spirit," he continued. "Now she is a soul forced to care for the many remnants of lost or abandoned crews. She collects them and hooks them together as they float by." Victoria was again perplexed, "How can someone, even a spirit, be forced to build a floating pile of wreckage?" Lucius held his audience, "Strictly speaking, she is not compelled into service, yet something in her past keeps her working day and night till eternity." "She might like some company," Victoria put in. "She might," Lucius offered. With Lucius's grin, George touched down at the center of the flotilla. "You still haven't completely explained the view?" Victoria beckoned. "Does she ever completely relax?" Lucius put to the chancellor. Irony filled the chancellor's cheeks as he caught site of the spirit. The spirit darted back and forth from ship to ship and the curious bunch slid off George and followed her. "Maybe she doesn't want to speak to us," "No," Lucius cut her off, in a polite manner. "She is just really busy; if you want to get her attention just jump in the water." "Jump in the..." Lucius pushed Victoria right off a barge in a very uncharacteristic manner. Victoria was more amused then most would have believed at first. The Spirit rushed to her side and began harnessing her to the ship. "Wait... Wait," Victoria called out. "I am a person not a board." The spirit righted herself on the deck of the barge where Lucius and the Chancellor watched. "And so you are," the spirit replied to Victoria before addressing the others. "Hi Lucius... why have you returned to visit?" Lucius's eyes softened as the whole trip was more a reflection of him then his occupation. "I was wondering if you could show my friend Victoria, the Subsa wreckage." "You know where the wreckage is I'm busy." The apparition darted off the barge and onto another, "visit again, "The specter invited as departing. The thin veiled persona disappeared on the far end of the next ship into a rapidly appearing mist and the three were alone again. Victoria was still wringing her feathers when Lucius led the group to another ship. The seeping of the feathers tapped against the wooden planks and a uniform rhythm accompanied their advance. Lucius and the chancellor for once never addressed business and all were entranced with the experience. Lucius began to lead the others below decks of a Tantamount trading vessel. The late morning sun shone from below them. Victoria was amazed to see a glass hull revealing hundreds and even thousands of underwater ships and Subsa vessels. The Subsa vessels dated to a time when Subsa actually had an underwater fleet akin to the long shadow. For the Islands of the Fog, the revelation amounted to a wonder of the world. The connected above and below water ships reached to a depth of over 2,000 feet below the water line in a great pyramid. Victoria was going to speak and then held her silence, hearing for a second a foot running across the deck above. The moment held them for a moment. The wooden structure encapsulating the rounded edges of the glass and the light piercing the waters edge created a funnel of bright luminance in constant blue. "Let's get to Cat's Wall, shall we," the chancellor motioned. Silence captured their walk to a very calm winged bird. The boards of the ship creeked in echo to each footstep and a bounce could be heard as the wood met the air. Lucius was the last to leave and sighed on his boarding of George. "No more distractions," the Chancellor charged. "We are off to a mystical island of strange traditions and magical happenings, away..." The Chancellor made the other two smile and laugh slightly at his over indulgence. The three began to behave more like their normal selves? George didn't want to leave the vessel either and ignored much of the chancellor's prodding and prating. George was comfortable resting after his feast. Less than an hour had passed between their arrival and departure. Victoria felt privileged at the site and spent many hugs on Lucius's grateful arms. The chancellor pushed them both on George and then lifted the bird to his feet with the waving of a stick. "How will we arrive?" Lucius asked. The chancellor was last on George, eyeing the rear dry spot of the bird. "Cat's wall is a strange world, having announced business will give us an advantage. We will fly straight to the hills and put down at melmo's residence. The bird leapt into the air and powered up into the clouds.

Chapter 8

Cat's Wall
"Island of Wizards
and Humanoid Cats"

The Legend of Ature and Ack

Cat's Wall was obviously not named after the wizards who reside there; although fair numbers of them do own cats. Cat's Wall was named for the humanoid cats that live in the mountains above the shoreline. It has been said that cats always land on their feet and the humanoid cats of cat's wall are no exception. In fact, they took the words a little too literally. The humanoid cats of cat's wall have a sort of inverted leg which allows them to fall hundreds and even thousands of feet, in some cases, completely unharmed.

The story goes that the wizards of cat's wall once inhabited the mountains and the cats the land but a fire of determination and a spark of pride propelled one lone cat to conquer a mountain. According to legend, A Wizard named Ature rose to be ruler of one of the major mountains on the island. Ature did not like any company at the top of the mountain, even Wizard Company. Yet, a most determined cat named ack decided one day to climb to the top of ature's mountain. When Ack reached the top of the mountain, he found a wall. The Wall was an almost impenetrable fortress built by ature. Ature upon seeing ack, climbing his wall, threw him off. Ack climbed the mountain a second time and before ature had time to act, ack stated boldly, "No Matter how many times, nor how far I am thrown off the mountain, still, one day I will sit on the mountaintop." Ature was furious and in one bound threw the cat almost to the shoreline. With each throw ack's determination grew and one day he decided before he was thrown to hold onto one of the bricks of Ature's wall. So now with each attempt Ature made to rid himself of ack, he slowly destroyed his own wall. On a misty day while ature was sleeping, ack claimed the mountaintop and sent ature to the bottom of the peak. In a strange twist to the story, Ature didn't mind living at the bottom of the mountain because he had never actually seen the whole island up close.

Cat's Wall unlike dragoon is a grey and white desolate landscape. If not for magic most of the inhabitants would have starved. Few crops, if any, can be grown on the island and then mostly spices and useful magical powders. Unusual fish living off the western coast and spotted cranes make up most of the main stay diet of those residing on the sixth island. There is a theory from off islanders, the reason the cat's and the wizards valued the mountaintops were due to the nesting sites of the cranes. Another unusual inhabitant to the island is known as a land beast. Land Beasts are six-legged fat flopping lizards and they provide a means of carriages for individual riders to navigate the muddy and harsh terrain.

Why either cats or wizards settled Cat's Wall is a mystery. Most believe the wizards settled as a result of being expelled from Ignis, Tantamount, and Scio. Others believe the location of the enigmatic seventh island is the reason for wizard colonization; since, no one has ever been believed to have reached the seventh. The wizards are thought to have cast the protective spell keeping all island people from the seventh island. As for the Humanoid Cats, They are thought to be the only actual original inhabitants to the island, surviving for centuries off the fish and the cranes.

The cats live in caves on various peaks and have become so fond of fire; all the peaks on cat's wall are lit up both night and day. The wizards gather at the base of the mountain in land based caves and huts. When visitors fill the island, the mountains glow from top to bottom, creating a virtual daytime in the night sky. Based on the story of Atture and Ack, visitors to the island are also astounded by the good natured friendship between the two races. Pride is the real glue holding Cat's Wall together. The Island's residents may have internal disagreements from time to time but when the island is at stake, the wizards and humanoid cats are one of the most surprisingly powerful land armies in all the islands.

Most of the trees on Cat's Wall are the famed Bog Fodders. The Bog Fodders grow out of the muddy and swampy terrain. They fill most of the visible landscape from fresh water swamps to salt water shallows. Bog Fodders live on a one-thousand year cycle and 500 of those years finds them dead in place until they open up and deposit new seeds. Currently, The Bog Fodders still have another one hundred years until seeds. With no leaves, they sparsely make a collective imprint on the panoramic site. Bog Fodders were the second homes to the cats when the cats were on the land. Only one bog fodder home seems occupied, at the moment, and most wizards and cats have never seen the resident.

Far from the western shore, a ship emerges off the east coast of Cat's Wall. Few ships make the long trek to the eastern shores of Cat's Wall. For one, all the island's inhabitants live on the west coast, not the east. For another, the peace on Scio was early to take effect and most of the combatants found northern routes home. Only one ship held the solace of the seas on cat's wall's east coast and," The Long Shadow of the Deep," liked being uncontested, as did its crew. "Captain, why are we on the wrong side of the island?" John being second in command was allowed a few mission specific questions when they were underway. "We are not as well known on cat's wall, as Subsa. There is a specific wizard, who might help us and the less we are seen the better. I'll move a small group through the island while you meet us on the northeast corner. John with all luck, we will be off the island before tomorrow night."

As the Captain's words echoed through the night air, a wizard appeared on the western coast. On either side of Pembridge, stood an angel and a humanoid cat curling the side of Marcus. The Archangel Spring Shine soon appeared before them on a land beast. "Quickly now, none of the wizards yet know of our presence and I would rather we all be about our business for the moment." Marcus and Magis followed quickly assisting Herbert and Pembridge. Five is about the maximum a land beast can hold and even then Herbert had to lock his legs on the tail. "None of the wizards would typically object to Tritons on Cat's Wall, unless they knew the true nature of our mission," Spring Shine put to the cherubic lot. A gesture of silence, with one finger to the mouth, from Spring Shine saw the five quickly through the bog fodders.

At approximately the same time, George was landing in the foothills of the tallest mount on the western seaboard of Cat's Wall, a place called cliff hanger. "Why is the place called cliffhanger?" Victoria questioned. "Little one, the place is called cliff hanger because of the steep slopes to the top and the sudden ledges." The Chancellor pointed to the many ledges of the mountain with fire and smoke. Lucius scouted the area and then settled in a bog fodder to view the proceedings. Melmo's House was built into the largest foothill and bore his family crest emblazoned on a slate rock, directly above the sanctuary. Melmo had a cat, not a humanoid cat, an actual house feline. The Cat greeted the guests with purrs from its white and tan chest. "Everyone seems to assume the contract will be honored, I hope for all our sakes the dragoons make good." Melmo seemed more comfortable with his tongue being at home. "I am sure there are no worries, Melmo," The Chancellor seemed to be a grandfather to the treaty and represented Triton, well. Melmo was beginning to invite Victoria and the Chancellor to sit down when Kur's Party drew attention from those in viewing distance. Melmo moved everyone out the door, "Let's get to the meeting site before some unhappy accident befalls the event." The chancellor couldn't have spoken the words better.

The Triton society bore some resemblance to Cat's Wall in both were administered with mountain governors. The Chancellor recognized signs of his own temperament in Parseval's Eyes as Melmo took them to a landing and introduced them. "Parseval is the governor of the mountain." Victoria didn't know whether to pet the humanoid cats or shake hands. "The magical overseer of the proceedings is a wizard named epoch." Melmo motioned the pair to a long curved bench. The small party sat around a huge fire pit with a stand in the center for the administration of ceremonies. Kur only brought one other dragoon, as hostility might have been higher if too many dragoons were present. Indilep traveled on his personal ship and nearly missed the start of the ceremony. Epoch asked for Kur's copy of the document. Reluctantly, kur agreed. Kur looked extremely uncomfortable considering the way wizards were treated on dragoon and the recent skirmish. Epoch raised his elbows and then laid the document on the platform in the center of the fire. Moving to a place where all could see him, melmo sprinkled a potion on the document. The dry powder turned to droplets. The liquid pooled in the center of the document then spread to cover the whole parchment. The fibers seemed to absorb the fluid completely in the manner of a dry adhesive. The document split and multiplied until enough documents for Cat's Wall and the others were in existence. He added his signature and parseval's document seal. Melmo held the pages in multiplicative form and then leaned a passing for each participant. "Not to be a nosy nudge, but what about the town where they are still fighting?" Victoria had grown as comfortable as Lucius to the chancellor's side. "More than likely, little one, on our last trip home, we will see the newly garnered peace. The Scions are more than capable of self-governance. The charge really falls to the outer islands to assist them on their way." With Robbins words, came a look from Indilep. Indilep was not going to let the northern coast of Scio go and Triton might well be heading toward a war with their neighbor. Indilep was the first to leave, followed by Kur and his many onlookers.

Victoria got up her courage and walked over to parseval. "Can we visit the top of the mountain?" The question came as a shock to the ears of the chancellor and parseval. Neither dignitary wanted to step on the other's toes. "Enjoy," the chancellor pushed. "Come I will show you the view from my office." Parseval purred in Victoria's direction, as if a feline cat. A quite strange motion for Victoria, she just laughed. Victoria being a bit forward grabbed parseval and flew him to the top of the peak. "Whoosh," Victoria powered hard straight up, giving parseval the feeling of an express elevator. Victoria set the humanoid cat on his feet at a stone crossing on the top of the mountain. "Wings are certainly nice to have, "Parseval stated with some astonishment. The governor's office was surrounded with oil from the sands of the coast. The oil burned and illuminated the office, accenting the view over tan stone rocks. A small bridge across the trough led to the office. On each side of the office was a statue, one of Atture and one of Ack. "Are the Wizards allowed up here?" Victoria broached as a foreigner. "Oh yes, the wizards are always welcome but both societies usually keep separate business activities." Victoria having an unusual assessment of people seemed very serious with parseval, "Melmo seems friendly." Parseval felt off center from the statement, "I have not known a better island representative in many generations." Parseval put his chin forward with genuine regard. Victoria began to push parseval, in the same manner as she pushed the chancellor. "Why do you war with the dragoons?" As a true politician the reply was automatic," We do not war with the Dragoons; the dragons have sought combat with us." Parseval continued in a more reassuring tone, "Cat's Wall is very safe and we have had peace for a hundred years." Parseval offered the Triton girl, Crane's feet. Crane's Feet is a delicacy but Victoria wasn't eating rare motheaters and not anything with feet in the name. Victoria looked at the view from the mountain and could see some movement in the bog fodders.

Land Beasts strictly speaking are fast creatures with very sloppy and sometimes nauseating awkwardness. The Arch Angel's group arrived at a clearing with five very old bog fodders. On the side of the center bog fodder was a door. "The resident, we are visiting is the oldest wizard on Cat's Wall." The Arch Angel only told some of the tale. Acumen was a student of Atture, surviving for hundreds of years on a magical potion. The potion enabled him to spend time as other creatures, extending his life ten years per transference. The total is tremendous, as Atture's legend is the oldest known story, on Cat's Wall. Many years had seen Acumen make the personal choice to avoid Cat's Wall Society. Acumen cherished his solitude and his respect. Spring Shine knocked, as his age and wisdom showed him the oldest of the five. The door was slightly ajar and the knocking pushed the old hinges further. Then suddenly, from a very old magical spell, the door closed again. "Maybe he's not home," Magis offered his elder. "He's here, although I am not exactly sure where?" Spring Shine puzzled turned toward the other four bog fodders. In an amazing and yet not all surprising nature to Spring Shine, the land beast, they were riding, changed into acumen. The Aged wizard looked to be about eighty years old. Pushing them aside, the old wizard made his way to his dwelling and shut the door. Spring Shine knocked another time out of respect for the legendary magical man. Spring Shine was not without his way and yet being an angel meant only using a power necessary to be used. "What do you know of use to me, winged creatures?" Spring Shine's reply was right into the keyhole. "We seek a spell to secure our wings, The Wings of Triton!"

Acumen was old and yet the wings were older. The door swung open and the group slowly filed in. The meager home disguised a very cushiony yet small several rooms with benches and comforters. "Do you have them with you?" Acumen allowed the travelers his sitting room and then questioned them. The furniture was made from wooden stumps and all the cushions were crane feathers. Wizard homes were very comfortable. "Why do you wish to secure the wings?" Acumen questioned more to see spring shine's awareness then obtain information. Spring Shine, although reluctant, knew the company he was in and imparted a small piece of well-known castle knowledge. "There has already been one attempt on the wings and we believe some interested party, may be after the seventh island." "The Seventh Island is forbidden," Acumen seemed well rehearsed at his statement and accompanying grimace and he stood stiff and still for every syllable.

Marcus, being quite impetuous for an angel, took the floor. "Pembridge is going to put a spell on them; the castle needs the added benefit of an aged wizard." "1,491." Magis gave a perplexed look, while motioning for his compatriot to relax. The wizard continued, "Few know my real age, 1491." "You think protecting the wings will protect the seventh?" Pembridge suddenly seemed alive in the conversation. Marcus again spoke up, this time to Pembridge, "You said protect; why does the island need to be protected?" "The Island is protected from without, of the contents which come from within." Acumen cleared his throat and moved to get tea and biscuits for the gathering. Herbert moved as close to the tea and biscuits, as etiquette would allow. The Arch Angel being the authority in the room removed a bag from his satchel. The wings were displayed in a solid spherical bubble. The glow of the wings grew and illuminated the dwelling.

Approaching from a few miles to the east, Rider and Hanz led a group of four men through the bog fodders. The clay soil muddied their boots and the throng held to the tree line. "Shouldn't we use land beasts?" Rider and the group walked in a line and passed branches to each other for passage. Hanz was a pragmatic man of the men and as such, rarely had rider's undivided attention. Rider didn't turn for the answer, "The beasts are loud and if you haven't ridden one, then valuable time would be lost to the men's acquisition. In any case, stealth saved us once and may yet help us again." Rider talking partly to the men and partly to him-self gave continuing conversation, "We are seeking an aged wizard who will give us the exact coordinates of our destination." Rider passing a branch in

Hanz's direction; let the officer grab before letting the limb swing, "And the atmosphere," Rider looked slightly displeased with the openness of the question, the gathering began moving through a covered clearing. "The atmosphere will only be utilized, once we know where our coordinates need to be." Hanz fell silent, except to usher the men forward and rearrange the point guards, forward and aft. Hanz making crossing guard gestures, gave repositioning salutes and waves. Directly beyond Hanz's vision, along the tree line a student in uniform walks with a backpack. "I hope my school isn't far," the student tells himself.

Meanwhile, acumen having treated his guests to tea and biscuits, now reached for a parchment from his den. He spoke, an enchantment, causing the map a flattening and stretching showing a three dimensional portal hovering above the sea. "You are correct," as answering some previous question. "Flying is the only way to reach the portal. How long do you need the wings protected for?" Spring Shine found an establishing voice on the progress, "A one year spell and the protection of Pembridge should be sufficient to avert any disasters the wings might encounter. They will be brought to our castle and our business with you concluded." "Very Well," Acumen's hands clasped together as he spoke a loud spell. Blue and White chips flew from his hands. These chips seemed to dance in a circle above the observers. The lead chip led a helical dive onto the curvature of the sphere. None of the chips touched the sphere; they only hovered when comfortable with a placement. Acumen pushed at the sphere as if the wind between him and the chips would stable them in place. The chips seemed to scatter to ash and when the last one dissipated, Acumen's Family crest was marked as the wing's protection. The crest glowed slightly and then faded to a clear indented mark on the sphere. Spring Shine returned the sphere to the aforementioned satchel. No one spoke and acumen followed the group out the door. The party hurried out to catch the nearest ship for Triton.

As their backs were turned the magical enchanters were not aware of rider and his shipmates in close proximity. Marcus was shimmering down a bog fodder when rider's group caught acumen waving. "Well what are you doing here?" he questioned with an about face. "We seek knowledge of the portal?" "Why?" Acumen was more apt to question a seeker then a protector. "To find the passage to the seventh and the riches therein;"

Acumen resumed his theatrics. "The seventh is mysterious and appears different to different people at different times. One must not just enter the seventh; one must also enter at the right time." Rider didn't know what to make of the man's riddle and said in a somewhat disparaging voice, "Just the Coordinates." The aged wizard looked as if he was just going to return to his bog fodder and ignore rider. When acumen reached the door, the strangest notion occurred to him. "Count the number of your buttons on the left and right side of your shirt, Mr. Rider." Acumen never actually turned and then went into his home and shut his door. Rider was confused, he got acumen's meaning but what are the chances rider's button count would be the numbers and why would he even partly assist them. "I expected a little trouble?" rider uttered. Hanz reassured his boss, "The angels will most assuredly not come quietly." Once again Hanz and rider were on different pages. Rider was more concerned with why the old man helped and the amazing coincidence of his shirt and how he knew his name. Rider wondered if he was on a path to nowhere. In any event, the captain was the kind of person to find any nowhere or somewhere that he sought.

"What about the time?" Hanz was of use to his captain after all. Rider counted his buttons. "I have six on one side and seven on the other. The six and seven must be the longitude and latitude coordinates and six is the hour and seven usually means thirty-five after the hour. "Do you really think, he would give us the coordinates and the time?" Hanz questioned. "I do." Rider stated.

The Archangel hailed a fishing vessel at the Cat's Wall western shore dock. The docks were well established being built only from and for Tantamount captains, although cat's wall visitors and residents frequented the docks when need permitted. "With the cats on the island now, cat's wall might be building new docking facilities," Pembridge believed his words informative but they were really more a hopeful inspiration, as he loved travel and the wooden planks could benefit with an upgrade. The feet of the gathering made soft creeks on the sloped entrance ramp to a large wooden platform, from which dozens of ships could birth. The nearest ship bound for Triton was a Tantamount trawling vessel named the brine. The craft was large for a fishing boat and was equipped with an upper helm deck for passengers, as well as a cargo hold for transport. The captain of the ship was friendly to Tritons. The common sense of the day seemed to point to Tritons as reliable trading partners. The fair was negotiated reasonable and the five-some were allowed the entire passenger deck for the journey. Marcus was instructed by Magis to place the wings in the hold of the second deck. As the group leisured on the front of the ship, the beautiful seascape caught their notice and tapered their concerns. Herbert seemed to relax the most, curling in a reclined deck chair.

Victoria and Parseval returned to the mountain floor where Lucius and the Chancellor were getting a cat licking, literally. The Humanoid Cats routinely licked the hair of the heads of wizards as a cleaning and bonding ritual. This accounted for the shiny hair each of the wizards displayed. Lucius seemed quite uncomfortable with the gesture and would much rather have had his hair cut. Victoria laughed in amusement, "Me next!" "You can have my turn," Lucius offered. After much fidgeting, Lucius's orange and white cat friend had finished the ritual. Straightening himself, Lucius approached the chancellor, "Either of the routes home will put us in Ignis waters. Either we intent on the west side of Ignis or pass the armies of Ignis off the northern shore of Scio." The chancellor sensed fear in his messenger, "Are you worried for our safety?" Lucius put off the chancellor's assessment visually and yet spoke to the discussion, "The Other Islands can be combative under fairly predictable circumstances. Messengers have been known to be lost crossing the eastern coast of Ignis." "Well, don't worry yourself, the people of Ignis may lack a certain direction but they are as concerned for the sake of the islands as all of us." Lucius took comfort in the chancellor's words and brought some shame to his demeanor for relaxing his discipline. Lucius prepped George for the second time on their journey and requested Victoria let him drive George. "Sure, you're trip. You shouldn't have any trouble, besides I think he likes you." The Chancellor patted Lucius's shoulder signifying their unity. "You will let me know?" Lucius asked of the Chancellor. "Of Course, let's just put a few miles on our journey first, the night is gonna be a splendid time to fly." "Splendid." Lucius returned. George didn't need Lucius's beckoning; He seemed always eager to get to the sky.

As the sun began to set, on the north end of the island, two ships almost passed in the twilight of the waves breaking in the distance. The Wings of Triton sat in a lone sanctuary on the upper deck of the fishing ship. One wing lit then the other, as if the wings were on fire. Sparks traveled up and down the feathers in the clear view of a spherical protective shell. Only the wings weren't on fire, the wings glowed. The glowing was not bright enough to cause any alarm, as no beings were within visual sight of them. The glowing wings pulsated and began to slip slowly through the walls of the vessel. This most unusual magical item was passing unharmed through wooden deck after deck and hovering in mid-air. Each of the decks, offered obfuscation, as the sight would have caused any person on the ship alarm and yet no one saw them. After the engine room, the wings drifted into the ocean and right through the rim of captain rider's vessel. The wings drifted and came to rest right next to the atmosphere. The two magical items began to glow together. The only creature with even the slightest chance of recognizing the magical meeting was Flink. Flink didn't see them. Flink just noticed the glowing. He only saw the illumination and went deck after deck turning off lights. "Must be under the hold," the man concluded but did not stop in his pursuit.

The brine supplied the magical group with fish as the most appropriate meal to most islanders. The dining cabin was glass enclosed and provided a circular view of the surrounding waters. The captain couldn't provide the group with servers and so brought the plates himself as a gesture to the group. Pembridge carried his and herbert's possessions around as if in not complete trust of the angels or else to protect some of his secrets. "Thank You, for your wonderful hospitality," Herbert offered to the captain, being polite. "You are all quite welcome and remember the brine on your next outing to Cat's Wall." "We will," assured Spring Shine. The captain exited with an enjoyable look on his face. Marcus was getting tired of coastal food and sought the refuge of his cabin. Magis decided to not eat for the purposes of self discipline, as angels needed to be light fast flyers. Magis couldn't sleep without first checking on the wings. Feeling the ledges of the small hallway with his hands, Magis entered the room with the wings. As quick as he went in, he flew faster out and appeared almost instantly in the dining cabin. "They're gone," magis stood still when having others attention. "What's gone?" questioned Pembridge. Magis turned to Spring Shine in an official reporting status," The Wings of Triton have disappeared or else been absconded." Spring Shine turned to instruct his friends," Magis get Marcus and conduct a thorough search of the ship. I will inform the captain of the importance of our cargo." He then turned to Pembridge, "Is their any assistance you can provide?" "I can locate them due to my spell," Pembridge suggested while still eating. Spring Shine raised a hand to Magis's exit of the room. Magis stopped. "Proceed Pembridge!" the archangel folded his arms and looked directly at the portly gentleman. "Very Well," Pembridge pleaded. Pembridge put down his eating utensils, reaching down to his side was his satchel full of potions. One of the bottles read spell locator. Pembridge lifted the bottle to gazing height, his not the gatherings. "When I name the spell and drink the potion, I will be able to see as if the spells target had eyes." Pembridge moved his food tray to one side and cleared himself a space. "Very ingenious use of magic," the archangel observed. "Poten circum," Pembridge chanted and then drank the potion to the last drop. His eyes became white and cloudy from the perspective of everyone in the room. Herbert made a nauseous look to Pembridge and then went out for some air. "I see a cargo hold with very unusual metal siding. Wherever, the wings are they are not on a fishing vessel, looks to be some kind of military ship and something else." "What?" The Archangel felt at a loss. Pembridge reached his hands out as if the objects he saw were in his grasp ", The Atmosphere and the glowing!" The captain upon hearing the commotion of the dining cabin rushed in to see Pembridge's eyes and reaching hands. The captain took a few steps back to assess the situation. Spring Shine turned to the captain, "I am commandeering your ship in the name of the Castle de Angelis and the Triton Delegation." "What For?" questioned the captain. "Someone is going to use the wings of Triton to enter the portal to the seventh island; I will purchase the use of your ship for one day to intercept." "I thought the seventh was a myth, I've been on these waters many years and not seen a seventh island." The captain was amazed at the new information. "The seventh is very real and we need to stop whoever is trying to go through the portal." Marcus moved into the cabin as the captain responded. "The Tritons have always been good to us; the ship is yours for twenty four hours. One day isn't going to hurt my fish." The captain left the room calling out," Get me the first mate." "Should I ask?" Marcus offered. "No," Magis put out.

Rider and his small party began to walk toward the north-west corner of the island. The ground was muddy yet the dark rocks provided a sure footing with each step. The scarcity of trees slowly led to large bushes and scattered shrubs. Rider could feel the cloth of his clothes with a slight cool wind and pushed his neck forward with the motion of the group. "You can," Rider motioned to Hanz and pointed to a small group of land beasts in a clearing. Hanz took on a serious and commanding demeanor to the other men. He got on the land beast to show the technique. "AHHHH" The beast was startled and bucked Hanz to the tail. Hanz seemed to be doing a Flink impersonation. "After him," Rider commanded. The Other land beasts followed through the few bog fodders to the beach and then north. "You're going in the right direction," Rider stated in amazement. "Do not worry yourself, Hanz. None of us know how to ride these. You must have the lead beast." Hanz waved to his screaming captain and struggled to the top of the lizard. Pulling on the lizards jaw flap, the beast flopped to a stop. "What the..." Hanz pointed at Kur's Party moving in the distance sky. All the beasts flopped next to Hanz. "Dragoons are not our concern, to the ship." Rider slapped Hanz's land beast. Rider needed some enjoyment in the day and here was the moment. The group of lizards made fast time flopping to meet the ship in a lagoon only known to John and him. "John must have made good time around the coast," Rider pointed out, as he could see a signature water disturbance of his ship in low tide. The Long Shadow never beached. The foursome had to swim to the ship and enter through a side entrance in the middle of the ship. Only one person could enter at a time as the passage was flooded and then pumped out before each person could enter. There are better ways to board the ship. Yet, rider never stopped ship operations for a small boarding party, not even one he was commanding. John didn't salute but came to attention for Rider's entrance. "The ship is ready for motion and the seas to the north are clear," John didn't realize the appropriateness of his account as he escorted the captain and Hanz to the atmosphere. The pulsing of the light had increased since the wings first entered the ship; meaning The Wings of Triton was a second surprise. "Where did you get the wings?" Rider questioned as Flink began to scratch his head at the glow. John's face went blank with astonishment," ahh, Flink where did we get the wings?" Flink stared at the captain, first mate, and Hanz," ahh...

nice huh" "John conduct a search of the logbooks and see if anyone left or entered the ship." "Yes, captain," john prodded Flink out of the room with Flink still scratching and looking. "Hanz tell Robert to head to the portal coordinates and then get the men ready for above water operations." "Yes captain," Hanz stated with an official exit. Rider scratched his head for a few minutes and then accepted his good fortune.

Chapter 9

The Portal

Marcus paced the dining room as Magis sat in waiting on the opposite side of the table. "What if this military ship has a hundred dragoons or Ignis elite? We should be more prepared then intercepting on less than an hour's notice." Marcus paused his steps only briefly for magis. "You are right and if worse comes to worse, the Triton Mark will be given." Marcus stopped pacing. The Triton Mark was the strongest magical spell of the angels and was dangerous for the target and the angels. The Triton mark required at the minimum three angels. "You realize if one of us loses concentration or the spell is interrupted, the spell could cost us our lives." Magis didn't slow or quicken his speech as even keels brought fair sunshine. "The Triton Mark when successful will give us control of the leader for long enough to retrieve the wings. Spring Shine has been through these scenarios. We will always, as angels, have the element of surprise." Marcus approaching the glass enclosure peers into the distance. "Let's hope surprise equals success." The last of Marcus's words seeing Spring Shine walking the perimeter of the ship.

Archangel Spring Shine calls for the attention of all on the small Tantamount trawler, wearing a cloak with the crest of his castle. Many seem interested, either never having spent time with Tritons or never having seen an angel. The archangel cleared his throat and began his speech," The reason many islanders have never crossed the portal to the seventh is because the portal does not reside in the water or below it. Rather, the only way to cross through is hovering in mid-air. The rectangular portal is large enough for two adult Tritons, yet none has ever tried. To my knowledge," he added in thorough conversation." If the wings were to fall into a human's hands, one human might be able to enter. Our duty is to retrieve the wings and make sure the portal is protected from those who might seek harm on the seventh." One of the Captain's mates on the trawler raised his hand for acknowledgement. "What's on the seventh island?" The Arch Angel shot him a glance, "Nobody knows, yet there is probably a good reason for the portal being protected for so long." All agreed and left the angels to their business. The decks shuffled and the engine could be heard picking up steam as the Brine disappeared from the side of the ship and gave way to the ocean.

The Long Shadow had a reputation for speed and with the water presumed clear; rider ordered the vessels to the surface and powered along the waters' tips. Hanz, John, Robert, and Flink gathered on the conning tower with the glowing magical items in a bag on the deck. The approaching night was still with a slight overcast and no breeze. "Who's going to where the wings," Hanz asked, when the officers were gathered close. "I will, I won't ask any of you to do a task of such risk." Rider faced his companion and the horizon. "The sun has set and the time is 6pm," the deck man called out from below. "Why are the four of us here?" John gave to listen. "Since, none of you can tell me where the wings came from, one or all of you may have to use the atmosphere... if we have any visitors of the winged type." Rider posed in place. "We don't even have a visual of any ship for miles," John added. John called down to make sure," Deck man report any ship sightings," John waited as the report chain was in effect. "No... wait... yes, one fishing vessel on a 90 degree intercept course. E.T.A 10min." John not wanting to lose face called the specifics," Do you have a name and some populace data?" Another ten seconds and the deck man yelled from the scope," The Brine, appears to be a Tantamount Ship." The captain approached the look. "Well, fishing vessels usually don't extend this far into Ignis waters, just in case, Flink get some binoculars and watch the ship." Flink almost tripped falling into the deck hole, and then a very strange coincidence, the passing crew member was bringing binoculars for the group. "Very fortunate," Flink rolled the binoculars up to the conning tower and awkwardly stretched to the stand. Steadying himself from the officers, Flink gave the brine a complete look. Several lights illuminated the brine, "They aren't sneaking up on anyone with all the lights on," Flink observed. "I see a humanoid cat and a Triton, no three Tritons and they seem rather lanky." "Well, this might just be an interesting few hours," Rider ventured. "Should we arm ourselves," Robert asked. "No, the atmosphere will put them on human terms with us and we should be able to secure the ship with our large crew. I should be in the portal when the Long Shadow is directly below. Keep the angels a few feet away from the atmosphere." "Do we even know how the wings work?" Hanz asked. Rider seemed not put off with the question," From what I have read, the wings are put on similar to a costume and then when they are removed, the wearer has a new set of wings." "What about this spherical bowl around them?" John pointed to the bag holding the magical items. "Hand me the wings and the two of you grab a hold of the atmosphere. There is no trick to the atmosphere, strictly a proximity effect. Make sure one of you has hold at all times." Rider began to bang at the sphere to no avail. Flink raised his hand still looking through the binoculars. "Yes, Flink," Rider offered while struggling. "Even if you get the wings on, won't the atmosphere block them?" Rider struggled toward the edge of the tower. "Good point, Flink, You three head to one end of the ship and I'll head to the other." Still, inquisitive his officers called questions. "Exactly how far is the effective range of the atmosphere?" John asked. "Well, we will see." Rider stated while moving the wing's sphere. As if in resistance to the separation, the atmosphere and the wings slammed together and bonded. "We might have a problem," Hanz gave to the crowd. "Two problems, the Tritons are flying here," Flink cautioned. "The flying is only temporary; here comes the answer to john's question." Rider joined Flink with binoculars. "We have reached the coordinates," a bridge man called up. Hanz and John pulled with all their might to separate the two magical items and received little recompense for the effort. The wind picked up as the skies darkened. Flink pointed to the quickly approaching Tritons and something else on the horizon. "A whirly bird? Might be a few more Tritons then we anticipated." Rider advised his men to put the items down and waited for the atmosphere to drop the approaching Tritons. Several moments tolled rider's nervous tension.

"One-hundred yards, they're still coming," Flink issued from his forward facing posture. "The Wings must be limiting the effect of the atmosphere," John after making his statement, heroically grabbed the wings and atmosphere; running over the conning tower to close the distance. John paused at ten feet off the tower's bow. "They're falling, "Flink updated to the officers. Rider turned his head toward Flink, "Shh. . Listen, we'll here a splash." Seconds passed with wind on moderate seas being the only backdrop. Rider straightened his head forward. "Angels!" John threw the wings and atmosphere to the top of the conning tower as Spring Shine brought him to the ground. The Fearless captain jumped to the port side and snagged the two spheres in mid-air as he landed on the bulk of the vessel. Flink jumped after his captain as Hanz went to secure the ship. Marcus and Magis anticipated and blocked the forward progress of Rider and Flink. Rider stepped back. The Two began to chant and soon Spring Shine was next to them chanting as a T begun to form on the Captain's Chest. Feeling weakened he could utter a phrase and make a motion; one phrase and one motion. "Flink," Rider threw the spheres to Flink who dove to catch them. Flink put his feet under the spheres and inadvertently booted them off the ship. The three angels kept chanting as once initialized, the cessation of the spell could have disastrous effects. Flink positioned to dive after the wings as john grabbed him from behind, bringing the lanky mate face to metal with the bumps in the surface welds.

John after recovering from his head blow saw the swirls forming in the water. A water funnel had begun to form off the side of the ship. Rider's movement slowed as he reached to his companions. John brought Flink to his legs in the same motion as using the man's body for a ram. John and Flink pushed right into the side of Marcus and Magis. The consequence was an utter silence for the incomplete spell. The three angels grabbed for a breath. "Boom!," The Three Angels, John and Flink were blown into the metal hull and rider being the center of the explosion was blown over their heads and off the ship. Rider's chest was the epicenter pushing down any obstruction in the path. The Result was actually safer for the captain then if the spell had been completed but leveled the angels and crew to the deck. Rider's exhaustion made him a float toy in the swirling seas. The captain eventually spiraled to the center of the funnel and almost submerged. As his body reached the inner circle drop off, the funnel sprung a spout right in the center. The spout slowly grew in length and diameter, holding the captain aloft yet drowning. The water spout grew quickly pushing rider into the air. The water spout and explosion didn't go unnoticed, yet notice came too late for the whirly bird. Lucius pulled and tugged on George as the spout hit the bottom of the bird. The Chancellor slid off George and dove into the water. Lucius followed after, leaving Victoria and George being pushed higher in the sky. Next to George, Victoria saw rider slipping in and out of consciousness as she reached out a hand. Rider didn't reach her hand but pulled himself up by the wing of the bird, who was no longer flying. Victoria and Rider held onto George; hoping the instincts of the bird would protect them. The Spout reached the exact height of the portal at 6:35. The bird was helpless entering the rectangular portal.

On the other side of the portal, the sun is shining at noon day. The exhausted man, woman, and bird tumbled through a clear blue sky. Victoria pushes and pushes on the George button. Rider barely has enough strength to hang on, as he places his holding. George with only twenty feet of sky, let's out and flaps his drenched wings, pulling the couple inches from the waterline before collapsing on a beach head. Just enough above water for the bird and passengers to breath, George rests as if a duck or goose. Victoria having the most energy walks and rests on the beach while staring at the mysterious stranger on her now exhausted whirly.

On the otherside of the portal, Pembridge and Herbert stride onto the surfaced long shadow deck tracking closely the captain of the brine and crew. Approaching from the conning tower, Hanz and Robert, with the crew, move to meet these strangers, as the medical teams of both crew break ranks to help the survivors. "What is the meaning of this?" questions Pembridge as most were in confusion. "Are you attacking our ship," Hanz put forth. "Certainly not, "The brine captain steps forward. At the same moment, Lucius and the chancellor climbs the side of the boat, where the two companies join. Herbert stares and stares at the sky. Both crews notice the cat's persistent look up. For above them, a rectangular shape stands revealing a sunny day and a clear blue sky. "We'll I'll be," states Robert," There is a seventh island!" The Chancellor recognizing the archangel motions in Lucius's direction for attendance. The pair runs directly, finding the side of the aged angel being put on a stretcher without any wings. "Did anyone enter the portal?" Spring Shine reaches out to the two Tritons. "A man, a woman, and a bird," The chancellor seems marveled and disconcerted with his own answer. "Well, what do you make of this?" the chancellor asks Lucius. Lucius looks at the mystifying phenomena and states with blank wonderment," A historic moment; a historic moment."

Chapter 10

The Seventh Island

Victoria lets the stranger sleep, as a big burn hole shows where his shirt and coat hold an attachment. Victoria picks up a stick and begins to poke at rocks in the surf. Rider slept for near a half an hour. George didn't mind or didn't notice the weight with the bird half in slumber. Rider reached out a hand stretching for a clock. The maneuvering caused him to find the beach, quite abruptly. "Where am I?" the awakened captain stood rubbing the water from his arms. "As I can figure we went through some kind of portal in the sky. Look!" Victoria pointed to the rectangle portal revealing a night sky. Rider looked as a smile beaded on his face. "We're on the seventh!" The smile remained as he looked around at the huge ocean in front of them and the large land mass behind. "You mean there is a seventh," Victoria interjected. "Do you have a better explanation?" Rider prompted the young Triton, who still had her wings." Victoria," she answered. Rider fashioned himself the captain of a one Triton and one bird crew. Victoria on a regular day would have found him stodgy but spending time with Lucius and the chancellor had relaxed her. Rider straightened himself and made various motions to his non-existent shirt. "The bird can get us through the portal; we are on an expedition to visit the seventh." Victoria hesitantly raised her hand," Do you think Mr." "Rider," the man lifting his legs through the surf related. "Captain Rider," he stated being formal. "Do you think... Mr. ... Captain Rider, the portal is gonna just sit up there in the sky. I've never heard people talk about a portal and one with the opposite time of day is very noticeable." "Well now, let's think, maybe the portal is only noticeable if a person/Triton enters." "Should we fly a return," Victoria questioned. "No, we will explore for two hours and when we have gotten what we came for then we will fly a return." Victoria went into a water shallows and tied George to a palm. Being considerate of Birds, she left him enough rope for him to get fishes in the shallows. Rider examined Victoria's walking stick, as he presumed, and fashioned himself a stick. The Two were about to step foot in an island jungle when rider stopped them. "You're not hurt from the explosion." "Thanks for your concern, captain." "No, I mean you can fly over the island, give us an assessment of the situation." Victoria was tired at the end of the day and yet she launched into the sky higher and higher. She passed the portal and flew straight up. Rider kept looking at her to figure the distance she could see from her height. Victoria turned at her maximum height and made a helical dip fall to a glide. The young Triton relaxed a leisurely pace across the seas. The Triton turned to almost the exact spot she had left. She stood to report," First the island is huge, the island keeps extending. I didn't see the other side." She didn't bring herself to a qualifier yet she kept motioning to speak. Rider waited. "The Island has everything." "Everything!" the captain always put fish stories in context. Victoria pursed her lips while talking," The landscape is every landscape, I have ever seen. There are dozens and dozens of dozens of animals. I did recognize a few animals from Triton but most of them, I have never seen before. The Island seems to revolve around a grassy area maybe five miles from here. "Victoria's wings brushed against the foliage as a nervous tension moved her side to side. Rider searched for each question, "Did you see any buildings?" "Not one," Victoria stood still and put her hands on her hips. Rider wiped some excess sand off his arm, "Any People?" "There might be some in the glade, to far to tell." Victoria's matter of fact attitude did level the captain's indesiScion. "Point the Way," rider had a guide and a stick.

Victoria marched through the jungle at a rather brisk rate, yet the five miles took them almost the two hours held in reserve. Rider never gave time unless he could keep the time. Yet a strange persistence slowed the walk. There were all kinds of small and large land creatures. Victoria went to pet some but they moved out of the way, then the animals began to follow them as if a parade put them in front. "I've been working with animals my whole life, and I've never seen them behave in such a manner." Victoria turned around and with every turn she could see the animals stop. The animals didn't stop; they seemed to stop from the edge of her vision and must have been following to all be close.

Then it happened, the marvelous and extreme light brought forth from a garden. A man and women stood in the garden, naked. The animals who seemed to respond to rider and Victoria were actually responding to the man and women. The Man and woman appeared to speak and yet didn't appeared to communicate and yet didn't. Yet an amazing amount of communication must have been happening for every life form seemed of such a happy nature. The Man and Woman didn't see them and there seemed to be a distance from one to the other. A voice stirred in the two travelers and in a flash; they were being drenched to the side of the ship known as the long shadow. Rider grabbed the ladder and assisted Victoria to the top.

The two crews almost didn't notice them until they realized the portal had disappeared. The Angels, John, and Flink were ambulatory and had joined the on deck gazers. The sudden appearance of their compatriots gave each of them pause. "Well help them up," the archangel rang to the ears of listening crewmembers. Five of each crew ran to drag a bird, a man, and a woman to the deck's surface. Several moments until the two were actually on their feet. The angels still needed their wings. Adjacent to the island visitors sat the atmosphere and wings of Triton separated. Magis reached for the wings. He then handed them to Marcus. Magis then reached for the atmosphere. John grabbed at the other side. "Wait," Rider got to his feet. "The Atmosphere is Subsa property." "The wings are Triton property," Magis put forth. In this conflict a neutral party didn't exist. John and Magis put the atmosphere at half distance between them. "With your blessing archangel, Captain Rider and I will discuss the matter, as diplomatic solutions seem to be my specialty." The Archangel recognized his own partiality and only suggested the meeting be held on the Brine. "There is another matter," the Archangel held attention. "The Triton Girl, the angels, and rider's officers will meet about the events we all were in observance of," Will meet on this, what do you call this?" "The Long Shadow," Hanz handed. "The Long Shadow," repeated the Archangel. "Agreed," Rider answered for his ship. Pembridge not being neutral, he found more to be gained from the discussion of the seventh. Leaving the chancellor and rider in solitude, as Lucius stood next to Victoria's side, believing rider was not a singular threat on the fishing trawler.

The angels and officers make a procession along the perimeter of one of rider's interrogating rooms; a surprisingly little utilized compartment. Pembridge and Herbert stand on the edge of the room as John, Hanz, Spring Shine, and Magis move to ask questions. The group didn't really choose as only four chairs plant the floor opposite the interrogation seat. Victoria sat, as Lucius stood at her side. John looking at the archangel found himself engaging in a melee of polite hand gestures. "You get the first question," John states with some reservation, the archangel seems to nod as he moves on his right elbow, looking at Victoria. "The Seventh Island, would you tell us what is there?" Victoria almost held her breath before speaking," All," "All," the archangel replied. John put in for a point of clarification," You mean everything?" Victoria's words went fluid," I mean all... all the animals, all one could want from a moment." "Explain?" Pembridge didn't wait for a turn, as he called from the doorway. "The Island is the happiest of places where everyone can have what they want and need from nature." Hanz looks confused, pushed the question," Should we attempt to colonize?" "Up to you," Victoria replies. John keeps with the clarification," Do you think the seventh will be able to be colonized?" "Anything is possible there." The angel's felt a renewed sense of purpose from Victoria's explanation. The long shadow crew deciding a return trip would be the ideal plan.

Magis observed Lucius's demeanor and then gave the look of someone recalling a face. "Lucius is your name?" "Yes, Angel." "Word has reached the castle of your speed and dedication. Do you think, you might consider life as an angel?" "Maybe," Lucius being polite, felt slightly off guard. The idea romancing his sensibility's for only a second. "Maybe," Magis replied. The angel didn't push the issue and Lucius never mentioned the occasion. Lucius did head in Victoria's direction. "What did you see there?" Victoria gave an adoring look," Joy, Perfect Joy." Lucius shrugging his shoulders gave a sigh, then he led Victoria out of the room. Victoria and Lucius led the others above the deck to see where rider's discussion had taken the group.

Rider and the chancellor's discussion occurring alone, they sat on the second deck of the brine. All the dining ware had been removed and a white linen cloth filled the décor of the meeting table. Robbins convening the meeting, across from rider, waited for silence before entering any discussion. The brine crew meanwhile became busy on lower decks maintaining ship status; sufficient silence came in an attainment of seconds.

"You do understand captain rider, the angel's guild is most powerful and could perceive your possession of the atmosphere as a threat." The chancellor realized the kind of man rider was and put the words as blunt as might be effective. "One could also perceive angel presence on the Long Shadow as a threat." Rider didn't concede to people who cut him. "What are you're plans for the atmosphere?" the chancellor was becoming a professional diplomat. "The atmosphere is Subsa property." "Would you allow the angels to accompany the return?" Rider grew slightly defensive at the idea. Rider stood and paced, then looked out the window as he replied, "Only if they brought the wings." "Why," the chancellor lowered his voice and softened his posture. "The Subsa people will be wanting a new artifact for maybe a month and the wings would allow me to stave losses on the trip." Putting a finger to the brow, the chancellor replied "I'll ask the archangel but he might request the atmosphere" Rider usually had the last words in discussions and the chancellor went for the order with the solution. "Then the fate of them will rest in Subsa hands." The two men shook hands and a strange sort of progress was made.

Once again the two groups met on the above deck of the longshadow. The brine staff brought chairs; an odd meeting table drifting in the middle of a night ocean. Pembridge grabbed a potion and dropped the bottle on the deck. The table was illuminated, a lit room in a dark sky. Since, most of the members attending to the findings were bound in machinations, imagination, or frustration, Spring Shine turned to the chancellor for a ray of good news. Rider sat being comfortable on his own ship and allowed the angels to converse. "The atmosphere will be allowed to be accompanied on the return to Subsa. Captain Rider and I believe Triton, Subsa, and the Long Shadow might have a unique opportunity to help Subsa and Triton. The wings will be displayed for a time in Subsa and the atmosphere for a time in Triton. Captain rider believes the decision should be left in Subsa hands. What are your thoughts', archangel?" "Well, chancellor, we have no qualms or historic disputes with the undersea people to the south. The Wings are agreeable for display in Subsa on the provision the atmosphere accompanies us home." "Would you be willing to leave the approval in Subsa hands?" Spring Shine didn't hesitate," Agreed, with our accompaniment." "Agreed," rider stated.

Marcus and Magis were eager to retrieve the wings. "The Wings, Archangel," Magis seemed always succinct in purposeful matters. The Wings were brought to the table as trust was emerging on the ships. "The Protection spells do not allow us to get our wings," Marcus observed in a sort of minimal panic. Archangel took on a fatherly disposition as he sheltered his friends. "Do you know the light-wing spell?" The light wing spell was a temporary spell allowing non-Tritons to fly. The Three performed the spell giving them very identifiable wings for a time. The wings glowed fire in a sort of light outline. "Perhaps this might help," the chancellor walked over with the three robes from emote. "These will allow you to move between wings and non-wings." On the top of the robes the angels put on cloaks to maintain appearance. Pembridge laughed," You look very akin to wizards." Herbert found a ball in one of the longshadow holds. Herbert bent down on the deck of the Longshadow and revealed a quite unusual cat nature. Herbert pushed the ball with his nose over to where Victoria was starring at the meeting table. The ball hit her on the left reverse calf. Victoria grinned and began to play ball with the strange humanoid cat. Herbert being a Subsa resident, occasionally had the smell of fish. Victoria didn't expect how good a ball player he was and flew in the air to catch each bounce.

Lucius never broached the subject of inclusion in the angels. He spent some time considering a position with the chancellor. Victoria, finishing with the cat, kept silent and tended George. The chancellor stated the obvious thought," One of the strangest side tracks, I've ever been apart of!" Victoria smiled and put herself in lead of the bird. George had a running start and took his time getting off the ground. "With our stop here we might continue on to emote." Victoria knew only the compass heading and took off in an easterly direction.

The Archangel pulled pecuniary notes out of his under robe. Currency was never a problem for the angels and the castle is always free to pursue more lofty concerns. The notes totaled 5,000 hugs. The Hug is the base unit of the Triton money and each 1,000 hugs is called a Kiss. The brine captain being well compensated, with five kisses, departed the ship. The Long Shadow was not use to guests, let alone guests of high rank and ability. The quarters of the ship were tighter then winged people would find comfortable. Yet these winged people weren't actually winged. The guest quarters were at the rear of the ship, as rider valued his space, even to his guests. "I have appointed one of our top men to be your liaison," rider assured the angels. "Anything you need just ask Flink." Rider left the angels and their accompanying Subsa guests. The bunks were small and yet very spacious for a submarine. Marcus felt all the mattress edges and searched the undersides.

"Are we going to have to wait a year for our wings?" Marcus always being less discrete then Magis usually kept silent. Marcus continued his preoccupation. "There are two ways to look at the circumstance," the archangel instructed. "Moving forward we could obtain our wings in a year or," "or," even Magis's curiosity was peaked. "Or we can undue the atmosphere's effect and leave the wings protected," Spring Shine's words sat better with himself then his companions. "If the castle knows how to undue the atmosphere then where was the threat from dragoon?" Pembridge being almost exclusively silent, engaged the discussion. "We don't as of yet but we will." Magis resumed his serene disposition. Magis's serenity seemed to calm the room.

"Have you ever been to subsa?" Marcus asked of Magis. "No, most Tritons stay out of Subsa after 'the peace over the water.' I think the idea of neither dragoons nor Tritons in Subsa maintains the Subsa agreement." "You mean the Subsa agreement for the atmosphere," Marcus rarely had magis over a point of logic and quite enjoyed the moment. Magis moved the subject to a deeper level," The Tritons and the dragoons weren't the ones most affected with the peace treaty." Marcus pondered the thought as the gathering set up a quiet table with stationary chairs.

Quandor's meeting with the Subsa council

The Subsa council is the main diplomatic legislature of the Subsa people. There is no central authority, only representative members from every major section of business, transport, manufacturing, cave management and the populace. All the members are elected in each sector and serve limited terms of office. Only in Subsa is business and human affairs given such equal shares with such a pleasant result. The Subsa council occupies the far side of the cave from rider's entrance dock and is surrounded on either side with ocean business, such as perfume extraction and algae tending. The daring Subsa people built the chamber with an iron face and painted over the metal with one of the ocean dies. The Subsa council building resembles a Scio lab with a very human architecture and a glass entranceway. The plaque on the side of the entrance read,' The Subsa Standard – The best utilization of any item in the air or water is the value we put there.' Quandor was alone reading the sign and the glass doors revealed an empty and dark entrance. The portly man sighed. The council is quite intimidating as any speaker must stand in the center of a darkened room surrounded by all the council members and address them simultaneous. Such was the dilemma of quandor. He occasionally on such nervous occasions groomed himself as a shin would. His prior life, as a shin never completely left his system and maybe never would. "Why do you trouble the council today," a voice rang from the darkness and echoed in quandor's ear. Quandor checked each ear before addressing the voice. Quandor thought drama, a wise course. "I gave the atmosphere, away." The darkness became quite loud and many minutes passed before they were silenced and the voice continued. "For what purpose?" Quandor could have fashioned rider as a scape goat, yet his popularity could be problem. Quandor went with the straight answer." The atmosphere is on loan for an expedition into the seventh island." The voices of the darkness again poised an exhibition. Quandor silenced them. "The Atmosphere will be returned in a month with no adverse effects to the dragoon." Silence came quickly as the whole chamber had the same question. "The Tritons!?!" Quandor raised his hand realizing, he actually thought highly of the endeavor. "The Tritons are not the possessors of the atmosphere." "Who is?" "Captain Rider." "Do the Subsa people get any recompense for the imposition?" "We will get credit, with the exhibition and the scuttle center is negotiating artifacts." Quandor didn't know all the specifics and would have kept the information to himself. The possibility of political implications weighed heavy on his mind. "Very Well," the voice dissipated and the lights came on revealing an empty chamber. Quandor sat on the ground, considering the choice of siding with rider.

On the far side of the ship, rider called an officer's meeting and included Flink. "Flink, you are officially ship's liaison," rider didn't wait for replies and Flink wasn't quick with an answer. Rider paced the deck. "Ship... Li... son?" Flink muttered to the officers. Rider answered to his aside," You make sure the guests are happy but you don't let them roam the ship." Flink slapped his head, considering the company. The captain's direct words were to his officers," Hanz and John, each of you is on guard duty for the two magical items on the ship. The items are to be kept as far forward of the deck and out of site." Hanz turned to John," We are moving up in the world," John's shoulder declined as Rider rose above his brow to the view of Hanz," Exactly, and reputation is important." Salutes were usually only for the officers, yet suddenly the boat was official. Everyone saluted the captain.

George found the trip invigorating having rested once on the sub and again on the seventh. "Home," Victoria. We will find each of these situations in quite pleasant order when we arrive home. "Are you sure," Victoria asked. The Chancellor didn't answer, Lucius did. Lucius said, "Sure," The Wind dipped the flying bird and all the passengers felt their stomach jump. Victoria laughed, as far below the long shadow disappeared under the wake of the waves.

Chapter 11

Angels and Outcomes

A wind scoops a bird off the coast of emote, and lifts the small aviary high on a westerly wind. Below the bird could be seen a man coming into focus, very distant to the ground. Celebus arrived at Captain Skimmer's Estate in the early morning light with dew covering branches and a brisk breeze. The breeze gives way to rain in a light graduating and sideways manner. The butler being attentive, as usual, sees the High keeper one-hundred yards early. The large frontal plantation always allows him the luxury of informing the captain and making necessary preparations. Thus all visitors got the grand tour. Captain Skimmer being informal with known guests usually wears a robe. The pace and vigorous manner of Celebus allows the sighting, since skimmer's knowledge gave recognition this being a formal meeting. "Morning High keeper," the men shook hands on the columniation with the wind blowing leaves across their chests. "Morning Skimmer, I am here on Emote business of the greatest import." The captain removes leaves from his face while leading Celebus to the study. Observing the papers brought with him in his left hand, skimmer cozies in his chair and offers Celebus liquor. Celebus refrains. Celebus's words explode in the curtaining study with mix lighting," Ignis is attempting a full scale seizure of Scio. According to these documents Tumult is in agreement." Celebus places the papers on skimmer's desk. The High keeper grips the cushioning guest chair in the study. "We are the only men in emote with the necessary scrutinizing consideration." Celebus gets air, looking from the liquor stand to the captain. "I have instructed the temple security. The security is forming a perimeter on the border of emote." Skimmer believing the High keeper as quite militaristic for a temple official agrees with a pursing lip, "Are you suggesting emote declare independence?" Celebus sits in skimmer's guest chair. "I am offering the position of general. Emote must remain free of Ignis; until the grand parity get's some sense." Skimmer reads Tumult's correspondence. "Tell me Celebus, what do we have at our disposal?" Celebus wiggles his head and anxiously speaks, "Well apart from as many people as we can muster, we have my security forces, your artifacts, and all the magical items in the temple." Celebus removes sweat from his brow with a handkerchief. "What's in the temple?" Skimmer being a man of influence on the island; at present didn't fancy himself a tourist. The corners of Celebus's mouth upturn a patting. "I wouldn't have come here..." Skimmer halted with his hand and finished Celebus's thought," Consider me General Skimmer."

Several miles to the west a much darker setting on the Scio volcano provides for a much more solemn discussion. The volcano assembles in a room holding the leaders of Ignis and Scio in consult of a rainy morning. A solitary drip can be seen falling from the ceiling to a point at the very heart of the room. Tumult and Indilep share a view from the center meeting chamber at the volcano's center. "The armies are advancing," Tumult locates into the chest of Indilep. "Exactly," Indilep states to Tumult. "Ignis will assure there aren't any disruptions to life on Scio. You and your scientists will have plenty of time to come up with ponderous new inventions."

"You said for a month only," Tumult moans his temple. "One month only." Tumult moves in his chair finding posturing for his remarks. "You do realize any longer; at the very least, Triton, dragoon, and cat's wall will knock on your door." Indilep's hands separate in open arms. "You have my assurance." "Well then, I appreciate your help, as long as you are helping." Indilep gave his feet attachment while standing in place; talking to the exit door. "Agreed... Mecos is quite capable in the field and will make sure the southern coast is free from strife."

As Tumult looks at the floor, a lab across the hall looks out the window. Mecos and his sixth battalion are at full parade dress. The army marches in uniform lines and displays their nickel-plated swords for the populace. "Not again," a lab technician viewing the scene comments. The man in a pale white coat pushed his seat closer to the viewing window. The scientist in charge of the lab puts a hand on his coworker's shoulder and grieves the window.

The Long Shadow could be particularly quiet when underway. The fin-tailing design stream-lines the water molecules into a shear water-wind. The Long Shadow is even fast by submarine standards. As the crew begins to feel the calm of the journey from the portal to subsa, rider calls Flink to the command room. Flink almost trips entering the room as the doors are raised a full foot, yielding the crew's impetus to motion. "Yes captain," Flink enjoying his time with his commanding officer, looks to him as a father figure. "Flink, let the angels and their friends have some space. I still want you to be attentive on them. Don't let them enter any secure spaces on the ship. If they move toward the engine room or the helm, you let me know first." Flink salutes and moves to the galley for food the officer's guests can eat.

The food in the galley usually consisting of fish in a fine paste with crackers and the guest's choice of tea or ale, usually became silently sufficient for rider's visitors. Flink isn't a cook's mate; gave notice to the kitchen staff. "The captain's guests need food and refreshment," Flink reversing directions in absence of a salute; the staff just stood in awe of how fast the young seaman seemed to be given officer responsibility. The kitchen staff didn't scratch their heads; they just wiped their brow and proceeded with 'The Vittles!'

The captain never saw Flink inform the elite passengers. His first notice came when a person's imprint made a connection at his door. "Good evening captain," Magis spoke while entering the officers' area. The wings of the angels causing them a slight sideways incident step. Marcus entering from behind but slightly to his left gave an opposing turn. "Evening... Angels," Rider didn't dislike the angels apart from the trident mark incident but he usually only cleared his throat for phlegm passage. Still, having one's chest explode; doesn't make for a fast friend. Rider chose to be ingratiating while keeping his control. "Sit for a minute," rider stood up and called to the nearest deck hand. Marcus and Magis didn't sit but chose to wait standing. "Deckhand," the captain expelled in the diagonal of the hall. "Yes captain," came the immediate response. "Watch the door. You are assigned door duty until I relieve you." "Understood," the discipline on the ship hadn't always been as well instilled but recent times met kindly on rider's chin. As for his chest, he needed to maintain a guard during any angel meetings. "Will you have a seat, at least then you will have to stand before you begin chanting." The angel's thought the captain in jest but he was completely serious and unaware the trident mark required three angels. "You do understand captain," the spell is to protect the seventh. Rider not being sure he did understand; the angels likewise not sure they wanted to sit. Marcus and Magis unearthing an acquisition, as most times; in luck with two chairs easily provided on one side of an oval table. Rider sitting opposite with another pair of chairs garnishing each flank, glances momentarily at his flanking. "Are you here to discuss the seventh?" "No," Magis replies. Marcus gives a shocking look with his agreement of rider. Magis rarely ever shocked Marcus. The two usually maintained a close symbiotic relationship. Magis voicing his opinion, as an observer of spring shine," Captain, we are here on a cordial visit; to learn about the wondrous long shadow." Rider forwarding a sly grin sat back in his chair. "You want to know where I got the ship." Magis mimicking the captain's face with his partial repeat," I want to know where you got the ship?" "Yes," Marcus called out with an approval of magis's reasoning. Rider looking each of the angels in the eyes took to exercising his vocal chords. "Most of my crew doesn't even know," Rider found himself being honest. "I would have told the crew but they all thought better of asking." Rider's face contorted a storyteller persona," I'm not from here originally." Marcus and Magis gave subtle hand gestures indicating the information; known. Magis relaxing the captain's concerns gave a slight overlook to the walls. "She is a great masterpiece of a metal ship and the only submarine we have ever seen." Marcus shook his head, again, in agreement. "The people of Subsa used to have submarines." Rider and the angels were in sync," Many years ago, I am told." Magis unlike Marcus knew when to stop asking questions and listen. Rider sitting on his left elbow put one thumb to his speech," Their used to be Subsa dominance of the waters until they became businessmen and recluses. Subsa is a fascinating culture." Magis in a rare occurrence shook his head, "We here you are quite popular there." Magis's offering became quite receptive to the captain's view. "Popular for a ship captain," he gave as a qualifying remark. Rider sat up in his chair,"

To answer your question more completely, I brought the ship with me and I wasn't the original owner." Rider pausing on reflection put his forearm to the table," The original crew disappeared and I am not sure where." The angel's eyes grew wide. "Do you mean vanished?" Marcus queried. "I mean we were all on the ship together one day and the next I was alone. I first appeared in Tantamount and recruited a crew. Paul of the 'TOLS' gave me an old submarine map of the seven islands. The map is some of the last known possessions from the last human submarine captain." Rider reaching to his left found a straw; he could twirl in his left hand. "We figured out how most of the systems on the submarine work and have been transporting cargo and seeking out magical items ever since." Magis looking for a clarification put his arm on the table, "When you say vanished do you mean before your eyes." Rider stood for the question, "Exactly, there is something strange in these waters, very different from where I am from." Magis and Marcus accepting the answer gave thanks to the serious captain. Magis continuing to leave paused himself reaching a hand to Marcus. Marcus knew what magis meant and the two bestowed a return to their demeanor. Magis chanted a brief two words," salve animus," The captain made two paces back holding his hands in the air," Wait now." Rider thought of the deck hand at the door. "Look at your chest captain," magis gave only those words on his exit of the room. Rider marveled as his chest had healed.

The deck hand began bracing for movement in the hall. "We are arriving in Subsa captain." The captain called out on the ship, "All hands to the ready." The Subsa dock venting an eminent approach.

The long shadow delayed any leisure activity choosing to focus the entire docking in Subsa on only one meeting. Rider alone grabs attention in Subsa. The captain's entourage being larger than usual got an eye from Subsa women on the stone and water streets. The four wizard, looking men, herbert, and rider shown in distinguishing colors in the strange cave light. Herbert is a famous water volleyball player in Subsa. Many of the adoring fans halt to get herbert's autograph. The cat signs four autographs, as a dimly lit sign displayed his face. The fans are beautiful Subsa females. They let out an, 'ahh,' at the cat's signature look with his tongue on a diagonal. The archangel motions a carriage driver forward when the women were satisfied with their papers. "Cat Celebrity," the driver scoffed to herbert's smile. The carriage gave a sloshing with each entrant, rider being last in closed the door for their departure. The carriage swung side to side and sloshed through the Subsa waters. The light in Subsa makes the travel seem almost at night. Day or night really depended on the person's perspective; as the streets weren't crowded and the carriage had two fast eels, giving a fast and even pace. Subsa seeming somehow brighter to rider, as his eyes seemed marginally used to the dim. The billboard lining on the top of the cave, gave a phosphorescent glow with Subsa shoppers darting in and out of stores.

The angels didn't usually have a reason to be in Subsa but took in the spectacle with quiet approval. The stairs to the scuffle center presented a busy opening. Rider paid the driver, as he seemed to be the host of this expedition. The Archangel didn't mix pleasantries with the rest of the group and headed straight up the stairs. Rider caught up with him right at the door to Quandor's office and opened the shell covered enclave. The moist official rose to his attention. The scuffle center was experiencing a moderate flow day. "Tritons are a rare sight indeed. We are honored by your presence." The lack of wings not withstanding, Spring Shine was a known figure in magical circles. Standing directly behind the archangel was rider. "Captain Rider," the stout and sometimes awkward man didn't immediately assess the circumstance but knew the meeting would be important. All of the office personnel were dismissed with a scoot of the blockade's underhand. The three Tritons took seats adjacent to quandor, Marcus and magis on the left of quandor and spring shine on the right. Herbert and Pembridge being residence of Subsa found a more familiar seat at the edge of the table. "Captain Rider is this in regards to the atmosphere." "Yes," rider responded. "Well, have you been troubling our dear Tritons?" Quandor shouldn't have patronized the angels but he was prepared for many contingencies, angels weren't one of them. "No, remember the trinkets, I spoke of the other day." Rider's facial grimace flattened. "Well, the atmosphere is desired on Triton." Rider seemed pretty proud of the situation quandor was in and yet he didn't see the next move. "Absolutely, not, The charter for peace, given to us from our ancestors specifically forbids the atmosphere falling in to dragoon or Triton hands." Quandor seemed confused with his own words as he was born a shin. Marcus, at Magis's prompting, un-wrapped a bag containing the wings of Triton. Quandor took his seat. "I'm listening." He corrected his stance. The captain had quandor's undivided attention. "The Angels wish to procure the atmosphere, as part of a peace agreement between the two peoples and only for a month. I figure displaying the wings should settle our agreement, as well."

"Just a minute, captain, the circumstance could cause an international incident among the dragoons. A long standing peace could be shattered, if the dragoons learn the greatest weapon against the Tritons is in Triton possession." The archangel enters the discussion, not as a diplomat or an angel but as an astute observer of business savvy. "The castle would allow a one month's dispensation of the wings to dragoon, in exchange for a mutual agreement of angel possession of the atmosphere." "Agreed, "The Angel signed a document to the effect, allowing the public knowledge and allocation. "You do realize, we will have to bring dragoon into the discussion, "the administrator orated. "In due course," came the archangel's words, "In due course."

At the moment when the archangel finished speaking, A large figure emerged from the side of quandor. Quandor looked quite satisfied with his bit of boardroom know how. Kur appeared before the meeting quite unexpectedly. "Kur has come here to discuss trade relations and wishes to see the atmosphere." Kur being most amicable for a dragoon and the mysterious seventh raised his curiosity. "You have been to the seventh?" Rider related to dragoons better then most, as he held some of their more charming personality traits himself. "Paradise, simply paradise," Rider eyed Kur's response. Kur grunted. Kur knew the importance of these artifacts, yet he held the populace non-magical view and as a representative of NEA became taught to favor Tritons. The archangel stood for Kur, "Captain Rider has used these artifacts for a curiosity. We can benefit to improve our relations. Would you agree to hold 'the wings of Triton' for the atmosphere's visit to Triton." Kur as a diplomat was the simplest of creatures and very rarely made important decisions alone. He would have to make this one and he did.

Quandor signed a piece of paper, Marcus moved across the table. Kur's signature marked a contract the angel had written on the voyage. The Three Angels stood with open smiles while shimmering an exit with the atmosphere. Quandor reached for the wings, Kur's tail flailed from the floor halting the progress. "Month," Kur grabbed the wings and left the room. As the door shut, the four remaining men gave each other a bewildered look. Pembridge thanked the captain for his hospitality and motioned herbert outside. Herbert rubbed shoulders with rider. Rider began wiping himself to get rid of cat hair. "Well captain, you keep life interesting," Quandor offered the famous captain. "Til we meet again," rider waved. Quandor shook his head. Rider gave a flat palm to the entrance door leaving quandor in his office setting.

In a contrast, far above the water, the swift-footed bird was breaking altitude records with the three Tritons. A clear sky enabled George's passenger almost a complete look at the center of the islands. Lucius nudged the chancellor and pointed down. From the ariel view, the volcano on Scio seemed to be erupting.

A red carpet swept over the geography as a bright opaque hue." I thought the volcano on Scio is inactive." "The volcano is inactive," The chancellor blurted. The scholar leaned as far off George as he felt safe and used Lucius for a hold. The chancellor pointed at red appearing to pour over the southern half of the island. "Look, there are breaks in the red." "I see," Lucius didn't but he really thought he could. From the height the two men could see the southern shore of Ignis. "Look, Ignis." The same red appeared on the southern shore. "An invasion, as quick as you can little one," Triton is where we are needed. Victoria pushed and pushed on the George Button. George had himself a steady pace and gained ever constant speed with an ever so slight dive into the canopy.

Rider tolerated a few waves at his carriage on his return to the submarine. He looked at the marvel of the prosperous microcosm and pondered the nature of Subsa success. Rider thought about the simplicity of the people and keeping to the very essentials of what forwarded their success. The light seemed brighter in Subsa. Maybe Subsa was in a daytime.

John met Captain Rider at the dock where he had the look of a man with determination. Branch sat waiting for rider on a stool and lifted several legs to get up. "Sir, all the records are in perfect order," rider waved his hand forward then down. The Shin realized the captain wasn't in Subsa on dock business. John and Rider's thoughts were in sync. "We'll the cruise has been adventurous." Rider offered only a smirk and held the door for his first. John paused at the entrance to the submarine. The captain immediately sped up and through several halls of the ship. Rider paced several decks with john in pursuit. "Tantamount will give us some trade business." "NO," Rider answered. "Ignis doesn't have a navy; those warriors need some means of transport." "No," Rider turned to John's face. "Set course for Emote, This time will use the front entrance, will get some work from the temple and make this voyage as prosperous, as adventurous." Hanz could be heard calling," All hands, man to ready," as Rider turned into his cabin.

After many hours of exhaustive flying, George found the chancellor's mountain. Both the chancellor and Lucius were asleep on the bird until the landing. "Home," Victoria stated giving the men an abrupt awakening. The Triton skies were setting and the sparse clouds gave magnificent colors. The 'Triton Highway' in the sky could be seen in the distance. The pyramid gazebo left enough of a ledge for the bird to flop a landing. "Door to Door service, very nice," Lucius was impressed. Victoria made a confession to the group, "Actually, I had heard of you both before you came to the bar and I knew where your mountain was, chancellor." Victoria put one wing to the right and slid off the surface of the bird. The chancellor stretched his arms from the journey. "Little one, do you think you might stay with us, as we are moving in the direction of the Triton Delegation." Victoria put a finger to her chin, "I'll need to rest and feed George." "Of Course, we all can relax for the night." The chancellor was happy to have his friends on his mountain. "Well, will you be requiring my presence," Lucius flared his wingspan on the gazebo flat and remembered his formal duties with the rank of Robbins. "Lucius, we will need you." The Chancellor motioned Lucius to one side of the gazebo leading to thick marble doors and the entrance to his residence. Lucius patted a response and spun his wings in a stretching posture. As Victoria plucked George's feathers, she began to lighten her spirit. Victoria noticed the chancellor's walking toward his residence. Plucking only the necessary feathers, she tied George to a pillar of the gazebo and hurried in pursuit. An attendant to the chancellor opened the door and then disappeared through a side passage in the wall. The chancellor's home was immediately off the mountain top and was a huge and luxurious mansion with large open doors, large enough for the expanse of huge wings, fully stretched. The white marble cubed rooms held plenty of space for all three travelers and the most delectable food in all the islands. The furnishings consisted of hard block surfaces smoothed with grand cushioned bags. Outer island food was tolerable, yet, the food of the mountaintop included every known dish from everywhere. Victoria didn't wait for the chancellor's approval as her favorite dessert rested on a white countertop. The chancellor feigned an approval and then sat face to face for eating. Victoria put on quite a display, as the chancellor ate slowly. Neither party had enjoyed these delectable desserts in many months, they would enjoy them now.

Outside the Triton messenger stood as if posing for a grand picture of a panoramic view. Lucius meditated on his duties, sitting near George on the ledge of the gazebo. The highway, above the mountain, maintained business day or night. Only a few wings on leisurely flight pierced the exquisite view. Lucius looked at the flying people in the sky. He was happy to be home.

The Long Shadow broke dock and made for open water in record time. The entire duration, rider remained in his cabin. John held the helm of the vessel and surfaced the ship. The surfaced submarine accelerated the speed. The weather was rainy and John and Hanz dawned rain coats to get the view in the open ocean. The conning tower view being only open for officers; allowing people to learn the appreciation of fresh air. "Do you think there really is a seventh?" Hanz brought the strange question to the first-mates ears. Shaking some binoculars and then reaching them to his eyes, John talked to his junior. "You saw the portal." Hanz stood looking at his binoculars with a shifting hand. "Most of these magical happenings seem to make some sort of sense. The portal should have stayed open. Is anyone going to make a return trip?"

"Hanz steady your motion." John put a hand on the fidgeting officer's binoculars. John brought his binoculars to mid-chest and continued. "Here is some advice from a senior officer, and a friend. Life is always forward. Make the most of every day and head in the direction of your dreams." Hanz smiled as John could be as serious as rider and in some cases more. "... and we never had this conversation." Hanz noted his friend's affection and then bent to open the hatch. Hanz left John alone on the conning tower and climbed the ladder. The crew officer felt motivated and went to prepare a team for a meeting at the temple. Swimming in view of the ship a woman can be seen in a white bathing cap. The thin and grey woman counts the number of her strokes, laying, floating in the surfing wake. "I hope land isn't far," she says as the submarine's wake nestles her concentration. The woman slaps the water for attention.

Flink calls the watch as Hanz enters a team preparation room. "All hands salute." Hanz doesn't notice the change in the crew since the seventh and marks the progress. Flink and five men stand for the motions of Hanz's imitation of captain rider's pacing. "We are journeying to the temple on emote and we are working on an official capacity. The team will give respect and above all keep quiet. The captain will ascertain the situation and forward instructions, understood?" the five man team saluted. Flink rubbed his brow as Hanz left the room.

Rider awoke from a day dream as he figured the sun was bright on the conning tower. Rider left the ship, unaware of Hanz's preparation team. The formal water entrance to the temple held actual stairs and rider put a repetitive pace. The main channel between Scio and emote had an inner estuary for a temple walk to the landing and entrance. The stairs were granite rock, native to emote and the walls above the waterline in clean brick condition. When rider reached the level of the temple stairs, He halted. The view from the land facing side of the temple was quite expansive and emote was a long flat plateau. "Where are all the people?" Rider noticed such moments being an observer of life. Rider entered the temple through the main door and realized the security wasn't present. He had to prod himself down the hall to the location of the main office. The door was slightly ajar and the captain pushed the door open. Celebus wrote on papers and busied himself with each parchment. Rider didn't always pause as many of the island formalities instructed, "High keeper?" "Captain Rider, an unexpected pleasure." Rider didn't know he was on friendly terms with the high keeper, neither did the High keeper. "The Long shadow is seeking an assignment for the temple." "Very fortunate, as I have one," the High keeper stood and left his papers on the desk. "Tell me is the 'Long Shadow' equipped for battle?" There were many men in the islands rider felt would be the first to ask him; Celebus wasn't one of them. "I thought Emote left war to Ignis." Rider didn't sit and busied himself discovering the various parts of the room. The Captain moved from the doorway to a bookshelf. "My dear captain, Emote is now a free protectorate and we are organizing a campaign against Ignis." Rider, reversing his direction, went to leave the office as he thought he entered the wrong door. Celebus moved around his desk and grabbed at rider. "The Long Shadow won't be put in any danger as Ignis doesn't have a navy, only battle boats." Celebus cared for the safety of his people, any people... with him. "The Temple will also need as many weapons as the long shadow can supply." Celebus ventured a return to his desk, feeling assured of seising the captain's spirit of departure. "Have you met the men of my vessel, the Long Shadow has the best sailors in the islands." Rider wasn't selling his crew to Celebus, he was simply stating the rare treasure, he possessed. Celebus believed in monetary recompense. "The Temple will compensate you for your work and you will receive command over another ship." As Celebus finished his instructions, a thunderous clamor of people filled the temple echo chambers. "Captain, wait here for a few minutes and fix yourself a drink." Celebus moved the Captain to the side, as he walked from the desk to the door. Celebus looked to the rightside of his hall from the door frame. Giving a momentary look at rider, Celebus sped off down the hall. Celebus left rider wondering regarding the nature of Emote's Status.

Donald and his wife traveled via horse drawn carriage through the drunken towns of the ale factories, toward crescent city. Some of the towns were well maintained through city-state control, while others were only staging areas for sailors or production operations. On one sparse city street, one of the ale-makers is interviewing for the company. A man with a vest bolo and short mustache looks at each applicant. The first applicant is a Triton. "No wings, we need bigger doors," the man pushes the Triton to the side. Where he sees a poet with a pen and paper," no poets, we need some communication." The next man in line is a warrior. The man smiles an approving grin and waves the man close. Donald's carriage passes the hiring exercise. "Do you think this Subsa place is close," Donald's wife asks. "I have never heard of anyone taking a whirly there, "Donald gives to his wife. The frail woman steadies the rocking of the cab with her arms down and outstretched. "Is there someone to ask?" Donald sat up in his seat and felt in charge of his affairs. "There is a bar tender in crescent city named Paul, all the ship captains know him. He'll get us passage to this place, wherever it is." Donald's carriage dug up mud and several drunken sailors followed the carriage toward the sea's coast.

A few miles away, on the coast, the Brine reached the shores of Tantamount and the ship offloaded. The excitement of the journey kept the crew busy talking and working. The captain stood on the bridge, happy for his ship. Looking to his first-mate, the brine captain shared his enthusiasm," The fish and the angel money, a very prosperous journey." The first mate had made the arrangements for the fish and stood with a bag full of gold coins. "Give the crew, the full share and we will split the angel profits." As agreed, the captain gave gold coins to each sailor for their share of the fish. The crew upon release kept the bars on Tantamount busy. The sailors talking reached the ear of every captain on Tantamount's east coast. The gold must have reached the captain's head, as he found a bar stool in the Tavern of Lost Souls and told Paul the entire story. "There was a huge portal in the sky and angels cast a spell on a man. A funnel pushed two of them on a whirly, high into the sky, as two others flew to a submarine." The brine captain waving his hands at the ceiling made gestures of the ideas. Many of the captains thought, he was drunk. "You've been drinking saltwater," one of the other captain's yelled out. Paul not being one of the many, he starred down any critics and soon brought silence to his bar. Donald entered the bar in time to see Paul's bravado. Paul got to petting the bar's surface in unity with the brine captain. Donald's wife walked close keping contact with her husband's shirt; watching the ship captains' leering hands. Donald's clothes and demeanor spoke of the Tantamount countryside and Paul recognized these. "Is there something I might help you with," ventured Paul." Donald didn't reveal his letter only one of the tickets. The ticket read, 'Waterbowl Subsa Herbert/Poet Seat 3.' "You're looking for passage on a seahorse carriage." Donald had eaten seahorse from the Tantamount coast, yet didn't quite comprehend Paul's meaning. Paul smiled and motioned to a weed carriage man. The blue skinned man stood for the bartender. Donald and his wife had never seen a weed, she grew sick and ran outside. Donald kept his composure, "You are some kind of sea creature?" "We are weeds," the man stated making an open palmed gesture toward Paul. As the scaled man escorted Donald to the sea shore doorway, Donald gave a look at the fascinating gill structure. Donald feeling slightly pushed by the gilled man with blue skin, gave placing to his comment, "Can you breathe with those things," Donald stated while still observing the nature of his skin texture. "Quite well," offered the carriage man while waving at Paul. Paul waved again at the two men leaving and then put in some time examining the posts in his bar counter. Donald's Wife was still throwing up, as the seashore revealed an air tight glass and wooden water carriage. The carriage had two enormous sea horses and a hermetic glass oval door. "My Carriage will get you street level at the Subsa waterbowl. Have you ever traveled to the underwater city?" "No," Donald was amazed and gestured to his wife, as she recomposed over a barrel. A strange looking man in a foreign business suit gave an entrance to the bar from Donald's right. Donald's wife looked up wipeing her chin," The Fog!" The Carriageman kept conversing with Donald while walking toward the docking. "Subsa appreciates visitors not divulging all they see in Subsa and allowing the city some anonymity." Donald could relate having a similar feeling regarding overabundant whirly times. He found encouragement and ushered his feet from a rock pedestal and into the Subsa carriage as the floating mass shifted in the water. Donald's wife almost fell and grabbed her husband, to stand upright in the felt covered cab. Donald and his wife sat and grabbed on to wooden bracing panels. The carriage didn't move out, the carriage moved straight down.

The talks of the entire crew of the brine became ostensibly quite coincidental with the morning arrival of a letter on a far away mountaintop. Parseval received a dispatch on Cat's Wall revealing people had reached the seventh. He didn't disclose the signature as he valued information in the same extreme as Lucius. Parseval issuing an order to a secretary gave a tightening in his nose skin, "Call melmo to the top of the mountain!" The cat of the mountain didn't wait long, as wizards have many means of transit on the rock face. Parseval, counting the seconds, spent the moments rearranging stacks of paper on his desk. Parseval never placing the piles together, he found interest in separating individual pages and moving them through the piles. Parseval's speed in sorting grew with the moments. As melmo entered the door, Parseval tensed, a gesture of respect, and melmo sat in a chair. "Here," Parseval handed melmo the letter sent from Tantamount. Melmo read out loud his conclusions before finishing the letter. "Do you think we should concern ourselves with the seventh?" Parseval spoke in a serious manner, "The people of the other islands always figure we have been to the seventh." Parseval sat waiting for heads to bob before continuing," We have half the magical world on the island and not one of us has been there." The cat gave a lick of his legs. "Well, maybe someone on cat's wall has been there," melmo fashioning the cat in the same fur. Parseval's reputation accurate, he is a ferocious feline;" A Triton and a Tantamount captain are claiming to have entered the portal, ME-OW." Melmo almost laughed as the tone being in jest, the content seemed serious. "Do you wish me to invite these people to the island for an inquiry?"

Such matters were really out of melmo's jurisdiction as island representative and he thought offering might ease parseval. "No, I think we need to figure our own way in the matter. Tomorrow all the governors on cat's wall are convening a meeting. Cat's wall could be officially forbidding travel in Cat's Wall Waters." "I'm the Island Representative," the mere suggestion seemed an obstacle for melmo. Cat's Wall diplomacy usually being a straightforward matter; team atmosphere's became normal. Parseval's authoritarian demeanor stood him without a chair. "We will stay out of other island's affairs until we can figure the situation at home. A contingent of wizards are being sent north. Off Islanders shouldn't enter a portal off our coast. I want you to assist them and see if you can investigate the matter." Melmo agreed to parseval's proposal, as there wasn't much use in being island representative to an island without diplomacy. Melmo stood and headed for the fire circle surrounding the outside. At the statue of Atture and Ack, melmo braced himself to the door. "Maybe we should ask Acumen?" Parseval didn't answer, just pondered the idea as melmo left.

The mood on emote changing, skimmer's plantation stood vacant with most of his staff moving toward the waterfront. Only a small portion of the general's estate bordering the water, the estate dock placing being one of the finest and fastest sloops an island can produce.

The Bonzis maker of ships on Tantamount never attempted such a fast ship. General Skimmer's mobility being first rate as concerns his plantation and managing the sailing ship and staff. A strange considering, a better evaluation of his estate people, saw the general placing his butler as captain. As the last of his staff board the ship, Skimmer salutes while standing with a horse and cart. The horse has a cart attachment with several red and gold beading luxury luggage cases. Lifting a leg, the general boards the stallion a fine black and white horse. Skimmer's ride on horse back from the length of the plantation to the temple is a very elegant cantor. Both the man's plantation and the temple border the water, on opposite coasts. Skimmer rides for a near hour on dirt roads; with much involved in science on emote many of the essentials could stand improving. Skimmer never let the essentials suffer. The road leading to the temple boasts one of the few stone walls on the island and sustains one of the oldest constructions; even though emote presents, as the youngest province. Celebus beckons his security team to attention when skimmer begins tracking less than a mile from the divides. "Attention!" Celebus watches his issuing warning at the temple, internal and external occupants. The security force of twenty two men, managing a personal touch with their stance, gives a chant" E-mote." Skimmer commands them, "At Ease." Celebus runs down the steps and speaks to skimmer's ear before running up the steps, again. "When you're finished with the security team, meet me in the temple divide." Skimmer heard Celebus's words but was entranced with the idea of leading. "First in line give me your name." "Trent," the man gave an answer; the discipline of the temple being as good as any military team in the islands. "Trent, you are in command of the security team. Get two men to open these satchels. Distribute the barb guns, swords, shields; one per man, and then give every man one item from the second satchel." The arming of the team became a brief few minutes. The satchel buckles gave easy. The general taught each of the men the unique nature and function of each of the magical items. "All of them have sharp edgy natures, all but one," the general's statement reached the ears of all in attendance. The man last in line being given Victoria's favorite bracelet. "What does this do?" Trent went to correct the man and then stood motionless for the general. "The Bracelet of Immobility renders the wearer completely paralyzed until someone utters the magic word,' Please.'" The last man broke all military demeanor; being given a bracelet of politeness. "I'll throw this at the enemy, they'll never figure out the secret." The security team started laughing, please wasn't in the Ignis vocabulary. The general displayed one of the swords. "These swords are special as they hold a secret." The general even if he wasn't commanding would have held the team's attention. "The tornado sword apart from being durable extends an actual tornado." The general demonstrates on the ocean going part of the temple. "The tornado emerges from the tip of the sword, when activated, and grows to ten times the length of the metal." The wind at the edge of the general's tornado actually clears many rocks on ocean facing wall. "One heck of a sandblaster," Trent makes a strict motion and the last man seises his day's talk. Celebus being excited for the general's arrival calls the security forces, a return to their outposts on the border," Security return..." Skimmer gave an agreeable look as he dismisses the troops with a salute. Again, the team shouts their words," E-mote." Celebus reaches his arm to skimmer," The troops are yours still we need a few more." Walking up the temple steps, skimmer speaks to himself, "You read my mind." The temple held only the top magical items found in all the islands. Quandor's collection on Subsa paled in comparison. Many weren't applicable to an army. One was. One gave them an army. Several divides parted before the men reached the object of the high keeper's fancy. From a glass enclosed case, a beam of light spread to the ceiling of the room. Celebus put a hand to each side of the light and the light deactivated. The artifact is simple looking; exactly in the shape of a 'T.' The bottom of the 'T' tendering a spike. "General the 'T' is a most unusual object." The High keeper sees a momentary return to curator, although he now takes into consideration his being the actual leader of the province. "The 'T' arrived from Tantamount," Celebus pausing for a second while grabbing his chin," There must have been a wizard living among the populace." Skimmer cut him short," What does it do?" Celebus makes sure to gesture with both hands and speak over the object as if a microphone, "When put in the ground, the artifact generates troops out of earthen soil. 'General,' these troops are completely dedicated to the person who puts the T in the soil." "How many troops," the general became stolid in his words. "The number is not officially known and can vary." "How many," skimmer had become a general and grew impatient at delay. Celebus gasped a breath before speaking, "The number is based only on the pride of the planter, can vary from ten to 100,000." Celebus waited for Skimmer's astonishment, he was disappointed. "Excellent, next artifact," the studious general cased the glass cubes. The temple cradled the creation of the very roots of a resistance. A persistence, the people of emote would push. Some of the other artifacts of interest included means of shielding troops and turning others invisible. In the hall between the divides, skimmer broached an obvious question, "Do you know the amount of island residents volunteering?" Celebus gave a side smile. "I sent out flyers and as of tomorrow morning; my conservative estimate is all of them." "All of them," skimmer felt an empowerment with Celebus's words. "All," the High keeper spoke to their people's cause," Emotens may not be as logical as those on mainland Scio but we all value our own." The general took a tally, "Emote has a few thousand residents, with the earthen warriors; we will hold the line and return some Scio." Celebus exhaled a breath, "I knew I hired the right man. Is your warship combat ready" The sea gave emote a natural advantage. The general began a walk with the High keeper, "I have the one; be nice to have another." The high keeper realizing his office on quick approach," My guest may be able to lend a hand." Celebus opening his office door revealed Captain Rider fixing himself a drink. "I believe you know each other and I believe; I have already met your crew captain rider." Rider is a captain and few men in the islands could reduce him. Skimmer through his prior success led the way for rider and gave him hope. Rider rose up to his friend, "Skimmer, we are not a warship. We are gonna need some compensation?" The high keeper led through recruitment and finance; the temple endowment being slightly greater than skimmer's fortune. "The temple will fund your activities." Skimmer spoke to the captain, "Rider with your ship, we might even help Scio to independence." Rider never really knew the pride of a team. Only the pride of leadership; He did now.

Chapter 12

Tense Posturing

The wizards are known as the worst negotiators of the waters. They didn't get a large Tantamount vessel for the portal investigation, only a long wooden boat. The portal resided over two and half hours north with four wizards rowing in unison. Melmo didn't lead the expedition and stood as a participant. The trees on the north end of the island were maple and palm and the coastline gave to a rocky-sandy mixture. Three wizards in tight robes ran around preparing their wooden vessel for the journey. One of the men recognized melmo and handed him a card, then resumed his work. The card read, "OFF-ISLAND EXPLORATION CONSORTIUM." Melmo read the card out loud to the three men. "Archibald," stated the eldest, "Cortil," stated the youngest, and ", Aclute" stated the one in the boat. Archibald spoke for the group;" We discover new lands and explore the vast oceans." Melmo gave a second look at the long boat. "Any new lands, lately?" Aclute held a map and ran over to melmo's position. Aclute pointed to a smudge of a dot several miles west of their position. The dot read, "'Crane Reef' (Property of Cat's Wall)." Aclute continued," We discovered the reef, a year ago, and credit the success to our long boat, <u>The splinter</u>. Melmo's mouth puckered a ripple and he imparted, "Congratulations." Aclute nodded, and then all three of them nodded. Melmo smiled at the consortium and put himself in the last rung of the long boat. Cortil and Aclute piled gear in front of melmo until he stood up and moved all the gear to the farthest rung. Then aclute and cortil pushed the boat into the water with a splash. Archibald stood and stated, "Consortium, Commence Exploration." Aclute handing melmo an oar; all four men rowed north. The wizard's didn't complain at the rowing and only needing to row for one hour, one of the wizards calling forth a great fish from the ocean, moving the boat the required distance. The fish wasn't an eel or a seahorse just a big spotted fish with low centered gills. Aclute having watched the many Tantamount captains make a double rope loop; he began a lasso hold around a fish with a bowline. Cortil who was twiddling his fingers, after calling the fish, moved to the side of the boat and began to splash in the water with his right hand while making shrieks with the side of his mouth. Melmo felt compelled into discussion," What is he up to?" Archibald sat upright in the boat and gave an explanation in the representative's ear," Cortil can talk to fish." The leader of the expedition stood overlooking the operation," He is usually charismatic with them." Melmo called out to cortil," Is the fish going to the portal?" Cortil smiled and turned a reply," The fish says the air bothers his ears. He'll get us an hour of the distance." Archibald looked at his friend with a look of surprise," Did you thank the fish," Cortil seemed to nod, as the fish seemed to nod and then the boat powered north. After the fish had left the boat, melmo brought an intelligent observation in the group's direction. "How do we know when we reach the portal?" The immediate response of head tilting didn't fill melmo with enthusiasm then the trio pushing forward formed a huddle. Their whispers were low and unusually soft for melmo didn't hear the conversation at only a half a foot's distance. He did hear the clap. The group made a thunderous clap, as Aclute rose to a standing position in the middle of the long boat. Aclute held his hands covered and then opened them, revealing a tiny black box with a red button. Aclute pushed the button and lasers formed a grid line at the center of his chest and on each grid line read the coordinates. "Archibald, looked at the readings and then each of the passengers and in a strange coincidence announced, "We have reached the portal." Archibald moved cortil and aclute to the side as he left the boat and entered the water. The elder wizard lifting his arms in the air while flames sbegan surfacing from his undercoat. The flames extending from the wizard's feet gave him lift to the required portal height. The wizard hovered as cortil commented to melmo," I don't see the portal." Melmo couldn't see the portal and then archibald from mid-air shouted," Land." Melmo furrowed his brow as

Archibald dropped into the water. Cortil and aclute reached and pulled their leader into the boat. "Did you see the seventh?" Aclute asked. Cortil smiled and dried the leader with a towel. Gasping for breath, Archibald pointed west with cortil and aclute resuming rowing. Melmo got the leader's attention while he was still rubbing the cloth on himself. "Did you see the seventh?" Archibald put the towel to the rung and told the representative," I saw a coconut tree on a rock," we need to mark the location. Melmo fell on his knees and held his head.

Several hours south at a clearing where rocks and sand meet bog fodders, a meeting of the <u>Cat's Den</u> was commencing. All the governors of every major mountain convened on the ground and relaxed on a group of boulders. Most Cats' Den meetings were grooming only affairs. Occasionally, they are called on in matters of war, peace, or money. Parseval in a very non-humanoid persistence ran really fast in a circle and scratched every rock where the governor's relaxed. Then parseval sat in the center and waited for each cat to put paw over paw. Parseval licked his brow several times and then related his information. "There are off-islanders entering the portal to the seventh. Right now, the off-island exploration consortium is looking to the portal; we must send a message to the other islands. The portal is under cat's wall protection." Parseval paraded around in a circle and felt very confidant of every one's participation. When all paws petted the fur, parseval announced another of his grand ideas to the governors. "I am calling forth our fighting felines and wizards to return to Scio." A rather shaded black cat chimed in from a corner, "And our peace with the dragoons?" Parseval licked and pawed his ears many times before answering. "The dragoon peace is based on a war, we will send our unit with a general announcement to all the islands." The black cat became insistence on another opportunity," And the dragoons will be informed." Parseval extracted a claw, "Per our agreement with the dragoons, we will not send them to point rock. We will send an expedition to the volcano. Once the grand parity is informed, the other islands will learn." The other cat's grew in respect of parseval and rolled on their bellies in admiration. The governor relaxed and licked his fur.

Parseval isn't the only leader with tense posturing. The cat's wall rivals for Scio have similar considerations. On a lone mountain cave, lives nea and his advisors. The cave is the deepest in all the islands and the main entrance is always guarded with at least twenty five dragoons. The sides of the cave are gilded in gold and reflect any light straight into the sky. The enormous openings reside in a hole covering the mountain. At the center of the cave is a throne and treasure room for nea. Kur frequents the cave to give reports. Dragoon knew most outside reports from Kur and he was held in high regard. The throne room is huge and nea is allowed attendants, as he is king. The entourage routinely brings fish and ste'vans to the throne room for feasts. NEA has a full buffet on tables for any he decides to invite. Kur carries with him the wings of Triton and flew through the dark cave openings. All Dragoons on duty noticed him and none impeded his progress to NEA. 'Swoop,' the large dragoon rooted his feet in the dark sandy soil. The Cave was large enough for a full wing spread but the positioning of the lair, deep underground made most dragoons land before entering. NEA had a large gold chair in the center of the chamber where each entrant could notice his placement. Top the right of his chair sat Triton whirly bird boats filled with motheater meat and ste'vans prepared with sauces from off-island spices.

NEA's cave glitters with the sparkle of jewels and gold. The mining of precious ores is little known to outsiders and one of the mainstays of peace between the dragoon and shin people. At the chamber of NEA are passages leading to a shin mining operation. None of the dragoons save royals know of the mining operations. The Shin and dragoon relationship is symbiotic, the shin own the rights to all the woodlands in all seasons. A yearly dragoon hunt is allowed as shin forbearance and the negotiated peace between the shin and the dragoon nobility is believed as old as the story of atture and ack on cat's wall. The claim of longevity in peace between the two races is contested in age only on cat's wall and another source of friction in their claim of Scio ancestry and right. Neither dragoon nor the wizards have ever had open warfare, as the other islands politics and trade keep the boundaries. NEA's claim of kingship on dragoon is unrivaled.

Kur speaks usually in simplistic terms with NEA, many dragoons only relate with description or mimicry. Kur knows the symbols and gestures the ones regarding subsa, the atmosphere, and presents the wings of Triton. NEA's tolerance being pushed to the limit; his hands move in all directions, as a command is given. NEA dispatches a dragoon legion to retrieve the atmosphere and return the wings. NEA doesn't blame Kur and motions his friend to Scio and the obtainment of a new advantage on the Tritons. NEA's feelings shift from Triton. Kur's instructions are to get himself to Scio for an alternative weapon for the atmosphere. NEA wonders about the possibility of war with Triton. The King of Dragoon sits in his chair eating while looking at his spiced beef. NEA eats slowly on this night, as Kur powers an up climb from the chamber.

NEA not being the only indignant leader on the island, he had company on a near island. Indilep had all but put Tumult in a secondary ruling position on the volcano. Indilep didn't. Indilep and Tumult shared power; Indilep commanded his armies and Tumult ran the island. The volcano's main chamber bore a chair for each leader. On this day, Indilep was enjoying reading the reports of several lieutenants, while Tumult sat idle with a vapid expression on his face. Mecos entered the main meeting hall to update his report to Indilep. Mecos turned and made an official walk in Indilep's direction. "The Island is secure on all fronts?" Indilep asked the question before a formal presentation and then answered his own question," Excellent, then there is no trouble with the air of Scio." "Not Exactly," Mecos interrupted Indilep's posture. "What do you mean?" questioned Indilep. Mecos meant to clear his throat but instead coughed," Emote has formed a blockade, the leading general is someone named skimmer. He dispatched a note to my lieutenant." Mecos stood at attention waiting for Indilep's direction,

Indilep turned ravenous with confusion. He seized the note from Mecos. The note was simple and stern.

Indilep,

Your persistence on Scio is not recognized at the temple of emote. Emote is now a free protectorate until the day Scio stands apart from Ignis. The temple will produce over 1,001 legions of earthen warriors, brought up from the very soil, and will combat any attempt on emote.

Skimmer, Commanding General for the Defense of Emote

Indilep read the note and tossed it on the ground. Tumult picked up the note and read fast before trashing. Tumult's longstanding position on emote had changed. The Scion Leader felt a pride for the residence of Emote and a pride for Scio.

Kur arrived at the very moment when Indilep would have trounced Mecos's spirit. Indilep's confusion became contorted and he stood still as Kur walked to Tumult. Tumult was fluent in dragoon, one of the requirements of leadership on Scio, is a man had to be as logical as linguistic. Mecos followed Indilep's stare to the meeting. Neither Indilep nor Mecos knew the direct symbolic language of dragoon. A point of information not lost on Tumult. Tumult stood patient as kur relayed the events of Triton and dragoon. Tumult gave the sign for distress, motioning to Kur the island was now in the hands of Ignis. Tumult further signed Dragoon would get assistance with Tritons for help. The Predominate Dragoon feeling of conquest was benefiting Scio. Kur turned and suddenly realized, relaying bad information is a habit, he needed to break.

Grand Parity Tumult sat silent staring at the back of his hope, a great dragon man departing the room. "What did he say to you?" Indilep needed a distraction. Tumult smiled as he suddenly knew the tables had turned for the better. The Scion Leader gave the posturing of a man about his business. Stepping up and walking a way, Indilep's answer came, "The dragoons are looking to a war with Triton." Indilep smiled. He shouldn't have.

On the far eastern shores of cat's wall another pair of astute observers are giving their hands toward a reasoning defense. Cat's Wall Waters are usually filled with Tantamount boats on the north, as most cats aren't fond of water and most wizards don't know how to swim. Melmo knew how to swim and greatly enjoyed the many ocean trips his station encouraged. Melmo thought about his meeting with parseval and worried for his home island. The new stance of parseval spread through each peak on cat's wall. There seeming to be a tide of a wedge forming between the cats and the wizards. Most of the cat's believed the wizards had been to the seventh or knew how to get there and the wizards thought the cats took the opportunity to be 'King of the Mountain.' Melmo thought if there was an answer; acumen would know the best course to proceed. Melmo enjoyed the bog fodders as with a flurry of new boats being built on the island, he enjoyed a peaceful walk through a quiet area.

Knock, Knock, came the noise on acumen's door. "Be home for once," Melmo rarely talked to himself but he was nervous. "Who is at my door," Acumen finding himself up and awake for melmo. The aged wizard, not aware of most island dignitaries, knew melmo as his over cloak was much brighter then any other person on the island. The door opened and melmo entered acumen's surroundings. The ancient wizard invited melmo for a seat and cleared away some papers. "Let me guess, the seventh," acumen's years had taught him inquiries to the seventh always arrived in groups. "Yes," melmo replied. "Cat's Wall needs you to open the portal as there are some off-landers claiming to have entered the seventh and the cats are concerned." Acumen surprisingly faced very few direct questions, as most people either were eager for the seventh or eager to protect the seventh. The wise man straightened his back, "The seventh is protected and the cats shouldn't worry. Tell the cats on the mountain, acumen is protecting the seventh." Melmo felt more comfort in the old man's words then in parseval's demeanor. "Maybe we should both tell him," acumen shrugged and followed the representative out the door.

On an island catty cornering cat's wall two groups of people carry messages. The dual consignments hallmark very contrary purposes. 'The Swabbed Deck' had brought all the chairs and tables outside to scrub and wash, in between shifts. The bar workers ignored most outside events, as most weren't immediately discernable as important to bar operations. Today would be different. The angels had just reached the shores of Triton and climbing gave a best approach on the bar's landing. Shimmering is teleporting and teleporting is fast. Apparently on a bright sunny day, only a third as fast as a dragoon legion full out. The legion spotted the angels, a most unlikely event. A bar worker almost spilt his cleaning water with the appearance of the angels and then in a last minute move of the left hand caught the rag ridden bucket. The bar workers stood still for the event and maintained there eye focus between the dragoons and their cleaning. The dragoons were slowed owing to the overriding idea; the Triton defense could defeat them in the sky. The leader of the air wing gave a distinct eye and motion in the surface direction. Wings up and feet down giving an abrupt impression in the fertile soil. The dragoons landing on Triton soil brought their arms immediately forward, closing the range between them and the angels with the atmosphere. None of the angels spoke dragoon, being an angel is far less diplomatic then usually necessary. Marcus, seeing the dragoons approaching, uttered the feelings of the group," NEA's not happy." Spring Shine pulled out the atmosphere. "The idea of handing over a weapon used against Tritons on Triton soil doesn't seem the wisest of options." Then the Archangel notices something. One of the dragoons is carrying the wings, "A direct trade," Magis issues. "A direct trade," Spring Shine agrees. Angel secrecy is beneficial and then there is the benefit of Triton/dragoon diplomacy. Spring Shine placing the atmosphere on the ground in front of them, he begins to chant. The bar workers, now cleaning a chair, slip on a wet spot with the appearance of dragoons on Triton soil. Neither Marcus nor Magis knew the spell commencing and both stood in awe of the event. On a clear blue cloudless sky, a bolt of lightning pierced the atmosphere. Marcus and Magis held their breath. The dragoons snorted and the rarest of things breathed fire. In an imitating fashion each of the dragoons sought to destroy the wings, as dragoons didn't need 'a wing machine.' After many attempts on the wings, the legion returned to the offshore skies. "You might have just started a war," Magis explains. "No, I think Triton will be safe." The wings reappear on the backs of all three angels. The bar-worker faints. The angel's words echoing in the night air for their flight toward the center of the island.

On another island war became the main consideration. Rider reviewing a sheet with his supply listing calls to a group on the long shadow conning tower from the temple grass, "Find Hanz. Bring all weapons in the armory and place them in the emoten temple." Then the captain strolls along the green where skimmer is waiting. The crew forms a line and shuttles the needed items in a convoy. The general begins talking before the captain is within comfortable conversational range. "Do you remember the boat my plantation staff is building?" "Yes," rider standing motionless, sensing a clause in the agreement. "The ship is a sloop; is on the water; and you will be in command. Rider you're job is simple. If you can keep Ignis off of emote then we win." "Simple." The captain felt very close to skimmer. Rider not losing face, always added something to the conversation, "And will show you the capabilities of the long shadow." The general instituting a silent facial remark as rider leaves the conversation; Skimmer believes the captain should be in top form. Such is a military command to individuals.

Chapter 13

War, Peace, and Prosperity

Rider entered the long shadow for a briefing of the officers. "Are we hunting for some magical item or protecting one as temple escort," john became more talkative as positive sounds seemed to help rider's mood. Rider grabbing his hip, made a very awkward twist. "We are involved in a war." Although, Flink was present, Hanz hit himself in the head. Rider folded his arms, "The temple is paying the long shadow to lead the naval barrage." As if remembering Hanz spoke up, "The reason for the armory being cleaned out." "The reason for the armory being cleaned out," Rider repeated his exact words. John became a ray of sunshine again, "You have a plan," Again rider repeated an officer's words. "Skimmer is leading a ground defense on emote, we have an above water sloop and the long shadow. The sloop will get most of the boats crossing the water; our job will be surfacing under the stragglers." "Piece of Cake," Engineman Robert stated with a smile and bestowing enthusiastically, as the plan included him. "Robert, I will need you to man the engine room for ballast floods and clearing. The Long Shadow will give emote an advantage. We will make the advantage worth while. I know skimmer well enough to know we can hold the island. The Ignis armies won't be busy with skimmer, if they never reach him." John saluted the captain," Admiral." The other officers also saluted the," Admiral."

One of the yearly traditions on cat's wall is the "scaling of the fire." The fires on each mountain writhe up and down the surface of the mountain and create an astounding visual attraction. All the cats and wizards stand on light rotundas and await the signal from the governors of the mountains. "RAWH... RAWHH... HSSS," the lights beckon a flicker and then the light rolls the surface. The man in a circle on the ground commences the signaling then abruptly puts a halt to the lights; pausing the participants motionless. Melmo stands on the ground reiterating known information to acumen lingering before parseval's mountain. Acumen raises an arm with a sense of a connection between his arm and his back. "The display lures many visitors as all the populace of cat's wall manually make the lights move. Only visitors get the true picture." Acumen smiles, "I have seen the attraction, quite amazing." Melmo and acumen approach the mountain stairwell; continuing in conversation. "Parseval must be waiting for us." Melmo held the wall for acumen's entrance and then in continuation, spoke." To begin the scaling..." The stairwell being exhausting for young wizards and cats; melmo held acumen's arm up each rail to the mountain office. The stairwell's ascension became quicker with altitude, acumen's agility being in fortitude with his spirit. Parseval was busy moving stacks of paper on his desk when melmo and acumen entering from a lower rise in the floor. The day being overcast on Cat's Wall and the cranes marching at a high estuary, they sometimes could be seen littering the governor's door. Each crane towering above the wizards and cats, Parseval's view could see them at the entranceway and in a side window. "The tallest creature on the island is cultivated for food. Still, they are held in reverance and given the freedom of movement around and between the mountains." Parseval talking to the cranes or maybe himself, gave melmo and acumen a notice to not obstruct his sight. "The larger mystery might be the reasons the cranes stay at all. Some believe the cranes are much more intelligent then us cats or human wizards credit them with." Melmo and acumen eyed the almost human looking birds and sunk in their disposition for the taste of them. The lead cat became impatient with the matter before him and in decision decided progress needing to be imminent, began conversing with his guests. "Well, can you open the portal?" As if acumen's stance had been built into his character he responded to the cat. "Why?" The cat almost flew out of his seat with the aged wizard's question. "Because we should know the secrets of the seventh," the cat pawed at the desk top. A retraction of claws gave his paws a soft feel over the stone, still there being an urge to scratch, he consciously held his temperament. "And keep them in a filing cabinet?" Acumen hadn't felt as alive in a discussion for many years. Acumen stood above the questioning feline. Parseval gave motion to side chairs and acumen and melmo sat for the large cat. "Yes, the island needs to be fully in control. We can't have off-islanders parading around our waters." Acumen raised a finger to parseval's pawing of papers. "The portal is technically in Ignis waters." The mere mention sent the cat through the mountaintop. Parseval licked his paws for several minutes then posted a response. "Just keep the other islands out of our portal." Acumen didn't wait for an answer; he knew the portal would be cared for. Melmo looked at the aged wizard as a mentor. Parseval never broached the subject again. The pair quieted an exit with the dimming of parseval's channel fire and a crane flying into the distance from the lit doorway.

Lucius awoke on a perch to greet the morning sunrise. Triton messengers sometimes find perch chairs more restful then beds as the wing muscles need to be upright. "I don't know how you sleep on those things Victoria noted passing in the mansion hallway." Most Tritons sleep on their stomach and only the very disciplined can handle a perch chair while sleeping. Her feet screeched the marble and banked her in Lucius's direction. The tips of Victoria's wings fluttered on the edges and she rose slowly from the ground making a huge push up with her hands. Lucius smiling to her gesturing, he awoke. The cleanliness of the marble is usually the most eye catching sight in a Triton mansion, accompanied with the almost invisible nature of attendants who prepare and leave food but are never seen conversing with residents or even walking about. In the main hall, delicacies spread on a buffet tray for each to sample. Lucius and Victoria ate sparsely the snack. The chancellor preparing the days events found his thinking reasonably sure. Reasonably sure he is still leading a group. Victoria and Lucius met him in an enormous center meeting room with much food on display. "We will fly to the Triton delegation and decide matters from there." Victoria thought only of her bird," Is George going to be able to come along?" "Oh yes," briefed the chancellor. Lucius and Victoria both gave only a nibble to each of the trays. "Will need to lead him off the mountain top first and then you can all accompany me to the delegation building." Lucius issuing a small wave to the chancellor's attention, "Dispatches have never extended to quite such a magnitude." Robbins exhaling a sigh outstretched his arm to his friend. "Lucius, will figure matters from the center," Lucius wasn't entirely comfortable with the chancellors answer and looked more resolute in his personal disposition.

George didn't have any food on the mountaintop and remained at full stance for the Triton departure. The wind flew briskly and the mountain began humming with the above highway and morning enlivening. The large bird lumbered a few steps to the left and right and shook the feathers at the morning. George remaining the only resident of the gazebo level most of the entire night. "George will be happier with a short run, considering our travels," Lucius put in. "Is he up to the task," the chancellor didn't doubt, he was just being himself, a diplomat. The chancellor pushed on the birds feathers and George spontaneously gave a leap of the pyramid gazebo. The three flew fast with wings spread, on George's exponential arc of the mountain. The feet of the bird and tail feathers fit perfectly just missing the edge of the gazebo setting. The angle of flight extreming George at near vertical stature. The three passengers found a hold and then found a sealing with their grips. The bird landed tight on the ground with one of the frequent up currents from the Triton floor. "I think George has had enough flying," Victoria put to the group. "Then will walk," neither Lucius nor the chancellor seemed to object to ground travel. George gave a relax side to side move as walking meant George placed his feet calmly.

The chancellor walked to the Triton delegation with his entourage as escort and his presence was giving him celebrity. Victoria began walking George in the manner befitting a gentle personal pet. Walking Tritons, gave to waving and patting the group with a feeling of closeness in the central community on Triton. "Do you think they heard about our trip?" "They must have?" The Chancellor requited assuming of the mass of his fans. "Certainly the aggressions of Ignis didn't spark this sentiment," Lucius put his hand center through the drifting and separating crowds. The chancellor pursed a concrete road which kept widening to a large building in the shape of a star. Robbins gave tourist information," The Star is standing flat and upward facing, a vistor can imagine the shape or fly for a look." Both Lucius and Victoria were familiar with the delegation view from the sky. Lucius put his center hand toward the chancellor's move.

The chancellor began walking Victoria to a post where George could rest next to other personal whirly birds; the lawn sloping down from the birds and creating a huge nesting site on one side of the building. "I am amazed whirly birds do not have an aggressive temperament," Lucius noting George's restful nature with Victoria leashing him to an upraising pedestal mark, all metal rope and chain. "The first birds George has seen since the bar." Victoria patted her composure. "And yes Lucius, some have an aggressive temperament, makes them faster flyers later." The chancellor didn't pause on the time to praddle with his companions. "Little one, the bird will be safe here." The chancellor reassured Victoria as the group walked toward the center of the complex.

Celebus overlooked the proceedings at the temple on emote; the entire populace of Emote, 3,000 residents not including skimmer's plantation crew in the water and the temple security guards at post. Since uniforms and tailors were in small supply, most of the residents emblazoned an 'E' on their chest. The stockpiles of weapons were small considering only the weapons rider provided and the temple magical items. The General took center stage to address the crowd; a small wooden stand on the granite stairs viewing rows of people standing with surrounding security. "Everyone will form a line; the tenth person will receive a weapon or magical item and instructions." The lines moving fast, each tenth person received a weapon. "The rest of you will grab hold of a rope attaching to a pole. When the armies approach, you will all be cast invisible. A temporary shield will be in place for Ignis's push and the army will be allowing a five minute wait. Celebus turning to Skimmer," Ignis will only realize fifty-four of us, you have a very large advantage in perception." "Strategy," Skimmer resuming his post began harkening an elbow to his right brow. "In addition, we have a box full of tree shoes. The tree shoes are aimed at the feet of the Ignis troops, when activated the shoes will plant them in the ground with a root system. There are one hundred of these. Wait for close proximity. The tree shoes will be given to the invisible troops. There will be earthen warriors fighting on our side; these will compose the first wave. The Invisible troops will be positioned to either side of the approaching army. I will raise my hand when the invisible troops are to commence. Another advantage will be our navy, our ships will bring down most of the advancing troops and after the initial battle; there is the possibility of advance. My hand will raise out for an advance." The general's hand outstretching, a person in the crowd reached with a question," And the sign for retreat?" Skimmer looking at the man made an upturn of his lip and a resting of his arm on the post," There is no sign for retreat, we live here; only a sign for their retreat." The crowd cheering a wave, "Emote and Skimmer."

Only moments later, Trent ran from his security post at a full sprint. The crowd moved allowing him the straight run up the temple stairs; skimmer met him at the halfway point. "Ahah... Ahah," "Breathe," became the official general's command. After ten breaths and several motions toward his airway, Trent breached a word. "The Ignis troops are approaching the shoreline of Scio, The battle has begun!"

Indilep sat with an ambiguous expression on his face as he peered at the striped walls for solace. On this day, the grand parity was reviewing the new inventions of the island. The flat clean floors in the chamber clapped with the feet of technicians vying for approval. The parity's scientific advisor described each discovery as lab technicians demonstrated their utilization. "The first is a super strong all purpose glue," the advisor's words explained. White-coated lab technicians pasted their shoes together; and their goggled helpers held them suspended in mid-air trying to pull them apart. The Grand Parity signed some paperwork in his advisor's hands and waved on the next group. Indilep's gaze shifted and he slowly began to stare at the proceedings. Tumult caught the stare," Shouldn't you be seeing to your troop's activities?" Indilep didn't answer. "The next is ..." Indilep stood and walked out of the room.

In the backdrop of the hall could be seen scientists making finger gestures to their lips. Let me read states one of the men.

To all interested island delegations:

Ignis is appeasing the populace of Scio with food rations in exchange for their silence in regards the huge army engulfing the island.

Please Help, Patriotic Scions.

"Perfect," the man sent the huge mail stack down a shaft. The scientists moved off on tip-toe. In the wake of the scientist's departure came Indilep marking his steps toward the window.

The Shin celebration of nature usually scheduled for the fourth day of the unfreezing of the waterfalls had been moved forward due to the presence of Tritons on their island and the sudden increase in activities of the dragoons. The festival coincides with the dragoon ritual of the hunt. The Shin Celebration honors the natural world's food supply which unlike on Ignis is only plentiful on the northwest and northeast corners of the island. "Pitter, Patter," the feet rustle the leaves. The nearly invisible line of the shin became serpentine as the twigs and leaves scattered in the wind. The massive wall of legs broke the tree line and uniformly lined the edges of the tulba, dragoon's largest river.

On the opposite side of the river, the dragoon's blazed fires and hit each other in the chest. The Dragoon participants carried ritual scythes on furry sticks. "Zoom," the dragoon's crowded the air, leaving the shin in deep concentration as water pursed their lips. The Dragoons in their revelry of the hunt; scout dives on motheaters scooting along the forest floors. Unlike, a normal hunt the dragoons will not scout the creatures on the ground. The Dragoons get one dive per motheater and must get a single motheater before touching ground. In experienced dragoons don't notice the herds through the camouflage of the tree layer and the most acute dragoons usually take several hours before a success. The Dragoons each dive at full speed toward the ground. Only when the first has achieved success will any dragoons' land. The hunt is a test of flight stamina, visual acuity, and determination. The Shin pealing from the river line form a grand contrast as they spin in intertwining circles and chant low tones. Many shin will find mates during the spinning circles and a few of the celebrations last for days. The circles keep spinning dark or light and bond each of the shin to the herd.

Looming over both celebrations is NEA's lair, high on a mountain top. The lair has many openings for entrances to the central chamber, for dragoons believed in prowess not discipline. The returning dragoon detachment held in formation as they entered the view of the gilded cave. The dragoons flew at several hundred feet from the celebrations. There wasn't a formal command issued or instructions given from the leader, the dragoons flocked as birds might in a dive. The entrances were all down sloped with criss-crosses throughout the funnel. The dragoons had such perfection in the technique, near misses were frequent as each zigged and zagged without loss of speed. The walls of the entire mountain shake with the entrance of a legion. The first to reach the landing site is the first to enter the cave. NEA stands and moves impatiently waiting for the entire assembly. Patience is a practical leadership skill NEA hadn't developed a taste for. The leader of the legion earned his rank due to his aggressive and persistent nature. Retreat on Triton didn't sit well with him. The dragoon cluster makes a bow at the now sitting leader. The shape for angels being a very awkward and silly hand gesture with both hands leveled on straight down arms. There is always at least one cackle from an assembly. The dragoon relates the tail seeming confused in consideration of a sign for a lightning bolt during the day. The great beast slams his fist on the ground and the king understands.

At the very moment when NEA holds the fate of Triton in his hands, the island representative entered the cave. NEA smiles as he wonders about the great advantage his servant had uncovered. Kur spoke in normal words as symbology was slow even for a small vocabulary. "Scio needs Ignis gone and will help against Triton." Dragoons very much honored prowess and thus held Ignis as a formidable island. NEA held his jaw as war with individually Great Island powers didn't seem the right approach. The thought of patience again crept into the king's mind and he advised the entire assembly. The King stands flaring his wings and breathing fire as he both gestures the symbols and speaks the words. "Scio, help Scio, Ignis destroy." Kur being deepest in the cave next to the King was surprised when the gathering moved aside for his departure. They weren't letting him leave, they were following him. One by one each dragoon fountains an exit. NEA frustrated with his kingdom throws his chair on his treasure pile.

No one was allowed to meet with the leader of the Triton delegation. Representatives, Chancellors, and other important dignitaries met in solitary sessions. The Triton delegation building was shaped in a star shape and several landing ramps extended over the slanted structure. The meeting will only be a few minutes. Maybe, Lucius you could show Victoria where the messengers work. The Chancellor entered a big dark hall with an angle toward the sky. The Particle Center was placed adjacent to the main Triton delegation building. The place resembled a particle accelerator with a big curved circle where messengers entered, received dispatches and departed. A shoot conveyed the messages and instructions to the winged people and a deposit area received messages. "Victoria, the particle center is the fastest means of dispatch on any of the islands." Victoria's head bobbed side to side as all manner of messages moved through the center. "Where do you work?" "I have an office as an official messenger and dispatch agent to chancellors and angels." Lucius led Victoria to the opposite side of the building through a grand hall. The hall was completely empty, the opposite of what Victoria expected. The first door, in a right hand section of the hall, read," Loquacious Lentil." "What's a Loquacious Lentil?" Victoria smiled answering her own question," A Talkative Bean." "No, Victoria," Lucius palmed the door with an outreached thumb and forty-five of his right forearm. Pushing the door inward; Lucius led Victoria into the partially vacant space. The dimly lit room held a table, a lamp and a man sitting in a chair on the other-side of the table with a parchment and ink. "Lucius and Victoria visiting the particle center," Lucius spoke the words and the man quickly wrote them on a piece of paper and handed them to Lucius. "Lucius made a bow at the man's ability and turned toward the door." Victoria didn't speak until the solace of the hall. Lucius, answered Victoria's question before she asked. "Any time of day or night you have something on your mind and want the ink version, visit a loquacious lentil. They write every word said in the loquacious lentil office." "I should visit their again," Victoria placed a finger to her lips. Lucius's face sighed a smile. Turning a left and then a right; Lucius, showed the office, he had earned through years of service. His name was scripted to the door in a bold black font. The sanctuary resembled a mini-version of the house of the chancellor and a small owl perched on the side of the office. The Tritons funneling in to the particle center were numerous. The traffic did slow as Lucius's office was on the opposite end of the building. The side of the building Lucius worked on had big rectangular openings for important messengers to conduct individual business. Victoria seemed to relate well with the small owl as she had an affinity for birds. "Don't you have to report or something?" Victoria actually enjoyed prodding Lucius. Lucius moved toward his desk. "I am my own boss as long as each chancellor or angel receives the correspondence and I am an effective agent of the dispatch. Some of my dispatches may last for several months." Victoria's eyed rolled as Lucius stated the obvious. The Triton girl felt a coming breeze as she manipulated the bird. One side of Lucius's office had a rectangular hole large enough to stand a Triton with outstretched wings. Victoria examined the rectangular hole in Lucius's office. Peering around the corner she could see a section of the building where people were coming and going. "Looks very near a beehive," she observed. "You are awfully smart for a bird keeper." Victoria laughed.

The chancellor was very fast in his meeting, as the next event was his feet on Lucius's marble. "Lucius, the situation has deteriorated on Scio and Triton is preparing for war. The delegation has assigned you and Victoria to accompany me as my personal envoys for the duration. With your agreement of course," the chancellor leveled his hand to his companions. "Of Course," Lucius handed his words. "Are we going into battle?" Victoria's pride partly stemmed from her expository function. "Victoria, we are the special arm of the government of Triton. The three of us will accompany a large group of boats in a mediating function." Lucius dropped his chin and raised his nose. His thoughts, wondering, where the other islands were running into problems. Victoria's thoughts wondered if the adventure would continue forever. The Chancellor's words resounded as the only audible pitch, "Ignis must be stopped."

Ignis didn't hear the chancellor's words as the sixth battalion sent a detachment to cross from the western shoreline of Scio to Emote. Mecos and Skimmer were close enough to see each other across a very slim 1/4 mile channel. Skimmers view was more intimidating with thousands of Ignis troops entering battle boats. Mecos's view was deceptive as he only saw fifty four men.

Skimmer commanded from a high mound less than a mile inland and motioned Celebus to the shield. The shield emerged around a one mile radius surrounding the temple and didn't include the battle boats. Half of the boats were overturned in the first few minutes of leaving shore. Not due to the shield, due to a long black wake ripping through the surf. "Rider must have wanted the first move," skimmer observed as the sloop hadn't yet reached the boats. Rider swamped dozens of boats and the Ignis regulars put their effort in to treading water. The small sloop came at an angle to the coastline surrounded by trees and flanked the red skiffs. The sloop crushed the remaining boats aiming for their keels at full sail. Ignis soldiers didn't have to fall in the water, with the sloops attack, and many grabbed the side of the ship. In minutes, the sloop was swarmed with an insect attack from Ignis. Each troop didn't attack the crew. The Ignis soldiers ignited their torches and put them right into the hull of the ship. Only a few minutes and the sloop was a blaze with fire. The Plantation stewards had a very short life in battle; The Ignis troops with nickel plated swords and torches burned the sloop and had the entire crew swimming for emote.

"Very clever," Mecos observed of the boats and proceeded to put more boats in the water. The sloop was gone and rider proceeded onto his next stage. The troops of Ignis began to link the boats in a tremendous chain. A wave of an attack headed directly for the shoreline. The second wave commenced slowly and all the residents on emote patented their resolve. Thunk, the boats hit the shield just before the beach. Mecos remained on Scio with more troops and couldn't advise his boats at the shield's edge. Then a very curious Ignis troop went overboard and found the shield didn't extend underwater. The occupants of the boats all bellied under and crawled to the sand. Leathery Large the group began igniting drying torch cloths and assembling in detachments on the beach head. Skimmer didn't let them. From a raised hand the "T" was pushed far into the rugged turf. An earthquake pattern erupted in the terrain as far as a few meters from the Ignis landing squad. One of the invisible residents could be heard yelling as the quake knocked him over a boulder. Skimmer collected these magical wonders with much the affinity of Celebus, Quandor, or rider; yet one never knew the full impact of an untested item. Earthen Warriors reached up as if rising from their graves to walk the earth. The number matched the incoming wave at three thousand. Skimmer would have enjoyed more. He watched as the earthen warriors moved in his direction. Skimmer ran forward with a loud roar," defend the shoreline, destroy the Ignis troops." The dirt and clay warriors commenced combat. The first Ignis troop testing the earthen combatants found his torch extinguished and his body being engulfed. Skimmer would relate the tale," As if the ground swallowed up the enemy and buried them six feet under." Few of the Ignis troops were able to recover. The crusty creatures buried the group of Ignis soldiers landing on the shoreline. The gravel and dirt formed a line stretching from one side of the southwestern seaboard to the north end of the island. Each of these beings spaced out twenty feet apart and could dispatch an Ignis troop for every foot of separation. Mecos disappearing behind his troops, skimmer began a smile. Celebus walked over and smoothed the dust from his skimmer's shirt. "Nice work," Celebus relaxed. "Let the sloop in!" skimmer seeing his plantation crew began moving the soil essences; allowing them to the mainland. "Sloop Crew reporting," his butler managed with a salute. The rest of the sloop crew forming a pyramid behind their leader, skimmer returned the salute. "Relax on the temple grounds and will call if we need you further." The plantation crew crossed the green slope north to the temple.

In the swampy nest of a giant frog, a butterfly could be seen pacing toward a stone window. Lily pads were adjoined with tiny bubbles, as bushes could be seen outlining a tree line. An amphibian tongue barely missed the darting shape. The butterfly charted a jagged course, as the yellow and black wings moved into the de angelis hallway. With antenna raised the butterfly found landing on a brown paper package outside the minister of domestic and foreign relation office. Large for an insect, the butterfly sifted through bows and ribbons on the giant carton. There a small bit of sweet sugar resided just below the nameplate. 'To the minister of domestic and foreign affairs: The Wings. Archangel Spring Shine.' The ravenous tick engulfed the nectar before flying on down the empty corridor.

Further inland, the chancellor's fury had found purchase. The Triton delegation was adjoined with an attached side building known, as the whirly boat loading center. Those accompanying chancellor Robbins on his return to Scio would board their whirly boats in the giant warehouse structure. The warehouse holds huge bins of fish for all the birds and a large boat stockpile. The opposite wall from the bins houses the great birds in huge stables from the ground to a one-hundred story ceiling. Ten of the center's best whirly birds were on the ground with boats attached to their backs. Guiding the group in one boat were the angels (Spring Shine, Marcus, and Magis.) "The commander of the boats is a man named

Beak." The Chancellor may have been talking to the group and may have been reminding himself. "Beak is a great name for a boat commander," Victoria even made Lucius smile. The Three Tritons strolled into the warehouse and halted at the last bird. The Chancellor met briefly with beak and the angels. The Archangel and his two associates were already in a boat and beak and the chancellor spoke from the preparation floor. Beak turned to the chancellor, "the angels are accompanying us... you are still the leader of the diplomacy. Congratulations, Island Representative." "Nice to hear," stated Robbins. "Your presence here is most unexpected archangel." The representative faced Spring Shine in the boat. Only the Archangel and Magis could be clearly seen from the bird. "We are here in a helping capacity." The Archangel put to the representative and then relaxed in his seat. Magis turned to the representative," A Helping Capacity!" Marcus nudged magis in a strange turn of events. The Chancellor turned to find George and found Victoria right in his face," Can I help?" The Representative losing a slight commanding nature," Get on your bird." Victoria had walked the bird from the delegation building and with his beak full of fish, she felt assured of his abilities. Lucius slowed Victoria's stride," Wait, these are for you." Lucius pulled out a pair of goggles. "The messengers use these in inclement weather, the inside lights up and they can see through the darkest, wettest, rain." Victoria gave Lucius a hug. The three boarded George, as the fleet of whirly birds ran to the sky.

Rider's Crew didn't have the full information. Rider always kept certain details to himself and some he never divulged. In the thick of the campaign, Rider addressed the entire crew. Usually rider chose the cargo hold; today he chose the deck hall with seaman pouring out of every hole. "The Long Shadow is landing at a very close proximity to Ignis occupied Scio. I'm asking for volunteers to sink the hulls of their boats, the volunteers will use the conning tower to drop these spherical charges in the water." The questions grew numerous and Hanz kept the peace," One at a time, raise your hand," The Hands which were flying up were quelled and then reduced to only three. "Yes," Hanz pointed to the nearest raised hand on the deck. "Will the charges be active before the release?" "No, very easy, push the button and drop at least 14 feet from the ship; Next Question?" A second hand referring from Hanz, "Will there be risk from the Ignis troops." "No, if an Ignis troop gets aboard ship, seal the hull and will drop the ship a hundred feet, advance another hundred and continue. Next Question..." A man from the rear of the ship fumbled into the corridor, "Flink," Rider knew. "Will we hold the island?" Rider paused on the question for a momentary reflection," Flink the question isn't can we hold our island but can Ignis hold theirs?" The crew came alive with movement and the ship became an effective machine. Rider did an about face and headed for his command room. His officers followed in toe. John didn't let the moment pass. "Water Mines can't be our best plan?" Rider stopped his walk. "See if we have torpedoes." The officers moved at as quick a pace as the crew. Rider turned into the command room, the ship filled with shouts and calls.

John ordered the ship to surface just in viewing distance of the emote populace; now visible and watching behind a wall of humanoid dirt mounds. Mecos called the chain to an advance. The next wave of battle boats headed for the emote coastline, acutely aware of the obstacles. Each boat carried lines of ropes and manual pump hoses. The Long Shadow infringed on the meniscus, less than five feet from the line of boats. No sooner had Hanz opened the conning tower hatch to the outside air, then he closed the hatch again. "They're outside," Hanz nervously uttered. John stood confidant to hear his words," Good. Throw those spherical charges and will all get some ale." "No, They are just beyond the ship," the words reached the first-mate's lobes, as the thud of a dozen Ignis troops on the ships hull could be heard. John began shouting, "Submerge... Submerge..." Rider also hearing the sounds began investigating them down the hall. "Submerge," rider screamed, increasing his officer's authority. After several seconds the ship drops below the water's surface. The thing rider didn't plan for being the Ignis troops fastening their lines to his ship. Rider and his officers don't see the exchange. After several seconds the ship drops below the water's surface. "Flood the ballasts," Rider calls as the hallway remains a temporary command room. The Long Shadow submerges ten feet down and then ten feet toward Scio; twenty feet down and twenty feet toward Scio. The long shadow doesn't drop below twenty-one feet as Mecos's soldiers begin pulling the ship onto shore. John faces a dismal turn as he expunges his phrases," Torpedoes aren't gone a help a sideways submarine." Skimmer bore witness to the events and watched the Long

Shadow's reemergence with Mecos. The filtering sand scratches and nicks the hull as the longshadow pushes up a sand bank to a forest alcove. Rider makes a pensive look then issues an order," Keep the hatch locked." The Ignis swords and torches subsisting quite a mismatch against dirt creatures. The Ignis armory is quite effective against the hull of the longshadow. Each burning torch and sword makes searing weld openings in the hard clean surface. Flink, always being present for events is the first to see," They're gonna burn a hole through the ship." Flink runs in the engine room; his words begin echoing in the captain's ears. Robert immediately puts a slap of metal in Flink's hands and pushes him to seal the edge. Around the ship other sailors make similar conclusions. Robert moves swiftly from one side to another and the officers see them bobbing and weaving out of compartments. John grabs at the spherical charges; He moves at least one in hand. John pushes into the face of rider, his feelings reaching certainty. "What are your orders, captain?" Rider smiles and sighs in a most official manner," The standing order is prey." Contravening Rider's order comes the thunderous noise of thousands of men chanting," IGNIS... IGNIS..." Rider, John, and Hanz almost strain their necks listening to the swarms of feet running along the hull. The Ignis chants reaching an extreme, rider grabs his ears to ignore the aching reverberation. The Ignis troops begin to pound on the conning tower hatch making loud thrashing noises. After a second pound, a very unusual occurrence makes the crew uneasy. All gets deafly silent. The chants silence and if there were any soldiers on the hull, none moved a step; even the nickel swords vanish from an audible atmosphere. The three officers below the hatch stare at each others bewilderment. Almost to the count of three after a three-way stare comes a most unusual sound. "Ahhh, slap, swoosh." Several seconds pass then," Ahhh, slap, swoosh." Something outside helps rider lift these people off his ship. The crew stood holding hull bracings, equally stationary in their nervous endings. Rider recognizing his purposes got the crew in motion, "Quick now repair the hull." The crew moved to an uncertain advantage. Hanz recognized another sound outside, "Catapults and bows and arrows, whoever is helping us isn't on the ground." Hanz continued his lively talk with himself," One of us is gonna have to look." Rider moved to the ladder when his first mate grabbed his shirt, "My honor, sir." Rider reluctantly watched John. The first-mate climbed to the hatch and turned the metal wheel counter-clockwise. The two men witnessed him emerge to meet the light. Rider grew quickly impatient," Well, what do you see?" John didn't respond, he just motioned the captain forward onto a tilted conning tower platform.

In the sunset of a penciled grey sky, Tritons and dragoons battled on the blue. Each side lunged at the other. Several dragoons were breathing fire at a group of Triton boats while individual Tritons sought to level them to the ground. The most confounding site of all is both sides were fighting a two front war. Half of the dragoons and half of the Tritons were busy removing Ignis troops, first from rider's ship and next from the shoreline. The Tritons dropped each of the soliders, they picked up, into the watery deep. The Dragoons gave each Ignis solider a cart-wheel flip into the treeline. Rider turned and saw Mecos's eyes as he faded into the dark forest. As Mecos left the scene, he was concentrating his fire on the sky with arrows hitting Tritons and catapults smashing dragoons. Mecos didn't know which one to fire at, Rider's confusion stemmed from as Flink mentioned fourth on the conning tower, "At least they're both on our side."

George flew from combat and veered toward the emote temple green. As George barely passed the heads of the earthen soldiers, he ran to a landing adjacent to the general. Each of the walking dirt mounds turned to move at the bird. "Halt, resume your posts," Skimmer was fast with the order as his view was half-blocked with them. The advancing earth creatures began returning to the shoreline at a slow leisurely pace. Victoria, Lucius, and Robbins slid off the left side of the great bird. "Lawrence," Robbins was thrilled to see his friend on the opposite side of the island. "Robbins," a mutual friendship feeling pervading the adventuresome would be brothers. The scenes before them being unusual even to those who have seen combat and instead of hugging the two men moved shoulder to shoulder and viewed the carnage. Robbins began to review the circumstance as someone who was giving advice on a road map. "Apparently, a dragoon went out of formation at one of the birds." The scene didn't slow with their viewing as the angels could be seen casting spells to dislodge the dragoons from their whirly. Rider and his crew had to shut the conning tower, not due to Mecos but rather to protect from falling debris. Marcus was successful and sent half a dragoon wing into the conning tower while guiding the rest of the dragoon into the water. Skimmer grew tired of the feud," I think both of your groups were coming to help. How do we undue this?" Victoria and Lucius sit on a boulder rock near the two men and watch. "We wait," came Robbins to his friend. "What are we waiting for?" Skimmer being a matter of fact individual gave a statement, "Both sides fight a two front war; they will soon realize the mistake and come to meet us. There!" The birds and dragoons did turn and move toward emote, although they put a sharpie down the center line margin of the sky. Trent and his security team were flipping the remainder of the advancing boats with their tornado swords. The only question on Trent's mind was how far off shore put them on the wrong side of the earth mounds. The general was growing wise of his mystical control and ran ahead of the landing parties, "Resume your posts," as if in a comic gesture one of the earthen creatures shrugged a shoulder. The words were absolutely necessary, the spells having a lasting nature and the creatures were in their regard." Trent's team found equal time with the landing parties and avoids any terminal troubles. Robbins recognizes Kur with the dragoons and walks to his position on the field. Beak soon follows although the angels hold their positions.

Across the channel, Rider lifts a huge wing off his tower and the officers return to the view of the slanted overlook. John and Hanz are viewing the dragoon and Triton meeting on Scio. Rider doesn't. Rider is viewing the advance of Mecos. Rider grabs the back of both wrong facing officers. John realizes and with a gesture toward the sky, throws the spherical charge, he still holds. Then with tail between their legs, the group jumps down the conning tower shoot. The charge only has a slight delay and the huge explosion gives the long shadow a few minutes. More importantly, the long shadow is secure with the hatchway.

"We are here to fight Ignis." Kur couldn't have been clearer, as the woods explode to the west. The explosion isn't outward; the explosion is a push of sand in the air and clouds the wood line coast. Robbins and Beak raise their hands, as the dragoons are going to have an exhausting evening. Kur calls out to his brethren preparing to fill the sky, "ARRRR." Kur scratches his head and turns, "We could use some help." Kur really being an affable dragoon; the two sides decide to chase Mecos a fair distance from emote. Skimmer grabs for the air, "What about the Long Shadow," as he wonders, does the group notice a grounded submarine. Beak recognizes skimmer's command even without a word being in mention. Mostly beak recognized the island representative trusted him. "Wait," Beak didn't know if he could slow the impetuous dragoons. He did. Beak enters a semicircle formed from the dragoons. He points to the submarine on the banks of the river. Kur seems happy with the winged man. "Will get Sub . . ." "I'll help," Victoria calling in response to her overhearing the conversation, launches onto George, while Lucius thimbles a fast pursuit. Robbins deciding the island representative should figure the situation. He moves toward the direction sitting on the rock where Victoria and Lucius vacate. George followed the dragoons, as the boats prepared to leave the grass.

Beak's command flight doesn't run but make successive power shifts above the heads of the earthen soldiers. The last whirly, containing the three angels, moves anticipating the follow. Three fully expanded wings catch the up turned wind and breeze back onto the lawn. Spring Shine, first to the ground, waves the two angels toward Robbins and skimmer. Marcus and Magis make unusual faces at each other, as their feet just grip the soil. They were glad to be Tritons again. Skimmer's butler, a man of unusual make and stalwart dedication, offer the gathering glasses of water and puts a stand together for the victorious crowd. The residents gather around the group at the rock, as the battle for the submarine is getting underway.

Kur and his dragoons spend energy hovering, as George moves into position. Kur takes a moment and burns the ropes attaching to the ship. Victoria doesn't push flat on the George Button; she motions to the whirly's thigh with her legs and toggles the George Button on either side. George lowers his feet as a crane operator might, while gasping for breath. George grips but never lands on the conning tower, a most outstanding tribute to the trainer. The yellowish scaling feet wrap around the metal in a precision finger fold. The dragoons look to Kur as he ushers them to either side of the submarine. When the entire flight has some part of the vessel, Victoria flat palms the George Button. Each participant find the weight of the submarine light; owing to the mass of dragoons and giant whirly. George seems to carry the gathering into the air and then Victoria does something to leave little doubt of George's strength. As if in a ballet, George spins the submarine and dragoons a full one-hundred and eighty degrees. The Long Shadow crew being not unaware as an initial bounce causes a startlement in the officers. Hanz speaking more than he should; states the obvious, "Captain, I think were flying." John and Flink put on an athletic show, as the two men sideways brace their arms and legs to the bulkhead. They resemble the twirling of acrobats. Most of the sailors just hold onto the nearest solid structure. The activity has a most hushed overhang.

Victoria seeing her gaze mostly looks at the distance to the water. Her attention being quite in allegiance with her purpose; she relaxes in her position. The dragoons staring almost exclusively at the sky keep their minds on individual supports. Only George sees the flock of incoming whirly birds. Beak seeing the submarine at less than twenty paces, darts above the heads of the emote guardians, he leaps higher into the clouds. The aerial functioning seeming almost planned as whirly upon whirly skirts above George's feathers. Victoria feels uneasy with the passing birds, a feeling she didn't expect. The Triton girl considers dropping the submarine in the water when she deems the passengers in the metal vault, 'fragile freight.' With helical maneuvering, the submarine enters the greenish promenade. Swooping low, Victoria barely misses the masculine strong men protecting the island. Several of the dragoons retract from the direction of the dirt mounds. Once again, and even before the rivets are reaching the grass roots, the brownish bodyguards find animation and trot in the long shadow's direction. Only five paces off position and skimmer becomes comfortable in his command," Return to your posts." One of the mystical beings kicks the sod before returning the four paces to the sand. Victoria is extremely careful in her placement and lets the dragoons move away before relinquishing control to gravity.

As if at a Saturday morning event, the general's entourage calmly discusses matters, while in the back drop dragoons negotiate with a confused crew. Robbins still ascertaining the circumstances consults the general. "Lawrence, the Triton birds will keep Mecos moving but you might want to consider requisitioning to Triton for permanent independent status." The general doesn't answer, as Celebus feels the question his. "All of Scio should be free, and Triton, dragoon and all the islands should give us full help to rid ourselves of Indilep." Robbins doesn't disagree; he just always kept conversations in forward motion. Several of the Long Shadow officers struggle with the dragoons who chose to fly them individually to the ground, as the Archangel entered the afternoon tea. "The Angel's Guild officially recognizes Emote's temporary independent status." "Thank You, Archangel," Celebus bunches lips, being deeply honored, as the temple aspires to the angel's level of influence. George almost steps on Flink, rolling on the green grass, as the angels depart the gathering in anonymity. The angels leave to the northern edge of emote, in a steady slow walk. Captain Rider and Lucius cozy up to the rock of command while Marcus and Magis grip each foot consciously in the emote soil, gliding from the scene.

"I never thought I would live to see my submarine dry docked on someone's front lawn." Skimmer and Robbins being both amused at rider's comment. A lone resident approached with a question to the far side of Lucius and rider," General will you be in need of the citizen army, as we all wish to resume our experiments and crop tending." The man didn't speak for all the citizenry. He thought he did. So did general skimmer. Skimmer first looked at Robbins before answering, "Beak has sent word to another boat commander and the dragoons are still here." Skimmer almost shook his head and then halted a reply. "The day's activities are concluding. Make sure everyone is here tomorrow." Skimmer turns to Celebus, "The temple security remains on watch for the entire week." Celebus didn't shake his head. Celebus states an agreeable current with the island confidence. "The long shadow is resigning her commission and heading for open water." Rider being partly glad the long shadow is on the temple green, while the crew tests the ship's seams seaworthy. Lucius never volunteering for outside services; part of him felt the push of Victoria's enthusiasm. "We will help with the ship's repair." Rider suddenly found he was indebted on multiple occasions to Tritons. The captain managed a smile, not a comment.

The gathering was again moved to observation when the dragoons recovered the majority of the burned out sloop. Skimmer didn't argue with his vocal cords and just pulled the 'T' out of the ground and handed it to Celebus. The mounds of dirt remained in place and created a visual threat in the wake of the enchantment. Kur was able to recover the sloop with only three dragoons and most of the hull was waterlogged but intact. Skimmer's butler lost his composure as he grabbed the plantation staff for a rebuild. Before moving he turned to the general, "We will have the sloop afloat in three days." "I'm sure we will," skimmer like rider only chose people he trusted for close companions. A very affectionate scene appeared to the side of the dragoons, as Lucius and Victoria flew the Long Shadow repair team around the ship. Repair teams were all external to the dry dock and sparks flew initiating the metal in singular shear alignment. "Woo hah," Flink enjoyed flying and made several imitations of a bird to the amusement of Lucius and Victoria.

Farther west, Beak engaged an encircled Ignis camp. The Tritons held an ominous advantage, as the group hovered above Mecos's head. The trees on the northern part of the island were in small clusters and couldn't hide a force of Ignis's magnitude. Mecos looked to his lieutenant, the lieutenant gave the direct appraisal," Triton and Dragoon have a huge advantage in the air, we either have to take shelter and bring them down or let them have the land." Mecos expected an easy victory on emote and wrestled with himself regarding the current dilemma. "Move the troops to the center of the island and await my orders," Beak watched as Ignis marched south. "Not the right direction, but emote is safe." Each whirly waited for as long as hovering energy allowed before returning to emote.

Beak called the boats into a conference in the sky, "We will rotate lookout shifts and maintain a mile radius clearing." There were Triton boat captains saluting as their birds formed a squadron. Beak was prepared for the cooperative military strategy of Triton and dragoon, what he found surprised him.

Kur and Robbins were flying in the opposite direction. Robbins leapt into beak's boat with kur hovering outside. The boat commander sensed the reason," Do you need someone to go with you," "No, Beak will be discreet and fast. Watch over, emote." Robbins position didn't call for saluting. He saluted. Kur and Robbins pushed up on the next upturned wind and shuttled south as a curved warm embankment in the sky.

Robert ran up to address his captain. In the foreground, the light was drifting on emote's western shore. "The Long Shadow is going to need a few hours, maybe in the morning," Robert fashioned a palm to his forehead. "Excellent," Rider returned the salute. The official nature of the job did start to strike the captain as enjoyable. Rider believed Robert was dismissed from duty, as he came around for a second meeting. "There is one matter," Robert put one hand on his pocket as he voiced the question. "With the Long Shadow," Rider briefed the idea. "No," Rider wiped his brow at Robert's answer. "The sloop, I have some extra metal panels and the boys think we could give her a metal hull." "Good show," Rider was never cavalier with his formalities, yet his men were overworked, put in harm's way, and still helping others. Rider believed himself the beholder of the best crew.

Rider found the command rock and sat with some of his crew beginning work on the sloop and some relaxing on the cushioned lawn. A pair of emote natives ran over to the shoreline with buckets of plaster. The two poured the plaster over each earth mound statue and used flat stones to manipulate the fluid. They were making the earthen soldiers into stone statues. Celebus and Skimmer really were amused and brought several other buckets. "Maybe the look of them will give us all a reminder," Celebus put to skimmer. "No, will remember," skimmer held in his remark. A bird keeper could be seen on the island bringing out a big cage with a hundred hawks and releasing them, marking the occasion. Celebus walked toward the same command rock and made a declaration, "I hereby declare today, sloop shadow day on emote in honor of the brave crews. A few hundred of the residents were in attendance and cheered at the temple's decision. The officers stood next to the rock," We never had a day named after us," John mentioned. "Well, we still have to get the boat in the water," Rider asserted.

Many miles to the north of the temple, the seas gave to the larger crossing from Emote to the mainland of Ignis. Marcus emerged from a wooded shoreline and postured for a leap into the thin air. "Wait," the archangel cautioned as magis and Marcus appeared from the forest. Each of the three men had sweated hair and clothes and the momentary rest of accomplishment. Marcus didn't complain but he almost did. The archangel knelt on one knee and drew in the sands north of the waterline. "The wings are an advantage but even with a human island, the odds of detection are quite high." Magis steadied the pair's question," We can't shimmer over five miles." Five miles would be the required distance and well outside the limits of their favorite spell. "No, we are not just going to shimmer." The Archangel drew the edges of the shores and assembled ten dots in the center. "The shimmer spell will have to be formed together with swimming; you all know how to swim." Marcus brought out the practical observation," The wings aren't water proof." "True, Marcus, the wings aren't waterproof but the backbone is hollow and floats. A horizontal shimmer would enable us to keep afloat for the journey. The only risk is the shoreline will see us first if we reach a populated area." "You mean float on our stomachs," Marcus asked for confidence as much as confirmation. "Yes, stomach first and will float before we shimmer. And we might need to hold hands to assure the spells reach the same distance." In a more than awkward manor the three men put their heads in the water and relaxed their bodies to a float. Spring Shine's hand was partially noticeable to Marcus and magis. He raised and then lowered his gestures. The group shimmered to another spot deeper in the crossing. Again the group shimmered. Marcus and Magis felt the casting, synchronization, and floating tension. The number ten was amalgamated to twelve. The last shimmer put the group flat on a well hidden sand dune. "phww, phww, phww," all three men spit the sand from their mouths and cleared their palates. "There are easier ways," Marcus mentioned. "A water boat or bird might be spotted," Magis instructed his friend to the approval of spring shine. All three noticed the terrain change to a grassy warm tundra and gathered for further movements near a cliff facing.

Tumult paced the volcano heart as the scientific advisor sped an entrance. "Huh... Huh...," the man calms his nerves and gasps for breath. "The scientists have all left the building and are forming a circle around the volcano." The Grand Parity maintained his silence, and discreetly departed the central preceptory. The grand parity slowed his foot pace on approach to the glass curvature garnishing the outer hall. He pushed right and then left; discovering the central panorama, as his advisor looked on. Indeed a circumference of white jackets outlined the street below. Tumult might have starred for a few minutes; might, but then he saw Mecos's multitude moving straight for the volcano. At only five hundred feet from the white line, the soldiers ignited fire arrows. Tumult bolted for an exit stair and was caught from his advisor's arm. "You better read this before going out there." The grand parity put intellect and intervention on an even scale. Reading carefully, the letter stated:

To the leaders of the Scio think-tanks:

You will be provided with the necessary Ignis supplies at no cost. The food rations from Ignis proper will accompany each shipment. In exchange, you will not cause any obstacle to Ignis troops on Scio soil.

Signed,
Indilep

The advisor added to the new information," The men in white have been maintaining silence for many months and their silence is done." Tumult returned to his glass station. The clouds of the sky grew overcast and billowed toward the volcano. Then in a surprising occurrence, the arrows were extinguished, as the lab technicians unfastened their lab coats. Each of the thoughtful men surrounding the volcano were now dressed in Ignis Red. The advisor turned, also dressed in Ignis Red. Tumult felt the empty halls of the cavernous rooms. Bolting, he ran for the stairwell. "Clang," The stairwell ripped for the solid interior wall. He climbed one floor and then the next. Each foot trembled an elephant and each breath was a gasp. The leader continued his athletics until he reached the highest stairwell and pushed for the exit door. Despite his spending a majority of his time in the central hall or at a desk, Tumult didn't feel his body's needs. The outside air at the top of the building was moist. Tumult didn't give a moment's glance at the extreme slope in front of him. Climbing the precipice, he scaled the rock cliff until the leveled grips bent into a crater. Indilep and Mecos noticed and pointed at the Grand Parities Ascension. All of the Volcanoes Occupants were soon looking at only one man on the very edge of the highest crater tip.

Looking down, the leader saw something no one knew about. Hundreds of feet below his position a red pool filled and bubbled as steam began to rise. Tumult jumped as the crowd gave awe.

The few seconds between the leap and what came next caused the entire crowd a shock. Some of the scientists turned down and others couldn't look away. Indilep and Mecos were confused, as a winner trying to assess the other man's perspective. Indilep's focus was the first to shift as the steam began to rise from the depression. He wasn't staring at vent clouds; he was starring at some sort of comets shooting straight at the volcano. Flying in a fast diving posture, Kur and Robbins darted through the smoldering surface of air and eclipsed the center of the mound. The precision each man had for life was displayed in the exacting speed at which each would grab the parity's arm. The two representatives completed a parabolic turn. Rocketing the acidic bubbles, the grand parity did not yet comprehend his rescue. Kur grabbed the parity's up-stretched left arm as the chancellor coddled his right underarm. When, the three were ten feet above the last steam cloud, the explosion occurred.

In mid-air and at high altitude, Kur and Robbins observed as molten lava overran the center of the island. Immediately all in the vicinity were forced up and outward. Kur and Robbins didn't look to the fate of the Ignis Leaders or the scientists and remembered only their friend needed them. Kur put Tumult on his back, as they charted a course to emote.

The Grand Parity slept on the back of the great dragon man, as visible fatigue set into Kur's eyes. He was a dragon man and not a whirly. Robbins pushed up on the shoulders of the dragon man lightening the load. At the channel crossing, the men dipped low to the waterline and collapsed at a brief spacing between earthen stone statues. "The volcano is erupting," Robbins words paused skimmer and rider for impact. The men didn't see any signs of the eruption until the ashes began to rain down on the waterfront. As if the people of Scio heard the representative's call, a crowd began to form on the Scio's coastline. Celebus joined the gathering, lifting his would be leader to his feet. "Welcome to the free emote protectorate." "Glad to be here," the only words he managed before a forward stumble. Celebus realized; he would have to make the decision, regarding the Scions running from the lava streams. Several hundred residents of emote, heard the commotion and began to surround the long shadow and George. Celebus surmised an observation, "With no ships able to ferry all those people, they are going to have to swim." Some of the many balloon ships were racing across the steam and a few of them popped in mid-air, sending the riders into the water.

Others can be seen forcibly wading an entrance to the water and pushing the black soot boundary.

"Wait," Captain Rider grabbed skimmer's 'T' from Celebus and pushed the device into the ground. The moist soil gave easy with little much activity. The stone statues enlivened and awoke the plaster sediment. The plaster drifted off as masks of the huge hulken mantels. Rider spoke with his mouth and directed with his hands, "Form a line across the channel," The many clay soldiers converged from either side of rider and formed a double file line before entering the water. "Form a bridge across the channel," rider twisted from side to side as he wondered the amount of comprehension a dirt mound had. The many walking mud mounds stood on each others shoulders until the division toppled the waterline. Then Rider smiled a salute at the soldiers, as he pulled the 'T' from the ground. The dirt dropped straight and the land bridge was complete. The residents of Scio frantically hurried along the lifeline. Each person was ushered onto the lawn. Most of the northeastern island residents were saved. "Good thinking rider," Skimmer championed. Both skimmer and the long shadow crew were impressed with rider's ingenuity. Skimmer also thought he observed a few extra mounds as a result of rider's intervention and postulated the ferocity of the submarine leader. Each of the Scions were given blankets and food from the temple and nearby houses. The native emote residents were surprisingly well supplied for such a scenario. One of them called out, "Lava on the bridge... Lava on the bridge," as more Scions ran from the red line across the dirt. Skimmer put the 'T' in the ground in long enough duration for the waterlines return and the channel became couchy to the care units on the great lawn. Tumult began to recover from his near fatal regard and enough to ask a question," What about Ignis?" Robbins was close enough for an answer," Most of the residents, including the Ignis battalion, were lost to the volcano." Victoria and Lucius brought blankets for the crowd and handed one to the grand parity. Victoria inquired regarding the latest odd circumstance, "I thought the volcano was inactive?" Robbins beamed a half-up smile," So did the best minds on Scio, little one." "We all have something to learn from this," Tumult added before finding rest on the temple green.

Beak reported to the chancellor," Do you still need the birds?" "Send them to Triton," the representative answered." Then will send for any further needs." "Understood," came the reply from the commander. Robbins paused beak for a moment, "And let the Triton's know the leader

of Ignis and Mecos is thought dispatched in the volcano's lava wreckage."
Beak paused himself and didn't comprehend the information till an hour
on his journey north. Beak didn't need to wave to his Triton squadron
relaxing on the lawn. They moved in unison with beaks moved toward the
whirlies. Lucius watched from the command rock as the dragoons leapt
for their island and the birds fashioned a northern route through soot
filled skies. Robert walked an approach to the coast and filled rider in. The
engine officer reported with a full salute, partly due to his admiration for
his commanding officer. "The Long Shadow is seaworthy and the sloop
will get along with only the plantation crew." "Excellent," Rider returned
the salute. Before Robert was out of site, the captain called to him. "Get
the men and tend to any wounded or needing assistance." Robert nodded
as he went to inform the first-mate. A night full of activity relaxed to a
place of somber care. Most of the visitors, residents, and mainland Scions
slept in darkened tents and blackened grass. On the opposite shore a vein
of red spilled over the blue.

Tumult felt his gut sink, as his legs reach for the morning air. None
of the other island leaders slept on the ground. Most of emote and many
Scions filled the green waiting for him to speak. Celebus, Skimmer, Rider,
and Robbins stood on the temple steps. The temple security formed a
line at the base of the steps. The Grand Parity addresses the crowd with a
renewed sense of honor.

"My fellow Scions, we face, as we have never faced before the
responsibility to rebuild. Due to the courage of the people of emote and
the present condition of the islands; I declare emote the official capitol of
Scio. When the island mainland cools, we will build from one side to the
other our great houses of knowledge. I state to all Scions; we will never
let another island hold sway over our affairs." The crowd cheers and in a
loud roar shouts," Tu-mult, Tu-mult." "Well, I think the event we have all
waited for has transpired. Wouldn't you say, Lawrence?" Robbins always
did see the fluidity in events. Skimmer harkened a reply. "I wouldn't say
Scio is absolutely rid of Ignis, until the island starts tending its affairs. "To
Right," Robbins agreed. Victoria busy pushing her nose and making her
wings come out, found herself amusing. Only Flink found the activity
curious, as he pushed his nose a few times. Victoria laughed. As the temple

meeting adjourned, the last of the lava poured into the channel and steam rose over Scio.

Lucius decided to get some practice riding George, as he wished to put the submarine in the water. As Lucius plucked the bird in preparation, rider ventured to one side with a bag full of coins. The bag constituted the entire reimbursement to the ship and crew. Hanz met the captain on approach," Maybe we did rob the temple after all?" "No," rider curtly reprimanded. "We earned the money," Hanz shook his head in agreement. The Scions began cleaning the island and refurbishing the coastline. Rakes and brooms swept the ashes into large piles and over the edge of the channel, where each formed a mix with the ashes being pushed clean through the crossing.

As the channel cleared, several days later, Lucius became practiced and got ready to put the submarine in the water. What Lucius and George didn't have were dragoons or beak's squadron. Victoria performed the task of runway director, putting herself underneath a hovering submarine. George sensed the event and abided Lucius's instruction. George may have seen the look in Victoria's eyes or the posturing of Lucius. George tensed and held his stance firm. George grappled the submarine with the strength of his talons. Lucius, let George choose the pace, keeping the height of the bird where necessary. The submarine only carried Robert and his engine crew. The journey was short but memorable, as the submarine wasn't lowered. George could carry the weight to the water but when he reached a certain threshold; the bird dropped the submarine a near ten feet into the water. The longshadow put through the water film. The Long Shadow was unharmed but the passengers remember the sensation of the fall and crash. Only one side panel seemed to leak but the engine-man recalled the account as mere condensation.

Rider shook hands with skimmer and Robbins. Celebus ran with a pair of satchels in his hands. One of them contained the unused tree shoes and the other a parchment of scrolls. "The tree shoes are yours as a sort of extra payment to make your journey prosperous and the scrolls are a bit of business, I hope you would take care for me." Rider looked at the new terms being laid at his door with partial admonishment. "Business," rider questioned Celebus, as he wanted to be more clear in any official tasks. "Captain the scrolls need to be delivered to Ignis's western coast. Don't worry, I am reasonably sure, you will find few protectors on station. The scrolls need to be delivered to a coffee and corn plantation on the center of the western seaboard. The tree shoes should make for a profitable day for the Long Shadow." "Will deliver your papers," Rider was about to turn and commence ship boarding when a surprise to both him and the gathering found the captain. "I'll travel to Ignis with the submarine captain." Tumult motioned in rider's direction. "You do realize, you are probably not the most popular figure on Ignis with the leader gone," skimmer asserted. Robbins put a close second, "Probably more popular on the poet's side then most." Tumult discarded the remarks and spoke directly to rider, "We might be able to get an early start on a different relationship with Ignis, if we can ignore the experientials and directly relate to the poets." "Grand Parity," Robbins vied for attention. "Let us come with you, at the very least a unified Triton and Scio front could get the discussions moving in the right direction." "Agreed," Tumult turned again toward rider and his dual satchels. "The Scion government will owe you a debt for the passage and we will look to the long shadow for our future transportation needs." Rider didn't quite see himself entering into full business with mainland Scio but he approved of the trend the long shadow had met with. "Will give you passage, as soon as I can figure a way onto our ship without swimming." Rider started to understand the helpful nature of the Tritons as both rider and Robbins knew Victoria and Lucius would help. The words weren't even spoken as Victoria and Lucius ferried the entire crew onto the conning tower. Rider shrugged as the earthen mounds had when Robbins lifted him off the ground. Skimmer and Celebus waved at the departing group and faced their leader still held in reserve. "We will get the rebuilding efforts underway and I will give you the larger office in the temple," Celebus found himself more fond of Tumult then in the past. Skimmer obligingly realized his new role on the island had obtained some permanence. "I too will prepare for your return, the emote residents I can recruit for a permanent force will move to the mainland and form a perimeter. "Tumult's mood was light and friendly as he picked up several prepared satchels for his journey. "General, High keeper, on my return the pair of you will be added to my advisors and I am very proud of your initiatives. Keep Scio safe till my return." The Grand Parity feeling very eager at finding a new solution with Ignis, as Victoria lifts him off the ground without even stopping. The remaining Scions wave at their departing leader before setting to work on island business. Skimmer interested in the high keeper's involvement asks about the papers he gave rider. "I have been keeping the poets in paper for many years and for just such a moment as this." Skimmer gives a lip nod to the interesting events. Skimmer seeming happy with the black cloud obscuring his view, ventures a review on the waterfront.

The conning tower was finally emptied with Tumults arrival and Victoria turned to find George hovering above the long shadow. The trident girl knelt and knocked on the door of the conning tower. "How are we gonna follow a submarine with a bird?" Flink caught the question from the ladder and ran to inform the captain. Robbins intercepted and handed Victoria a piece of paper and shut the submarine hatch. Victoria unrolled the parchment with a map and the place of destination read," Tannon." Lucius reached for Victoria's arm and pulled the Triton girl onto George. "Where is Tannon," she asked as she got comfortable on her bird. "Tannon is a country settlement, should be quite pleasant," he added. George moved slowly and directionally to a skyward pitch and then slowly powered a climb.

Flink motioned to the captain from the deck hall of the Long Shadow. Flink didn't say a word and rider put a hand on Flink's shoulder. "We are going to the poet's side of Ignis, there shouldn't be any Ignis swords there." Flink had previously bruised his skin on a nickel plated sword. He wasn't eager for an Ignis landing, yet he was eager to meet poets. "Get to your station," rider stood at attention. Flink saluted and then rider saluted and then the sub sank below. Rider and crew set a north by northwest heading. Rider remarked to John in the officer's room," First angels and now the grand parity of Scio," John smiled," Maybe your Subsa reputation is expanding." Tumult entered the room in hearing the mention of his title. Rider questioned the leader of the volcanic nation, "Do we address you as Grand Parity?" Tumult raised his hand," Captain, you are at the command of a formidable ship, I should be asking your address?" Rider shook the grand parity's hand," will get you to your destination in one piece, Flink will show you the important guest quarters." The Grand Parity went for his items. The Grand Parity commented, "Strong Ship," Flink smiled.

The underwater maneuvers of the longshadow only lasted for a half an hour, as john called to the crew for an all stop. "Why are they calling an all stop," wondered the grand parity. Flink ran to the officers chamber for information. Rider already had Robert, Hanz, and john in a seated position. Flink stands at the door, awaiting information. Rider notices the partial entrance. "Come in and sit down, don't block the main deck." Flink finds an empty chair. "The official order is maintain depth and position for one hour." Rider continues staring at the blank faces before him. "I am leaving the ship for the hour, keep the crew busy, and inform the grand parity... we are on routine ship's business." John raises his hand for a question and rider nodds as Hanz and Robert look to him. "Will you be needing help?" Rider being very curt and very oblique," No," came the crew's answer. The captain waited for the officer's leave and then found the hatchway. The same hatchway the gathering originally found in utility on cat's wall. In his hand was some of the gold and tree shoes from emote. Hanz could be heard a few decks over," Is he going to drown, we are over a couple hundred feet under the waterline," Then rider only heard silence, securing the front door and flooding the compartment. The captain held tight his breath and dove straight up to a very fast approaching air pocket. The submarine captain quickly regained his senses in the rotunda of a huge cave with a giant metal vault door. Kneeling to a rise first with his knees and then with his bags; the surface of his feet find the landing in front of the door. Bags at his feet, rider turns knobs and switches. The rotating wheels in the door seem interconnecting and spin for several rotations before unlatching the opening from the frame. Rider moves to the corner of the opening and observes a well lit cave with two passages. One of the passages revealed a mine shaft with metal ore in buckets. Rider grabs at blocks on the wheels of a cart. The captain moves the cart a few feet and then re-chalks the wheels. The other opening is a huge room of gold and treasure. Rider puts the tree shoes and treasure in a corner of the room and then grabs for a picture hanging on the wall. The picture is of a Scion woman dressed in a submarine officer's uniform. The picture's texture and corners seem old and partially faded with water damage. Rider's momentary focus returns to the bags as he puts the gold in a pile and the tree shoes on a shelf. The room contains many shelves for artifacts. The shelves on the left side of the room contain captain rider's name on each level front. The shelves on the right side of the moist cave maintain gold placards reading,' Captain Sylvia Insula.' There are two tables in the room with log books. Rider pulls a writing implement from his garb and scripts two entries on the left side table log book. He then looks to the right side table log book with a similar picture of the Scion captain on the book's cover. The submarine captain salutes the log book and walks toward the entranceway. Locking the door with a pull verifying security; rider drops into the watery abyss and pushes his way toward the hatchway opening of the long shadow. Inside, the hatchway the air deprivation concatenates reaching a maximum. Rider seals the door and floods the compartment. Completely drenched and exhausted, the captain laid still before putting himself to his feet. The hatchways' secured, he enters his ship toward his stateroom.

The crowds cheers a loud roar at the Subsa waterbowl. A water carriage pulls alongside the opened arena and the driver opens the door for Donald and His Wife. "These are very strange accommodations," remarks Donald of the cave overhead and the strange bluish people around them. Donald's wife make an inverted sigh at the nerves in her fingers; the whole circumstance seeming other worldly to the rancher's wife. The coachman makes a gentlemanly wave to half oval entrances to the stadium. Donald moves a step and then slides slightly. Watching his leg he remarks," Let's watch our toes here, I wonder if the tale of elves living in the Ehleta posts on the eastern seaboard are true." Donald's wife smiles erratically at the man holding her reality and then the couple moves into the stadium.

The waterbowl contains a large arena for all water related sports. The arena has panoramic seating for the grand contests. The afternoon contest would put Herbert, the current individual champion, against an unknown new comer. The challenger was clouded in mystery, as he was a poet. The Poet's were as individually reclusive as the Subsa populace was as a group and all were eager to see the water ball. The attendance was near full capacity, as Herbert was in his prime against all Subsa competition. The minority of off-Subsa residents and the youth of Subsa provided Herbert a secure fan base and many t-shirts donned his signature tongue slant. Pembridge usually got good seats at the waterbowl, on the rare occasion of his appearance. The wizard seemed engrossed in eating algae and fish paste. The package of paste came with a spooning stick and as the crowds cheered he dug deeper into his snack. As Pembridge lifted his eyes a vaguely familiar sight approached from his right side. "What are you here for?" Pembridge questioned as he stood for Donald. "Whirly keepers aren't usually visitors under-water." "These have been some of the most difficult instructions." Donald indeed knew little of cat's wall and less of Subsa. On Donald's right stood his wife with frizzed hair and a half glazed look speaking to the unreality to which she perceived her perception. Donald motioned to his wife for a seat. Reaching in his pocket Donald presented Pembridge with his letter. Pembridge looked over the letter and then wrote a notation on the top. Pembridge put the letter in his satchel and drew a potion. "Here, give this to one of your whirlies and in the morning your whirly will become four horses." Donald being a rancher, in instances of uncertainty stuck to the known. "The letter states, this old parchment would be payment," Donald handed the paper to the relaxing wizard. "Let me see." Pembridge read over an old Ignis contract as herbert wound for his first serve. In a crowd pleasing move the cat serves with his tail in a forward somersault. On one side of the net stands a timid man; with a coach, yelling orders. The poet kept his pen and paper in a water proof bag and when Herbert's serve crosses the net, the poet swims. Herbert being the aggressor and the poet's technique seeming as if he was running away from the ball and yet always in the ball's path. Before the ball touches the water, the poet crouches into a fetal position. The ball hit the poets elbow and flies across the net. The ball in a tight defensive posture obtains twice the speed of herbert's serve. The cat would need finesse to approach the next serve. The ball landing in herbert territory causes the crowd to, "awh.". Poet 1 Herbert 0. Donald's wife bobs her head as she relaxes in her surreal setting. "Where did you get this contract?" questioned Pembridge. Donald crosses his legs and pauses as the crowd cheers on Herbert's first ace. Poet 1 Herbert 1. "Many years before you visited our ranch, Ignis solider's came to Tantamount's northern shore, facing Triton. They offered me this contract as payment for several months with whirly birds." "What did they need the birds for?" Pembridge put a finger to his brow as the conversation grew in interest. "The soliders said they needed the birds for transport. They never did get the whirlies and I kept the advanced payment in the form of this contract." Pembridge read the contract to his own ears and Donald's as the board advanced, Poet 2 Herbert 2. The poet's serve is quite gregarious; occurring as the strangest site in the bout, with him tossing the ball to his coach on the sidelines. The coach tosses the ball to the poet and he punches the ball over the net. The officials scratch their heads as to the legality of this serving technique. Poet 3 Herbert 3. Pembridge clears his throat before reading, "One militia of 1,000 Eastern Ignis troops for one month in the service of the notice." Donald immediately has his question ready, "Where does one get the militia, the parchment sounds as if the militia is a group of horses." Pembridge being worldlier then Donald imparted some knowledge of Ignis. "The Eastern shore gets militia protection as currency and utilizes the currency for goods; the protectors distribute the goods among the populace. Any 1,000 troops will honor the contract, as stipulated under Indilep's rule." Donald didn't say another word. He grabs the bottle and spirals toward the doors with his wife. Pembridge looks again at the paper, "Do I need a militia?" A whistle blares in the arena with shouts and hand waves. The waterbowl officials put herbert and the poet on the sidelines as they review the rule book.

Angels on Ignis

Far on the western shore of Ignis, a hooded figure mingles above the poets scattered on an agricultural farm hillside. Stiff rows of corn lean in the breeze. Poets of all shape and sizes move in and out of the corn rows and up and down the hills with several sitting near a couple of bushes on a ridge. The poets notice as poets notice. The stranger observes the crops seem well tended for some of the poets gather up corn and kept physically fit. The visitor wouldn't be easily discernable until the sleeves of an over garment slide slightly and reveal a bluish skin. The hand moves across the crops and then climbes a long trail to the center. One hand sees the foreigner reaching into a pocket and extracting a potion. The potion is immediately satisfactory with imbibing. The figure releases the potion, rolling toward the grass; on the highest point of the hillside in the longest field of grass. The alien to Ignis begins twisting and moaning while turning slowly and then quickly from one side to another. "mm... mmmm. . mmmmm," then the twisting increases to a marginally incomprehensible speed. Smoke lifts from the pockets of the garment and "whoos..." the vistor turns into a flame, a pure blue flame. Every poet within viewing distance and some from as far as several miles away could see the blue flame on the hillside. The blue flame encompasses several layers and burns cool. Crowds gather for hours. Some poets attempt an extinguishing of the flame with water or dirt and none were successful. They sit for hours and write some beautiful verses, even at these moments maintaining their engrained silence.

Three angels on the chimney highway would be a very noticeable sight to an island without Tritons, let alone angels. The three men donning their wizard outfits seemed very close to the traditional poet garb of the island. "We are dressed very near the poet garb of the island," Spring Shine explained to Marcus and Magis who usually agreed to the archangel's reasoning. Poets never traveled the chimney, as the poets were even more reclusive then the warriors. Still, there garb was immediately passable for Ignis wear and allowed the angels the flexibility of access to their wings. Spring Shine never explained the reason for the trip; all Marcus and Magis knew came in the form of immediacy in their silence and obfuscation. Silence subsisting imperative.

The roads reveal gave little options, the large grassy expanse between two mountains lacking in erudition. Shimmering had gotten them to the southern beginnings of the road; now they hoped the people would decide on other routes of travel. The three men walked for miles without seeing another person, then out of nowhere. "Look," Magis pointed to a single man sitting on the left rock ridge. "A Poet," spring shine smiled at the man on the ridge. "Why are they called poets?" magis asked, figuring they all can't have the same profession. "Marcus, the poets are indeed poets and live solitary quiet lives. They grow crops and build houses, yet their hearts lead them to writing poetry for near eighty percent of each day. Ignis governs them from a distance but there is a real spark of fire in their hearts. One day the poets will rescue the island." "Good day," the archangel called to the man on the ridge. "Day," the man returned. "Not very talkative," magis observed. "Well, the less one talks, the more one observes," Marcus nodded in agreement with the archangels reasoning. The three men continued there walk.

After the sun had grown comfortable to their forehead, the three men begin to see groups of protector's form on the road. "The protectors are most inquisitive. We will shimmer past." Magis was a little impatient with his instruction. Then the archangel outstretched his hand at the two men. Keep your heads focused straight, we will walk past. The Protectors did notice three poets walking north on the chimney. "Get to your own side of the border," one of the protectors shouted. "Poets aren't allowed on the road," gave another. The protectors did manage the western seaboard as well but with far less regard. As the three men passed the patrol, the protectors picked up dirt from the grass and hurled the dirt at them. The angels kept walking and held speech for over a hundred yards. "Being a poet isn't easy," Marcus observed. Spring Shine obtained a fatherly demeanor as he was a wise man. "You will find every profession in life has some obstacles. The poets are probably a friendlier bunch then the protectors believe." Magis maintained silence and shivered slightly on their approach to the northern mountains. The Archangel waved his hand at a large gate appearing in the distance. "We still have to pass the 'Gate of the Question,'" The Angel pointed to a gate the size of a city block between two rock walls. "Why is the gate called the gate of the question," Marcus frustrated toward the archangel. The Archangel walked in silence until the group had gotten closer to the center and then after observing the gates dark grey wooden slots with bowed metal claps, springshine answered to the ability of Marcus's observation. "The gate contains two guards and each person entering must view the question to move into the experiential's zone." In the center of the gate a door resides allowing individuals to enter without opening the main gate. Springshine walked left toward the door and motioned with several fingers in an attractive posturing. "Once inside, we will fly over the guards and exit through the other door." Magis gave a hand sign signaling their comprehension. Springshine removed his cloak, exposing his wings and entered the door, pulling on a metal ring on the left side. The other angels took off their vestments and hurried after springshine. Marcus hopped a few steps before his cloak came loose from his feet. The inside of the gate grew larger than the gate proper with a length of near another city block to the exit door. In the very center stood a cottage and on the far ends of the gate were seats for weary travelers although people on the road seldom made the most of them. Two women stood in the center of the great dirt brown expanse, a poet woman on the left and a warrior princess on the right. The three Tritons readied their wings for flight and flew right over the heads of the women. Before the Tritons had reached past the women, the warrior woman shouted," Is there, a problem?" and then she threw a bucket of water on the poet woman. All three Tritons made a landing on the other side of the cottage. Magis pushed his nose center and forward," Huh ... Tell me archangel the meaning of this." Springshine motions his compatriots to the door as they return their cloaks. The archangel spoke, "Tell me the question answered with a warrior princess throwing cold water on a poet girl?" The men seemed to believe there was wisdom in the thought though none mentioned the event.

The frozen northern mountains cupped a valley where the experiential meeting hall resided. The archangel could have opened the doors with his hands or shimmered into the chamber but spring shine reached for the highest peak of theatricality. Marcus and Magis opened each door while in mid-air. Spring Shine walked the center of the chamber while his associates flew to his side. The experientials indeed were in a meeting and they just stared at the great figure before them. One of the more diplomatic men stood and addressed the angel. "Can we help you with something?" "No, but I can help you!" The northern colony on Ignis is completely self-sufficient and didn't rely on command structure, as each experiential and protector was held individually responsible for assignments. "As we speak, Ignis troops are preparing a leave of Scio. You might want to consider the situation on Ignis." "Angel... Ignis is on Scio to keep the island safe." The experiential addressing the angel stood and clasped his hands. "Then maybe you can explain this," the archangel threw down a report from a science team on Scio. The experiential didn't have to read the report; he knew what the archangel was getting at. The Archangel didn't wait for a reply and pushed the matter. "Indilep runs ramped on the populace of Scio and Ignis is left in a bit of disarray." Another experiential broached a question," Are you suggesting Ignis get rid of Indilep." "No," the answer came as quite a surprise to both Marcus and magis. The archangel sat on a stool given to him from his associates. "Ignis should be divided to foster prosperity in the citizenry." All of the experientials raised their hands as if in grade school. Then the gathering stared at one another and put their hands down. The first speaking experiential made the groups feelings known. "We have heard this idea before. As everyone knows, the warriors, if left alone, will kill each other off and the poets seem to favor some sort of anarchy." The archangel outstretching his wings, as he speaks ", Explain, the reason for Ignis's involvement on Scio; when it doesn't believe its own people capable of logical thought." All the experiential's sat, as none had an easy answer. The government officials without a government gave their full attention to the passionate Triton. "Ignis doesn't need conquest of Scio," Spring Shine clearing his throat curtails his Ignis thoughts, "Ignis needs an interested citizenry. I can assure you when you win the hearts and minds of your people, Triton will stand with Ignis." Then with almost an evil stare, the archangel put fear in the men," Angels are everywhere." The words forming a shifting look on spring shine's face as he spins his head in a maddening aloof gesture. The three angels shimmer, the longest distance ever in an attempt. the weather being cold and frosty at the edge of the mountains, the three men gave purchase in their biceps. "Do you think the visit was enough?" magis asked. "Only time will tell?" The three men expanded their wings and flew east toward Triton.

Watching their leave were several experientials peering through the snow drift. The distance was great enough where there sight was as much imagination as reality. They returned to a highly involved session of discussions. The large cavernous hall escaped heat quickly from feet, even with all doors closed. Several experientials stoked the flames of a large fireplace. Before the first experiential grew comfortable to a chair, one spoke to the gathering. "Do these Tritons really believe a Scion scientist will mount a defensive against dragoon or the cats? And hasn't their involvement usually extended beyond their borders." Another in similar tone spoke of the grand parity," A leader is more than the smartest person in the room; he must also have a larger view." The meeting of several distinguishing experientials stood on the far side of the hall and moved toward the fireplace for warmth. The same experiential who once spoke against the leader's interest rose his hand. "Is Indilep returning?" Suddenly, the gathering realized the infrequency of angel visits and postulated the fate of their leader. The men at the fireplace turned toward the discussion. One experiential conceded to the wave coming across the faces, "Ignis could have a hand in prosperity, we are closer to three countries with similar interests then a single whole...." None of the others answered him, their thoughts drifted toward the ceiling and the last voice heard stated the obvious, "Should we choose a new leader?"

Tannon is a small village in two lines facing east. The ground is fine flat raked brown powder. The houses face north and south but the village points eastward. Rider's submarine has placement from a long dock reaching just above the waterline. The dock being better suited to a small row boat and being longer then strictly sensible. The observing sun provides a moderating back drop for the hatch occupants to clamor their feet on the dislodged boards. Tumult and the chancellor race on the metal enclosure which now beams with the rays of the sun. Flink arrives first and sees the light of day with George flying high above. Flink secures the docking as the two dignitaries approach the foreign soil. Victoria and Lucius landed just east of the dock and meet each occupants approach. Rider quickly catches up to the party, garnishing his two satchels; one with Celebus's papers and the other the remainder of the tree shoes. "Where are all the people?" Rider made the statement and very much spoke for all present. Although, Tumult leads a major island, he never has been to the poet's side and rider similarly had little reason to visit the western shore. The two men began looking in the direction of the aged diplomat for advice. "Well," Robbins calmed himself before continuing. "We might have to find some unifying factors before we can approach the poets. The poets need to feel a common interest in each other, as much as in our efforts. They are farmers and run these town shops when they are not in the countryside." "Great," rider stated. "Will round them up and give them the scrolls." Tumult sensed Robbins meaning more than rider. The parity reached in his pocket and grabbed an, "E," from Emote. In fact, the parity had quite a few as the people of emote gave them to Tumult as a gesture of good will. "Give them these," Tumult held aloft the letter for Robbins and riders approval. "Quite," was Robbins response. Rider just scratched his head.

Just then Victoria caught site of a man with a paper and pen. "Wait," she called out trying to get his attention. The poet turned and ran for cover. "I'll get him," Lucius answered to their astonishment. Only two paces saw Lucius off the ground and above the village rooftops. Lucius flew low and scooped up the man between two houses. In a fluid motion, he put the man feet first on the ground between George and the officers. The man didn't speak and looked frightened. Summoning up his courage, the poet up turned his nose.

Robbins went to talk to the man and the grand parity stopped him dead in his tracks. "I'll handle this." Robbins didn't qualm with the leader of Scio. Tumult eased his approach and halted to the man's up turned skin. The Scion leader carefully pulled at the, "E," he was holding and handed it to the man who was trying not to look at him. Tumult raised the 'E' to the level of the sun and then the man's expression changed.

The poets eyes widened and he grabbed the 'E', and held it to his heart. The poet sat cross legged on the ground and began to write every word of his brief experience co-joined with his life experience.

Rider was still scratching his head when Robbins decided to intervene. "Give me one of your 'E,'s," the chancellor asserted. When Robbins wanted to be direct, he could command a leaders attention. Tumult gave him one of the stitchings. Robbins put the 'E' low to the ground in opposition to the grand parities posture. The reaction was immediate and severe. The man got up and turned around running straight out of the village. The man ran the middle line of the village and over the first hill. On one knee Robbins faced his company," Well we tried?"

Just then, a rumble began from the other side of the mound where the man had disappeared. Flink's ear lifted up to the noise and then George turned. When all in the party heard the noise, George took flight without any passengers. Victoria reached to grab George but decided to remain of the ground. She was questioning her decision, as near two hundred people emerged running for the crew. Rider believed himself experienced in these matters and led the charge for the submarine, "All aboard." Lucius cried out to his companions," Don't, wait." Lucius suddenly realized he had immobilized the long shadow crew and felt a shock in his system. Lucius was a fan of the sensation. The crowd of men ran and Lucius cried out again, "Seas," The two hundred men reared up on the backs of each other. None were injured but Lucius put on his best smirk and stroll, walking toward the ship for relaxation. "Give them the patches," Robbins instructed the leader. One person at time The Grand Parity handed out his patches numbering one hundred and realized the deficiency could be a problem. A squabble started between those with patches and those without.

The quietest fight in history was in their presence, as one side made lude gestures at the other. "Mimics in a fight match," rider was amused but Robbins knew the situation could quickly escalate. Robbins pointed to rider's satchels. The captain grabbed a parchment to show the diplomat; Robbins shook his head. Then the sub commander realized the diplomats reasoning and agreed. Rider faced his nearest ten shipmates and waved them close. Rider and the Long Shadow crew threw the entire amount of remaining tree shoes at the feet of the poets without patches. The tree shoes grew roots and planted half of the poet gathering in the ground. The poets with the patches laughed and laughed. Then the most remarkable occurrence, they began to speak. The first words were meaningful; "We should be a village, again." Robbins directed rider to the planted poets. Reading from a scroll, rider made a magic a chant. The tree shoes were returned to their former state. The captain was going to collect them but Robbins gave a most disapproving head nod. The poets without patches were each allowed to keep the tree shoes. This caused some grumble among the patch holders and laughter among the tree shoe holders. Robbins in a most official manor bowed at the grand parity and then stepped aside. "My name is Tumult; I lead the scientists on Scio." The Grand parity held out his hand to each of the poets but they didn't shake his hand. They hugged him. The very largest group-hug ever seen in the islands, happened right on Ignis. Victoria, who was keeping an eye on George, couldn't resist and ran to hug everyone. Robbins gave another gesture to rider and a hand wave. The captain returned a why did I come here look. Rider distributed the scrolls to each of the poets and they were most grateful. Robbins then called to Victoria, "Do you still have that map I gave you?" "Yes," she answered while removing her hugging posture. Robbins handed the map to the grand parity who showed each of them where he was from and where they could come for assistance. The crowd of silent men said nearly in unison, "Thank You."

"This is the corniest thing, I have ever seen," rider and his crew grabbed their turn to laugh. They weren't laughing for long as some of the poets began to bring them corn. The fields just outside the settlement held vast stores of fruits and vegetables. The poets seemed to hurry themselves to the field and returning. A few bushels at a time and then a flood of yellow and brown landed at the gatherings feet. Rider looked around in bewilderment at the stack of corn mounting as high as George. "Flink, Flink," were the only words the captain could manage. "Yes, Captain," Flink answered. "Load the ship, we are paid in corn." The entire crew loaded the huge stacks of corn into the long shadow. When the crew was nearly finished loading the corn, rider looked at Robbins. "Do you need us for anything else?" "No, thank you captain," rider and the long shadow made a western exit. As rider reached the dock, his first-mate slowed his progress. "Are we gonna leave the grand parity with the Tritons." "Yes," rider answered and made his way to the conning tower. Victoria who was still standing at the side of Robbins witnessed Lucius landing on George. "You really have got the knack with him," Victoria puckered a grin. "He is really a nice fellow, aren't you," the love fest continued as Lucius hugged on the bird. Robbins literally through his hands up in the air at the upsurdity of the happening then he asked a most uncharacteristic question, "Do you think Scio and the poets will be able to help each other." Tumult rose as the expert," Our societies will help each other grow." It would be years before the Ignis poets actually reintroduced trade with Scio. Yet progress was being made. The poets actually had internal trading on an individual schedule.

The Emote 'E's weren't all the same size and one of them had near twice the diameter of the rest. A short yet stocky build of a poet became leader of the village due to the size of his lettering. Robbins opinion of the poets grew with the sudden marks of prosperity. The instance forced a question to the representative's focus. "Do you think these new towns will spread across the land?" Tumult answered for the poets, "The poets will over time see tannon and the western shore will move toward mercantilism." Tumult having spent more time with Indilep then the others posed a question to the town leader," Do you think Indilep was a bad leader?" The poet didn't even blink, "Indilep is a wise and beneficent ruler." Robbins pulled on Tumults clothing," Maybe let the news from Scio filter through the Ignis experientials." The Scion leader shook his head in agreement with Robbins thinking. Neither the Grand Parity nor the island representative expected the answer they got and both men paused for thought.

George rested in the center of the village and many people, pet the great bird. Tannon was far enough away to have never seen a Triton whirly. Tumult unraveled one of the scrolls rider had brought in his satchel. The Grand Parity showed the papers to Robbins, "These papers aren't all blank." The chancellor leaned in curiosity toward the papers. "This is a map to the temple." Robbins made an observation, "Celebus wanted them to know where there paper was coming from." Over Tumults left shoulder could be seen a small long boat on the shore. The village had a small ship and decided to initialize trade relations with a shipment of food. "Well, you've got your ride home, good luck!" Several of the villagers were putting oars in the boat, while the rest of the village looked to preparing their settlement. Robbins waved and prepared an exit with Victoria and Lucius. Some of the poets wondered if the tree shoes could ground the great bird and they just missed his left foot on take off. Tumult sat on the ground with legs crossed and tried to explain some of the many inventions, the Scion people can build. "We have machines, they fly over peoples heads and we have bonding agents capable of holding a person in mid-air." George's wings had a leveled fast approach to the windy hills of Ignis. All three waved on departure.

On the opposite side of the hill then the traveler's side stood a rather tall figure. The figure was garbed with a cloak and yet the skin could be faintly seen as blue. The blue skin uncovered an arm walking away from the tannon festivities. In viewing distance of the departing whirly bird, the ominous cloak shimmered.

George flew lower than usual as many weeks of flying pushed his posture in a monotone ensconce above the parapet of small hills and wondering villagers. "Ignis is really much nicer then the reputation." Victoria gave in to her impertinence as she had grown comfortable to the chancellors and Lucius's expectations. "The island residents are very capable!" "What are you talking about Lucius," the Chancellor forgot his station for the moment. Lucius eyed the Chancellor's look and grew comfortable with his words. "The poets perform three times the tasks of most citizens and with extreme efficiency." Victoria took to listening as she wasn't sure of Lucius's thoughts. "The warriors similarly are quite adroit metallurgists." "Yes, there is a symbiosis between all these island elements. They all think protection is the best means of survival and the Tritons and Scions need to show them otherwise. We will build on their strengths and get Ignis to productivity." "Is the warrior side much different then the poet's side?" Victoria's voice came from behind her forward face. "Night and Day, Victoria; Night and Day," the chancellor's face turned toward the sun's side as George banked toward the chimney. The sun was an afternoon sky as fires built on the landscape.

Victoria seemed more interested in the warrior huts and battles on display in the eastern quadrant. "The eastern side is more uniform then the poet's side," Victoria observed. Robbins peered over Victoria's shoulder to observe her comment. "Discipline, the warriors have a very strict discipline." "Well then explain... there," Victoria pointed to a mound where a crowd had gathered around a muddle of upraised grass; in the center of the mound stood a man and a humanoid cat. "Cat's Wall residents don't usually visit the warriors," Lucius observed. "Let's take a look," the chancellor raised his hand to the side, as George followed the grade of his hand to the slope of the mound. The Whirly had to both turn straight and negotiate high over a dip and the heads of the warriors before landing on the mound. "I think Victoria is having an effect on you Robbins," Lucius blurted before dismounting George. The chancellor shrugged as his and Victoria's attention were turned toward Pembridge and herbert. Herbert tugs at Pembridge's cloak as he did not notice the giant bird's landing. Pembridege kept patting the air in a calming gesture to the confused crowd of warriors. The Triton Island Representative nearly walked over Pembridges's glance before his attention dislodged from the gathering. Pembridge and the chancellor being not as familiar with each other as Victoria and herbert seemed. Victoria and Herbert began bouncing a small rock back and forth to each other. The audience seemed enthused and began throwing rocks at each other. Several gashes cut the arms and the legs of the warriors. The confusing behavior results in Pembridge placing a finger in the direction of his brow. Pembridge throws a potion on the ground causing a flash of light over the soldiers. The older Triton intervenes," May we be of some help, wizard." Pembridge becoming unusually talkative as ideas become appealing. "A Tantamount rancher gave me an entire legion of these soldiers for one of my potions. Now, they all look at me." As if echoing the wizard's words, the warriors sat on the grass and with arms in locking supports gave a relax in the sunshine. The representative makes a motion at Lucius. The gesture means scout the surroundings and only Lucius could see the visible communication. Lucius instituted a skyward approach while the gathering, observed the many soldiers encompassing the group. "You could build a fort and in the fort you could sell your potions." Pembridge turns to the side to hear robbin's words and recognizes the distinctive nature of the elder statesman. "The Tritons really are the wisest of races." Pembridge being honest gave a motioning gesture with his hand to the crowd. Pembridge beckoned to the trees and told the group to build a fort. "Knock the trees and make a pile." One at a time the group began rising from the dirt, grass, and rock covered soil. The warriors prized personal iniative over safety and individually groups of two and three plowed the great trees. Pushing the trees down and stacking them in a huge pile, the strong men groaned at the intensity. "Argh," the warriors, who had been combating each other earlier, now combined their efforts toward the brown heights. "Pembridge, right." The island representative recalled the meeting at the portal. Pembridge nodded as he directed and shouted to the engorged group. "Push the trees down; don't hit the trees with people." The trees weren't being hit with people; Pembridge seized the moment to caution against the falling woodland. "Do you think you could encourage other of these militia groups to build forts?" Robbins held tight to his words as Pembridge moved across his stage. Pembridge nodding again. "Right, a trade route in eastern-center of Ignis soil," turning again toward the men he calls," Stack the trees in a pile."

The lumbering men swing the logs in a circle and place them one after the other in the center of the huge landing, below the leaders. Pembridge pushes a potion into the chancellor's cloak as payment for the idea. Robbins takes recoil at the nature of the wizard. The island representative doesn't prod Pembridge and steady's a pace at George, while reading the label on the bottle. The label says <u>Bright Sky</u> and Robbins gestures to Victoria and Lucius, as Victoria remounts the lumbering George. Lucius calls from the sky toward the group on the landing. "There is a shelter near the trees!" The shelter Lucius began calling out with one hand to his mouth, mostly caught Victoria's attention. "Get the men to stop knocking down the trees," she gave in a concerting tone. George moving his beak from left to right in an animation of aviary expressions. Pembridge enthralling in his machinations begins pushing the men further into the woods. "Get all the trees," the stout wizard commences at nudging the positioning warriors. Lucius swept down from mid-air and caught Pembridge unaware. The messenger began lifting him toward the sky. Pembridge moving his arms caught a struggle with squirming, his gaze looking toward the potion bag still remaining on the landing. Victoria and Robbins give their wings an air breeze and soon meet Lucius in the air while herbert discovers his agility with a rock. Lucius doesn't drop Pembridge, Pembridge lets his feet relax on a landing and becomes one with the grass. Lucius lands to the right giving a signal toward some deer skins on upraising sticks in front of the gathering. The warriors can be heard getting near the shelter, in a small clearing. Lucius comforts the dear skin overlap entrance with both hands; he puts his right foot to the tent. Lucius's feet hesitate on the moist earth surface, he stands in mixing attention. A warrior, from the trees pushes in front of Victoria and Robbins, swaying in, near the messenger's sight. The singular warrior doesn't come alone. The entire grouping of 1,000 warriors stands with angry faces toward the three Tritons and the wizard. "Pembridge can you explain this?" the chancellor nerve-racking his words on the wizard. Pembridge being rather calm, while brushing himself of grass, shakes his head. An answer soon coming in Lucius's direction, from the tent placing. Lucius tightens his muscles, while guarding the sanctuary. A young girl with deer skin clothes can be seen soothing the fur side of the tent lining. The dark skin female gives a shout to the warriors. "atah, atah." The warriors immediately stand at her attention. The Triton Island Representative wincing at himself, waves a warrior near. The soldier looks at the placement of his feet in a very self-conscious trance. Only once the warrior comes in contact with his pacing near the island representative does he stand for a question. "Do you know this woman?" The warrior shrugs his arms giving small information," A night after a rain storm, the fog brought her and the shelter." The man watching his feet for placement with no external reason for precaution gave a most peculiar impression in robbin's direction. The warrior makes an awkward gesture while finding a place with his compatriots.

Lucius feels the grimace of the crowd, as he enters the animal fur. The girl is alone in a large shelter, the light entering only through seams in the skin lining. Lucius places each foot in a deliberate spacing and spreads the distance with his hands outstretching to invisible tent parts. The young girl chuckles for she has better tent vision. The soil giving to animal fur, the messenger watches his own feet's transgression. Lucius eyes the center pole, giving a reach toward the steady center for bracing his balance. In an awkward slight of hand, Lucius's feet give underneath him and his hand moves from the tent pole to the floor where he bangs his head on the firmament. Lucius reaches both hands forward, as he is immersed in a blue liquid of unknown origin. "Lucius get up from there," Robbins asserts, intensifying the light to the messenger's state of affairs. Victoria hears the noise and with the young girl lifts Lucius out of a well. The blue liquid is a heavy die and permeates his skin to his chest. "Did you fall in a blueberry soup?" Victoria questions. With a breath toward upward air, Lucius gives an answer, "this isn't soup." The young girl grabs a towel and dries off the messenger. Robbins and Victoria lend a hand with cotton clothes from a small bureau near the center. Lucius waves each hand free of a mix of animal fur and the blue liquid. Victoria asks the young girl," What is this strange substance?" The girl, not speaking the same language, she points toward a tub. Robbins calls to Victoria," Well?" Victoria makes an assessment of the situation," the liquid is some sort of bathing treatment." "Feels like glue," Lucius describes to the shelter. The young girl points to a part of her un-blue furs, as Lucius's blue glossing makes an impact on the white fur linings and floorings. On the clean furs are a huge bowl of blueberries and a huge bowl of white powder dust. Robbin's inspects the strange dust with a feel between fingers. "Chalk. This substance must have similar properties to a paste," Lucius found the statement agreeable, with his wings catching a tight interlacing in the blue seals. Lucius with a shake of his hair moves toward the brighter lights outside. The sun glares in Lucius's face while Pembridge and the warrior crowd stand in front looking at him. "Ya... Yeah... Ahhh," the crowd cheers in laughter and raising their hands to the sky, return to knocking down trees. Pembridge shaking his head in disagreement with the event moves toward the tent. Lucius renters forward of Pembridge and grabs for a bowl on the far side of the shelter. He then grabs a ladle, he finds near the chalk. "What are you doing Lucius?" Robbins gives with his hands. Lucius doesn't answer, just fills the bowl with the blue liquid and runs outside. The tent empties to look at Lucius. Lucius runs around the tent while dripping the blue liquid in a circle on the soil. Pembridge gives a thumb up to the wise idea and herbert a downward paw. "Good thinking," Victoria offers. Lucius gives a reticent smile and acknowledgement. The young girl seeing the blue circle around her tent gives Lucius a kiss on the cheek, causing him to blush. Victoria gives a bothering pout toward the scene and flies toward her George. Lucius and the chancellor give each other encouraging facial twitches and let their feet fall from under them with a concurrent ground to air wind sprint. Lucius with wings still in paste met the soil with his face, causing a flat roll and spitting of grass and dirt. Lucius getting hand from herbert and Pembridge, gave a welcoming to the ground of his feet. The messenger walks in a sideways position through the logging operation. Several soldiers cheer with Lucius's passing and the Triton man gives a quickening to his feet. George getting off the small plateau, found himself instigating a search for grass. The enormous bird sifting massive amounts of dirt, near the log stack, found some sustaining protein, flapping his wings in consent with Victoria's entrance toward his saddle. Several warriors either ducked or hit the ground, for George's displaying aviary bravado. Robbins hovered in a difficult landing on the saddle with the shifting movement. "You are gonna have to climb," calls Victoria to Lucius. The messenger grapples with feathers and ascends the giant with legs and arms in a slight head twitching disruptive manner to George. The island representative gives him a hand onto the saddle, observing the new blue feathers. Lucius becoming uneasy with the prospect of bonded feathers gave a tight gripping of the saddle leather.

Robbins, Victoria, and Lucius are unaware of concurrent proceedings on the island of Triton at the Triton delegation, as regards their findings. The Triton delegation consists of representatives of every lowland province and each mountain. The mountain representatives are independent of the jurisdiction of the mountain chancellors. Most representatives of the mountains keep their chancellor's informed; an unnecessary procedure with the advanced messaging system of the particle center. A delegation review board only requires 50% participation with a 100% of board attendance. "Call to order... Call to order," the wing tailing shoe gavel hit a rock, on a pedestal. A medium built svelte Triton man with a rather long twingeing mustache continues speaking in the center of a great starry chamber. "The delegation will now consider the findings of our new island representative and Commander Beak's Squadron." Beak stood and with a pound of his chest makes a half crescent symbol with his hand, the gesture of honesty and allegiance to the island. The gesture is returned from the leader of the board and all sit in the star shaped hall. The seats in the hall have deep slanting plates while marinating the room in layering star perimeters. The leader approaches a platform adjacent to beak and reads aloud beak's report. "A great battle commenced on the island of emote; for the freedom of the Scion people. The dragoons and Tritons pushed the oncoming troops to the center of the Scion mainland where a natural volcanic eruption destroyed the remaining troops, the leader of the sixth squadron, and Indilep (The Leader of Ignis)." Clamor erupted in the Triton delegation. The leader waving the gathering to silence and continues the report. "The grand parity's life was saved in part to our island representative and the dragoon representative. The angels and Robbins are still in attendance with an eye toward the middle islands restoration. The chancellor has a Triton whirly keeper and Lucius, the chancellor messenger, with him." Beak makes the introductory gesture as confirmation of a faithful read. The next report is a recommendation of service from the angels. "The Angel's give official sanction for the nomination of Lucius, the messenger, as chancellor of the mountain, formerly Robbins. 'Signed Magis'" The Angel's held in high regard usually bring consensus and a nomination is assured. A vote would still be required on the mountain of all nominations. The speaker rose again, "Beak keep your squadrons on the ready and will keep you posted." The star-chamber has star shaped entrances and exits. Beak forwarded a salute and then forwarded himself toward the outside hallway. The Triton delegation stood while beak rose up a slight ramp toward the entrance star on his right. Beak left the Triton Delegation building with a smile regarding the proceedings. The squadron commander giving no notice to the wandering crowds makes a right on the outer star with a brisk walk toward his whirly warehouse.

High in the skies directly above beak's position stands a 1,000 foot pole. On the ground the pole size seeming enormous, people would think the pole a support, for a sky platform. A person on the ground looking straight up would see a most unusual sight. There a man clamors from the top of the pole at the circling of Tritons around the cylinder. Triton's encircle the base in groups on several distinct height levels. "Who can stay circling the longest?" The man repeats incessantly to the competitors. The fatigue setting in to the eyes of the circling Tritons, the man holds a statue and occasionally laughs at the sky. A Triton flying from one of the sky highways grabs the man on the top of the cylinder and lifts him screaming skyward. The rows of circling Tritons smile at the gesture and then begin circling faster.

Chapter 14

Triton, Tumult, and the Cats

The Cat's Wall ninth was very akin to the Ignis sixth as neither had impressive navies and most cat's and wizards loathed the water. Many long boats carried cats, wizards and supplies. The ninth took a brisk ocean as the oars flew low for the occupants. The wooden vessels creaked with the retraction and extension of the crew. The lead long boat called forth a message, "Scio... Scio," The message relayed through a wizard captain on each of the ships. "Scio... Scio," came the return and in less than a mile the first long boats reached the western Scio shoreline. The cat's and wizard's rowed in unison and hummed on a shoreline approach. Tradition had the wizards throw balls of light into the air ahead of a shoreline approach. Steam poured from every orifice in the blackened earth of Scio and several cats were reticent to move off of their wooden seats. The lead wizard general stood hopping on the shoreline as not to burn his sandals. He was followed with a cat second in command. The cat remained in the long boat for speech with the leader. "Ignis, Triton or the Dragoons," the suspicious feline put to the wizard and then licked his paws. The wizard moved his hands in a sideways gesture as a hurried thought entered his brain. "We Won," the wizard leader pronounced in a low and syncopated tone. "We Won," he continued with the shouts growing with each continuance. "We Won," he pushed to the air." Victory on point rock." The leader shouts to the crowd. The crowd screeches and hollers, "Hoorah!" The still moving general's hands turn upraised and his facial demeanor turns flat. "Everyone in the boats... home." The general flopped one sandal and then another off into the water as he entered the long boat. The lead wizard soaked his blistering feet in the surf, as his boats turned in degrees toward cat's wall. "Our ancestral home will have to be rebuilt," the wizard gave only to the air diagnolly above him. The wizards looked at the general, the cat's looked away.

The very central volcano had not entirely blackened the surface and grass patches grew early across the surface of a hill near the volcanos center. Just beyond the hill, three women sat up in the grass growing in the charred earth. These weren't human women or even Scions; these were Tritons and the unknown survivors of the upheaval. Each of the women had blackened wings and partially stuck to the surface when their wings made contact. "You saw the dragoon, enter the volcano and then whoosh the island melted." The woman tendered and pealed her wings from the grass roots and let them flap once for air cooling. "No," spoke another. "Another one of Indilep's protection schemes, this one got him." The ladies all made twisting motions to cool the wings edges. The heat gave intensely from the ground swell. "The Triton was with the dragoon, maybe he started the eruption." In all their postulating, they didn't concede the natural event of the island process. The tar on their feathers put their demeanor toward aggressive protection until one of the ladies offered a productive notion. "We'll find the Grand Parity and we will rebuild Scio." The most astute students of Scio grabbed the wind and powered hard into the sky. One of the women noted to the others," Flying with dark wings is harder, yet we get more power with each push. The lead Triton silenced the observation, "We get Tumult and he'll make the right decisions." Sweat poured from each lady as the temperature of the island only cooled with exceedingly high altitudes.

On the far end of emote, opposite the cats. A huge wooden sloop lofts in the seas. Extending from either side of the decks seemed to be long circular storms. The turbulent air seemed to almost make the ship float in the water. The title keeling to the sea air, 'The Emote Protectorate,' the nomenclature of their home emblazoned in a crest and label on the ships representing panel. The air ran the tight skin of the sails and the hovering tips crested the light of the sun. The waters slapping the deck boards revealed the glossy board exterior and the newness of the reconstructed design. The bank of the turn with the ship leaning created a quarter mile arch, subtending the turn of the deck wheel. The crew could be seen viewing off the port and starboard main deck. They could be seen for an instant and then the crew all grabbed a center line and disappeared. In a few moments, the ship was sailing a return to the eastern coast.

Meanwhile, on the far southern coast of emote an important meeting commences at the now black topped town of point rock. On the charred and burned ground, the general parades his security squadron, wearing a white manifold display of achievements. His horse and cart carry supplies for each man's station, every three hundred feet around the perimeter of the entire darkened oval. After the first ten stations the preparations became routine and each group feeds the procession with perfunctory marches. The parade line motioned a parabolic arch around the outer positions of the stations. Skimmer moves his feet toward the slowly emerging waterline to a sight most unexpected.

The spirit of the barge is in sync with the general. Only her task is much different yet in an ameliorating style. One each she fastens her great barge in moorings to the elastic melting soil, a carriage here, a submarine there, and many ships of unknown origin and type. The sudden movement in the spirits direction seemed consistent and purposeful or at least intentional. She pushes in a counter-clockwise route of the steamed perimeter. Skimmer doesn't see the view at first; he puts most of his attention on the left or the right. Then as the view reaches the summit of unawareness, the general halts the line with a wave of his hand.

Most of the ships couldn't maintain water tightness without extra boarding or welds. The spirit wisely rests them on the sand shelf near the mooring plugs. Skimmer waves in a most egregious nature toward the spirit then hails Trent who now dawns a dragoon barb gun. "Trent, tell me have you ever seen this large a navy, anywhere." Trent shook his head. There were only five of the great ships within view yet the trail led to one cueing of the shore and with each step to the water more ships appeared to his far right flank. There was a galleon with cannons and a grand yacht with ornamental fabrics adorning an intricate face. The spirit, as Lucius observed didn't slow for those not into a meeting and for some odd reason the spirit made an exception as the white figure approached along the blacktop. The spirit of the barge ran to skimmers party and rather then being surprised at the apparition, skimmer sought answers. "What is the meaning of all these ships?" Trent waved a hand at the spirits incorporeal and semi-lucent appearance. She just gave an awkward sideways look at Trent's attempts at touching. "The ships are a gift to the great island of Scio after the great red spot fell over and turned to black." Skimmer being new to generalship wondered regarding his own protocol and made a half-bow of the head in acknowledgement to the gesture. Then the spirit didn't run off but dissipated into the steam rising around them. Skimmer raised his hand to Trent who silenced his questions. "Trent will move the remaining soldiers into rebuilding these vessels. Islands are always safest with a navy." The cart and company moved in unison to meet the unusual crafts in the breaking waves.

The first craft was the great glass bottom barge Lucius had shown Victoria and Robbins. The glass was undisturbed and the vessel was entirely sea worthy needing only new sails for propulsion. The general and Trent moved onto the first ship and explored the structural integrity of each wood and glass attachment. In one of the holds of the ship a huge piling of animal art was stacked and secured to the deck hatchings. Trent and the other islanders differed to skimmer's expertise. "A grand sign of the new Scio, sailing ships and submarines..." Skimmer spoke from the under deck of the glass ship and then rose to the view of the other vessels. Most of the crowd still on the shoreline gathered their belongings onto the main deck and waited the build instructions. The submarines were Subsa build and had eel and seahorse harnesses. "Get the boards on the galleon and will move them to the glass ship and the yacht; will rework one of the submarines for the other." Busy with orders and understanding, he got Trent, "Make camp and manage a crew for each detail and one for fishing and food; should be a productive day." The last remark was as much for his benefit as for Trent's. Trent acquiesced and the entire group entered the ship holds. Skimmer glimpsed at the sticky nature between his feet and the surface, pushing his legs toward up and down marching. After several reviews of his boots, Skimmer relaxes and enjoys the new productivity of his office, when the three black winged angels arrive at his position. One each they sweep low and dart the steam; each finding a perch away from the general's peripheral vision. "Scion leader, we seek the grand parity." The general felt a startlement and turned the one-hundred and eighty degrees to meet the ladies gaze. His face turned sour with intrigue at the darkened wings. "You ladies are survivors of the storm." "Yes," the one closest replied, standing at a review posture for attendance. "We will bring the leader to the islands center for rebuilding," The second lady spoke. The general grabbed his chin," Tumult is very well and working with the poets on Ignis." All three ladies held hands in gratitude for the safety of the grand parity. One of the women, saluted and the other's postured a sign of allegiance. "You can help put these ships together for the new navy. I'm sure there is some expertise you can put into them." Skimmer didn't speak another word to the trio and watched them power over his head onto the glass hulled barque. The ladies put to work finding new bonding agents for ship planks and metal attachments aboard the glass bottomed ship. "The Ignis soil with high volcanic content is excellent for strong rock holds," mentions the seeming leader of the Triton ladies. One of the other ladies brings a sand mixture consistent with their wings. She meant a similar texturing to concrete. Skimmer became fascinated with the ladies ingenuity, as he strolled the promenade of the deck, supervising the workers. Hours later Trent mentions to the general the grand contributions of these new black winged ladies. "Since arriving to work on the ship, the women have increased the strength of most of the ship levels with their compound." The sweat from the heat of the wings and the labor near the island kept the women undeterred and their esteem for the island increased with each tightening of the boards. "You ladies do Scio, a proud service." Skimmer wasn't the grand parity; however he represented his island well with approving manners to all creative solutions. The general's remarks were only in the air for moments when the surface of the ground brightened in view of the main deck of the ship, where the three women stood. The girls noticed and skimmer kept peering at the surface of Scio. Skimmer's face gave a widening smile," The ground is lightening... yellow... no gold." In a mild shaking gesture the general forwards a notion regarding the events," The volcano must have had high concentrations of gold in the hot lava." The gold glimmers and catches the attention of only one of the workers. The emoten residents were on a mission and there work on the mainland island stood paramount. The Triton women caught glance of each others wings and watched them turn from black to white. "Strange," states one of the women. "Shouldn't are wings turn gold?" The ladies seemed slightly disappointed and then they each found space on the deck of the ship and began to flap their wings in the breeze. The remains of soil on the wings were released to the wind. The gilding of Scio wasn't localized. The island formed a very intense daytime lantern. The intensity of the island increased in weight on the resident's view. The gold caught the notice of an approaching Tantamount vessel. The general waved across his arms for an attention to the incoming ship. Then the workers caught notice of the islands surface and ran to dig up the soil. "Gold... Gold...," Trent ran to skimmer's side and then laughed catching notice of the operational vessel in the waking waves. "I hope the ship is friendly," skimmer nodded in serious agreement and moved off the glass hulled deck toward the incoming vessel. The ship landed several hundred feet from skimmer and Trent's approach. A lone woman exits the ship with very formal attire. She waves forward her hand and two men bring a table and chair for her to sit on the gilded Scio soil. In her right hand she carried a ledger and the woman sat exactly in the chair while dismissing the men to the ship. Skimmer and Trent posed the obvious question upon reaching the visitor. "Are you here for a purpose?" "Yes," the middle aged woman offered. "I am here to see the grand parity." Skimmer gave another glance toward the woman and then put in his reply. "The Grand Parity is on off island business, I am one of his advisors." "Good," the lady didn't wait for long answers. My name is "Ms. Ehleta and I represent one of the five families on Tantamount. You have heard of the Ehleta." "Indeed," skimmer was originally from Tantamount and knew of her and her family. "Tell me, Ms. Ehleta are the stories about the elves in the Ehleta posts true." "Everyone asks," went her initial reply. The lady relaxing her chair forward, she gave a smile and a head tilt," Many years ago, my family experienced a labor shortage and a friend of the family suggested we consult one of the wizards on cat's wall. Well, we got a wizard. A most well kept man with a bright blue cloak and he was very knowledgeable about summoning magical creatures of all sorts. The family told him to keep the incantation simple. The wizard made an enchantment and several tan elves appeared. The elves worked well in the lumber and construction mills until one day one of the supervisors entered the mill and all the elves were gone. The wizard was recalled for questioning, yet he didn't have an immediate ready answer. Only several years later we began hearing these stories of elves in the elheta posts." Ms. Ehleta gave a head nod. "The story is true. Some believe the posts are gateways to the land of the elves. We encourage the stories generating interest in our construction." Skimmer looked at the woman's desk on the edge of the island. "And your business currently?" skimmer's question brought the woman's hands in a grasp. Tantamount usually remaining neutral in political occasions, the organizer found an opportunity. "We will contract the rebuilding of Scio with Triton marble, Tantamount ranches, and Ignis poet cottages." Skimmer being native to Tantamount measured the intent of the beautiful woman of business. "And in return?" Skimmer leaned on his sword.

"Some of the fine soil," "No," Skimmer shook his head with his remarks. "The grand parity will meet with you for technology or artifact payments." The new capitol is emote and you can direct your ship to the high keeper. Celebus will give you an audience. Here take Trent with you and good luck with your concerns." Skimmer pushed Trent toward the Triton business woman where he gave an awkward pause and a look to the hand, handshake. Skimmer seemed anxious to return to the ships and waved to the pair," Luck..." Skimmer seemed confused and walking a way putting his head down and up toward the word, "Ehleta." The confusion soon dissipated and Skimmer smiled at the emotens on the gilded archipelago.

An exhausted George grapples the front entrance of 'The Swabbed Deck,' nearly knocking a few of the drying tables off, yet far enough to allow the entrance and passengers room. George stuck his landing in the deep soil pushing an exact landing. The Island Representative shakes Victoria's hand. "You are more than a bird keeper, you know." Victoria kisses him on the cheek causing his cheeks to turn a rosy red. Victoria moves over toward Lucius. Lucius finds himself in close proximity and a little nervous for the standing wind and the bar smell. Maybe these aren't his exact thoughts. Lucius shakes Victoria's hand with a flat painted grin. "BirdKeeper," he gave with a twist of the shake. "Messenger," Victoria curtsies a bow. The bow doesn't finish as Lucius and Robbins make an upward back twist toward flight. Curving an arch in the sky, the men manage a wave to the young girl standing with her bird. Victoria can hear the hustle and bustle of the bar. Mr. Finkle Charm calls from the office.

"Victoria... Victoria," Victoria kissed her bird George and leads him to his home.

The longshadow crew sat on the top of their submarine in the middle of uncharted northern waters. The waves splashed and retreated against the streamline hull. Each of the crew had fishing poles and positioned themselves over the edge of one side of the enormous hull. Corn wasn't the best bait for fishing and some buckets' titled Subsa food were brought up from the ships galley and brought better results. The crews' poles had the barest of essentials with wooden staff and line. The officers fished on the opposite side of the ship and the center of the conning tower held several buckets for the sea going creatures. "Tannon is a crazier story then the elves in the Ehleta posts, I heard growing up." Robert smiled in approval," I rather enjoyed tannon." The two men went silent, realizing the implications of tannon with their crew mates. The officers formed a line look toward their captain and he quite acutely felt their thoughts. "We'll get them!" Rider was as brief as possible, letting John, speak for the ship. "We are an artifact crew and we have enjoyed the many artifacts we have..." Rider smirked at the suggestions. Hanz chimed in with an over-step," We are 0-2 with the atmosphere and the wings and 2-0 on corn and money." "Your right, Hanz." The captain stood as the only man standing and addressed the entire crew fishing on the hull. The feet of the captain gestured with his arms and hands. "We are an artifact vessel. We shouldn't be sitting on the top of the waters. We should be patrolling the deep." Rider conditioning his arm in the skyward direction, his face grew stark and his demeanor serious," All hands down the conning tower, all teams prepare the scopes... dive, dive, dive." Rider watched the entire ship move and the fish buckets and poles disappear into the vessel. The captain gave the instructions before entering the longshadow main. "Set a heading west of Ignis," John's eyes squinted as he registered the instructions. "Captain, there is only seas to the west." "Do they go on forever? Will only know if the boat gets moving?" "Yes, "John replied as he saluted the captain and went second to last down the hatchway.

The temple on emote with the cooling and gilding of Scio became a very busy place. Some of the native Scions were busy building a permanent bridge between emote and Scio while others built temporary shelters for their experiments. The main temple filled with the rush of crowds and designs. Those residents not involved with skimmer, Celebus, or the Scions, returned to their own farms and work houses, giving a sense of revitalization to the islands image. The main water entrance to the temple lay vacant yet filled with noise from the people on the upper landing. The Ehleta landing ship was slightly more ostentatious then most with a recognizing of the Tantamount house building trade represented in the design and luxury. The upper deck had huge draperies and comfortable couches for Trent and Ms. Ehleta's access. "Do you think Celebus will agree to us rebuilding the island?" Trent being a very loyal temple security man gave the patent answer," You will have to consult the high keeper." Ms. Ehleta shirked with impression, while lifting herself off a striped couch. "Over an hour's journey around the island and you keep giving the same answer. There might be an offer of employment toward you with the ehlata, although you might be busy here for awhile." She conceded her answer and motioned to the ladder enabling the pair the bottom rung of the temple stairs. Trent being a gentleman holds the business woman's hand as she steps onto the granite. Trent and Ms. Ehleta walk to the rush of the crowds above. Above the temple, a Triton messenger can be seen climbing the sky and rolling papers occupying the stairwell. Trent knew his way to the main office and usurped a line of people getting the high keeper's attention. The line consisted of mostly native Scions with inventions and building plans. The glaze of the walls glimmered brightly with the suns return to emote. Celebus's eyes were fixed on the door with the frequency of visitor's and his eyes became enlarged with the view of his head of security. "Trent, I thought you were accompanying the general on the security of the mainland...," Trent maintained a strong back in the face of his leader. "Security is posted on half the islands perimeter and the general is working on building a navy for the island of Scio." Celebus stood and walked around his desk. "A navy, well the general is really getting into the rebuilding effort and I've never seen your guest, she must be someone of great import." Celebus reviewed the distinguished business woman with a smart review of her possible connections. Ms. Ehleta reached out and shook the hand of Celebus. "I am Ms. Ehleta and represent my family's inclination regarding the rebuilding of the Scio mainland." "News travels fast," Celebus stated while looking from Trent to Ms. Ehleta. "The residents of Scio would be grateful for the most prestigious house builders in all the islands granting their expertise." Celebus moved toward his desk and Trent moved toward the corner of the room. Ms. Ehleta pulled up a chair and folded her legs, reaching into a folder she had brought with her. "The Ehleta are willing to rebuild the islands laboratories in the styles of the Tritons, the Ehleta, and the western poets of Ignis. I considered the gilding of the island would make for easy payment, yet the general seems to think technology or artifacts would be more inline with the grand parity's perceptions." Celebus went and fixed himself a drink while answering the prestigious guest. "The interest of the island will be forwarded through our own iniatives. We would look to the Ehleta for supplies. The esteem in the great state of Scio is increasing. The great minds will be leading the seven islands to the next stage in our prosperity." Celebus shook the ladies hand and put her proposal on his desk," Trent escort Ms. Ehleta to her ship." Celebus remained in his office and dumped his drink in a small side sink. He never took a sip.

Trent and Ms. Ehleta barely reach the water entrance stairwell, when the entire line of Scions, pour out of the temple. The crowds shouted," Tu-mult, Tu-mult." Celebus being the last to leave the temple caught sight of the returning grand parity in a long boat. The poets chanted," Left, right, left, right..." All building and experimenting continued the sign the residents were forward looking. The poets never left their boat and rowed in reverse with each leg Tumult put on the sands of the Scion capitol. "Left, right, left, right..." the poets rowed while the grand parity at the seashore and Celebus on the green, watched them vanish. Turning around the grand parity caught sight of the Scion mainland glittering in gold. Celebus slowed his pace toward the Scion leader with the crowd's silence. The high keeper formulated a statement. "The island spontaneously turned gold. There must be gold in the rock layers." Tumult put a finger to the air and felt the breeze across his face. "Gold is a decent building material." Celebus and the crowd began to listen. "Get several of our people and contract some of the warriors to turn the gold into beams." Celebus seemed invigorated with the solutions coming his way. "You have barely been here for a few seconds and already you're solving island problems. Let me show you to your office." Trent and Ms. Ehleta didn't wait. Ms. Ehleta was shown to her boat. Trent waved a hand at the retreating ship. After Tumults suggestion, the lines of people got in a race to the main office. Celebus and Tumult strolled in silence for several feet.

Tumult put in his authority," See to the metallurgy preparations and the redesign of the island. There are still hot parts on the mainland. You won't lack for heating surfaces." Celebus smiled in pleasant surroundings and moved toward the temple. The Grand Parity strolled to find his office.

The great expanse of water separating Ignis and Triton held rocking waters on a misty grey sky. A lone pair of wings emerges white on the darkened seascape. The distant figure enlarges with the waves crashing toward the Triton shoreline, a shoebox appears in the carrier's hand and his elevation seems much lower than normal for cross water travel. The man hits the slope before 'the swabbed deck' and maintains a close ten feet to the face of the rock. Whizzing past two men and a whirly, the messenger keeps close ground cover. High above the shoreline the Triton Cup is beginning with all whirlies circling several thousand feet above the ground. The whirlies appear in all five natural colors and hold only one rider each for the great journey on the outer edge of Triton. All the Triton onlookers hover in mid-air as an official carries a horn. The horn is enabled and the whirlies head along the coastline. The messenger darts the huge shadows of these birds, as well as the onlookers from the ground. The whirly birds lower their altitude on the cross over to the water's edge. The messenger darts parallel to the great birds with their separating distance increasing with the inner towns of Triton. The birds seem to reappear several times above treetops and house roofings before disappearing in lowland hills.

As the land lifts to the Triton mountaintops, the messenger ignores the above sky highways; choosing to skirt each mountain and divide each gazebo. The flatland houses on Triton mostly hold humans and they were each awestruck at the Triton's tactics. Passing low, a mother and her baby wave at the man before he startles a couple of horses," He must be training for a race," she tells to the youth in her arms. The box in the Triton's hands emerges outstretched as if facilitating his swimming in the sky. The mountains give to trees and a plateau, as the messenger barely misses the whirlies on the lawn before the particle center. "Swoop," the deliverer pushes the upslope and dives into the loop of messenger and packages. The package is dropped into a shoot, as the messenger catches another package and finishes his circle. The shoe box slides down a flat backed stone white slope, topping a large pile.

A man with glasses grabs the box and enters the long hallway to the opposite side of the building. The Triton carefully pushes maximum walking speed, as any faster and his wings might give him lift. Again the man turns a corner and begins reading the names on the doors. "Lucius," the Triton speaks softly to himself as he opens the door. "Greetings," Lucius offers with a monotone grin. The man hands over the package without explanation and Lucius doesn't ask. Lucius bolts out of his office toward the sky. The owl in his office does three leaps in the air before returning to his perch.

Lucius tackles the northern trees and swamps choosing a much higher altitude then the initial deliverer but then again, just above the tree line. The green is dotted with houses and a few hills. Then the green turns rocky and the houses turn to castles. The largest and most distant castle surrounded by a swamp, stands alone, amid a huge vacant land. Lucius flutters his wings as he lands, near a cross stone hallway. A flat piece of stone juts from the castle allowing him to place his feet and meet with recipients; he doesn't even wait a moment. The minister of domestic and foreign affairs for the castle appeared in the stone arch. "Lucius, what have you brought us today?" "Cat's Wall, important, Archangel," Lucius could have conversed with the minister but chose the minimal approach to his delivery, as he had another appointment. Lucius flew straight upward and got into an angle twist to forward his motion. The minister waved as Lucius flew toward the shoreline.

The minister paused a moment to examine the box, the shoe box had a center bow and a right side charm. The color scheme seemed familiar to the minister but he couldn't recall where.

The minister walked the stairs to the archangel's office and found the door already open. The human wasn't ushered in as before but found the archangel busy reading over reports of his angels. Spring Shine wasn't being rude but rather efficient as he never up turned to see the minister. The minister sat slowly and read the box cover, "To the Formal Angelic Administration from Cat's Wall." "The box should say who on cat's wall or else we must presume the writer means the whole island." The angel was clarifying a point of logic not lost on the minister. "Oh well," the minister smiled as he threw the box in the air and chanted quickly. The notion the minister was capable of the angel's spell, surprised spring shine. The mid-air approach was obviously to garner attention. Much faster than other chants the box exploded into a letter. The letter floated and coursed the air, sliding perfectly in the center of Spring Shine's desk. The floating letter covered a brown parchment with the sender's name Robbins and the addressee, parseval visible before eclipse.

The Archangel read:

To the Formal Angelic Administration:

The People of Cat's Wall wish all outer islands to know, the portal is strictly off limits. Any magical or scientific contrivance utilized to reach the seventh island will face the resistance of a unified wizard and cat consortium.

Pleasant day and season to all, Melmo,
Island Representative

The minister didn't wait for the archangel and got to the heart of the matter. "With the atmosphere destroyed, is there another way to get to the seventh?" The Archangel met kindly force to see the minister's face. "There are several, we guard each one." The minister seeming, as a man learning knew information. "I'm shocked; the islands' view the seventh as myth." The minister positioned his hand inward toward the archangel," Here you are holding the keys as a keeper." Spring Shine stood and walked toward his window, in the distance, he could see several whirly dancing in the sky. With his back turned to the minister, spring shine made his feelings known. "The people of the seventh aren't ready for us." The minister accepting the answer gave a retreat back faced toward the door. The minister put a finger to his forehead, just about to leave; he started remembering something in his pocket. Reaching in, he grabbed an envelope. "There is one more piece of business. It arrived shortly before you did. It's from Ignis," the minister stated handing the envelope to the archangel. The minister stood for several seconds awaiting spring shines attention. "Well, aren't you going to read it?" Spring Shine returned to his window, "No, I think, I'll let the mystery sit awhile." "Any other business archangel," the minister could see the angel had personal duties. "Day Minister," the archangel dismissed his highest ranking officer. "Day Archangel."

The next entrant into the archangel's office didn't walk. She shimmered. An empty office tingled with a bright haze and shiny surface. A dark cloaked un-winged figure appeared before Spring Shine. The dark cloak lifted over a humanoid shape, revealing Lily. "Off-Island Angel reporting," Lily put her arms behind her back and took on an official demeanor. "Continue, Lily," the Archangel sat for her report. "The steps' on restructuring of policy on the eastern side of the island is moved forward through Pembridge via an old Ignis contract, from the whirly center in Tantamount. The poets were gathered for officiating with the Grand Parity and the bar on dragoon was prepared for Marcus and Magis's arrival." The Archangel handed lily a group of beads. Lily situated the beads around her neck. The beads caused a bright light to fill the room; the light relaxing lily was transformed from weed to Triton. "See the foreign minister for your next list," the archangel waved and lily bowed an exit. The archangel stood before his office and shimmered. Spring Shine appeared on the long ramp to the leader of Triton and walked steadily toward the pinnacle.

Below the ramp, the chancellor moved toward his new office. The title on the door read, "Island Representative." Robbins paused at the door for entrance and then entered. The door gave way to a series of offices and an apartment for his residence. Several people greeted and patted his wings. There were no hidden people here and Robbins found the large office with beneficent colors, granting him a well deserved relax. Chancellor Robbins took off his collar and tried a perch chair.

Tumult stood in the temple for a meeting. Celebus and representatives of many emote and Scion think tanks were in attendance. The Grand Parity put in his plan for the island around a rotunda table in a smooth surfaced office with cold abasement seats and table. "The gold on the perimeter of the island will be smelted for beams. The volcanic rock will be brought to emote for fertilizing soil. Once the soil is revealed on the Scio mainland perimeter, we will plant palm trees. The trees will help cool the island exterior with the heat and the gold." Celebus went to raise his hand, when skimmer entered the room. Skimmer walked toward the grand parity and gave a salute. The grand parity smiled and relaxed his demeanor. Skimmer spoke to the leader," I have several vessels under construction and two operable. A glass hulled barque and a submarine." The grand parity grabbed his chin," Captain Rider?" "No," came an answer from the general. "The submarine is a Subsa build. We made the sides air tight and I am here for a fuel source for the submarine. I am considering Celebus's poet paper." Celebus moved backward at an angle. "Poet Paper," Celebus uttered to the general. "Yes, poet paper will generate steam for the ship and we can have both ships for supplies around the island." "We'll get to work." Those were all the remarks Tumult had on record for the discussions. On departing the meeting, Celebus led the group out of the temple. "Just a second," Celebus imparted to the grand parity. Running down the marble hall, Celebus found an entrance to the display forward his office. Removing the glass, Celebus re-exposed the 'T' to the light of the temple. Celebus put the 'T' in a satchel on the side of the case and moved forward to reacquaint with Tumult. Celebus raised the satchel as they left the temple. "What are you thinking," Tumult gave to the high keeper. The 'T' has more than defensive abilities; let's see where the earthen creatures can help. Tumult nodded and leaned his way down the steps and toward the nearly constructed bridge. The bridge workers ran to meet the grand parity when he was nearly twenty feet from the bridge entrance. A lab technician dressed in white paused with glasses in hand. "The bridge is made of the same granite the temple utilizes for stairs and we have gotten a volcanic mixture for mortar. The bridge shines granite, black, and gold." "Are you finished," the grand parity questioned the lead worker. "The bridge connects on the right side; we should have the left side in completion within a couple of days." "Brilliant," the lab technician nodded with Tumult's approval and skipped a hop toward his work. Celebus didn't let the moment pass," Should the bridge be widened for movement of materials." "Let the bridge keepers know the correct amount." The Grand Parity walked toward Scio along the right side bridge with Celebus watching the rock supports. The Grand Parity motioned for the 'T'. Kneeling and feeling the Scion mainland surface. Tumult put the 'T' in a hot spot on the surface face. Celebus looked intently as the grand parity produced over 10,000 soldiers spanning a large distance covering the eastern half of Scio proper. The earthen creatures came in an assortment of colors from brown and green to gold and black. Some of the creatures still oozed hot lava and fanned themselves for cooling. Celebus in a strange reversal of roles urged the grand parity toward the creatures. "Get all the gold you can from the surface of the rock faces on the ground and pile them in a central location." None of the creatures moved, although some turned their heads toward the ocean. Then in a sudden motion, all of the earthen creatures listened. Some of the creatures dug into the ground for the gold while others removed the gold from their bodies or others. Several of the earthen creatures reformed in black, brown, and green. The removal of the gold and the construction of the earthen beings left a beautiful expanse of dirt and fertile soil. "Amazing," Celebus stood in awe. "Melt the gold into plates and beams." Tumult reviewed the creatures injecting hot lava into the gold pile and manipulating the reaction with their hands. Several hours kept the creatures busy and Celebus and Tumult stood in silence. The Grand Parity led Celebus along the coast," get a crew to plant palm trees along the island coast around the perimeter of the island. Get the security stations participation and get the island built." Celebus found his nerves steady walking toward the first security station. Tumult clapped his hands; the island creatures clapped their hands.

The grand parity leaving the creatures admired their work for several miles, as he headed for the center of the island. Beams and Plates simmering within several minutes on the heat in huge fires the creatures began pushing and melding the heat plates into sheets with arms and bodies twisting. The island is hot with the working of the creatures and the motion of the lava. Tumult walks further than the last opening a creature's existence makes in the soil. The brown earth should have turned black to his recollection; yet something entirely of a different nature occurs with each moment. The gold soil at a radius of a half-mile to the volcano turns white. The volcanic soil also gives with the approach of Tumult's feet and in some places makes a crackle. The grand parity kneels in the white soil and pierces a gaze, while coming to an illustrious conclusion. "Calcium... calcium deposits..." Continuing his walk Tumult finds small trees growing in the calcium deposits with strange coloration. The calcium deposits continue right to the edge of the volcano and climb the cliff's face; The Grand Parity makes his own foot holds in the teeming soil. The volcanoes surface grows a steep slope with graduation and Tumult places his hands into the warm soil hoping for their preservation. At the very tip of the volcano where he had earlier stood in loss; the volcano still bubbles and churns hot with steam. Tumult stands for many hours looking at the red active volcano when above him he feels something cold. Small tiny flakes fall on his head and brow. The still wind cradles each of the flakes in small mounds and the volcano and the island begin to cool.

Lucius had just reached the sands of aboveboard, as he scouted himself a viewing dune. The sands graduated from a light white to a grayish and then darkened brown. 'Thud," the messenger's feet sunk into the giving of the dune's surface. Lucius peered right and then left and caught site of a familiar whirly bird, a mile down the coast. Adjacent the whirly were legions of northern Triton forces in dress uniforms. The messenger commanded his wings only slightly off the ground, a very difficult maneuver. The hovering arched and dust falling feet relaxed to a downward point. The wings angled and slowly increased speed. Lucius flew the sand at less than three feet and closing to the gathering on the other side of the beach. He sensed each breeze and undulated as the wake of a wave. Slowly the air lifted him and saw him subtle his regard to a straight and flat landing. He landed right in front of Victoria. Victoria had a huge grin on her face as she proudly displayed an official uniform of a Triton squadron. "I am officially a boat captain, as the island representative felt George an excellent whirly for the Triton force." Victoria blurted the words without inhale. Victoria's Triton uniform wasn't the only sign of regal familiarity. George had an official warming cloak signifying his participation. "Congratulations," Lucius managed a salute. Victoria kissed him. The pair sat down and watched the view of the birds approaching from an hour behind. Beak began approaching the pair with a downward pant of the air. "Don't get up, Victoria," Victoria wasn't getting up, still she enjoyed the approval of her commander. Victoria looked over her left shoulder as beak handed her a shoe box. Lucius's eyes widened as he was all to familiar with charms, colors, and designators. Beak knocks the box out of Victoria's hand with as respectful a rude gesture as decorum permitted. "Whoosh," the box turned instantly into a letter and cradled the air toward Lucius's feet. The messenger read the letter for a few minutes and then passed the letter to Victoria who returned the letter to beak. Beak stood at attention," Congratulations Chancellor!" Lucius reached over and shook beak's hand, as he returned to the squadron. Victoria grabbed for Lucius's side and the wind seemed warming.

About the Author

Thomas Terraforte was born in Yonkers, NY. In his youth Tom ran track and became an Eagle Scout. In the 1990's he attended and graduated from the Georgia Institute of Technology with a bachelor's degree in Electrical Engineering. After his school years, Tom joined and served honorably in the United States Air Force. Today, He lives and works in Bethlehem, PA. Mr. Terraforte draws inspriration from a variety of fiction and philosophical writings but especially those of acclaimed author Robert Jordan.

Lightning Source UK Ltd.
Milton Keynes UK
UKOW02n0617210815

257274UK00004B/34/P